PRAISE FOR
GREEN GROW THE DOLLARS

"As always, Lathen plays it cool, with low-key prose and a good deal of whimsy. Thatcher is as urbane and razor-sharp as ever."

—*New York Times Book Review*

"SELDOM HAS MURDER BEEN SO ENTERTAINING."
—*Washington Post Book World*

AND FOR EMMA LATHEN

"A masterful plotter, an elegant stylist, a comic genius, and an old-fashioned purist who never sacrifices logic for surprise effect."

—*Newsweek*

"PROBABLY THE BEST LIVING AMERICAN WRITER OF DETECTIVE STORIES."
—*C.P. Snow*

Books by Emma Lathen

Published by POCKET BOOKS

Most Pocket Books are available at special quantity discounts for bulk purchases for sales promotions, premiums or fund raising. Special books or book excerpts can also be created to fit specific needs.

For details write the office of the Vice President of Special Markets, Pocket Books, 1230 Avenue of the Americas, New York, New York 10020.

GREEN GROW THE DOLLARS

EMMA LATHEN

PUBLISHED BY POCKET BOOKS NEW YORK

 POCKET BOOKS, a Simon & Schuster division of
GULF & WESTERN CORPORATION
1230 Avenue of the Americas, New York, N. Y. 10020

Copyright © 1982 by Emma Lathen

Published by arrangement with Simon and Schuster
Library of Congress Catalog Card Number: 81-18395

ISBN: 0-671-45049-2

First Pocket Books printing April, 1983

10 9 8 7 6 5 4 3 2 1

POCKET and colophon are registered trademarks
of Simon & Schuster.

Printed in the U.S.A.

CONTENTS

GREEN GROW THE DOLLARS

1 PREPARE PLOT THOROUGHLY

ON Wall Street, where paper money is still highly regarded, flights into gold rarely pick up much speed. True, some venerable and blue-blooded brokers persist in holding the abrogation of the gold clause responsible for the Decline and Fall of the Republic, and otherwise respectable institutions harbor a few gold bugs. But, apart from these oddities, most of Wall Street, most of the time, looks on gold as just another precious metal.

At the Sloan Guaranty Trust, for example, weeks and months could pass with only routine mention of London fixings and Hong Kong closings, despite the considerable participation in overseas finance enjoyed by the third largest bank in the world.

Currently, however, John Putnam Thatcher, senior vice-president, was getting hourly reports about bullion. He was getting reports about other things too because, at the rarefied level at which he and the Sloan functioned, gyrations in the price of gold had implications beyond the melting down of candlesticks.

". . . the dollar's strong. Dwayne says that the Bundesbank is in with heavy support," said the clipped voice from the Sloan's Money Desk. "Also, there's a rumor in Brussels that Kuwait is raising the price of crude."

"Tell Wybell to check that out," said Thatcher, replacing

the phone and shifting from offshore chaos to the home-grown variety. "Go on, McAdoo."

McAdoo was detailing a disquieting outflow from savings when Walter Bowman, the Sloan's weighty chief of research, suddenly interrupted. "John," he called unceremoniously from the door, "they've just announced a three-billion-dollar error in M–2. There are rumors about Manny Hanover's reports, but I don't have anything solid yet. I'll get back as soon as I have more on it."

With that, he disappeared. McAdoo, blinking nervously, remained.

"Go on, McAdoo," said Thatcher.

In minutes, they were again deep in CD's, Federal Funds, and M's– 1, –2, and –3.

This tumult and shouting had been continuing for days now, and gave no sign of abating. Contrary to appearances, it did not mean that the Sloan was tottering on the brink of ruin. To date, performance had been exemplary and Thatcher, who had recruited and coached most of the team, had every reason for satisfaction. During uneventful prosperity, almost any bank or banker can flourish. There had been profitable doldrums in the recent past when Thatcher could have left the Sloan to run itself—or even left it in the uncertain custody of its president, Bradford Withers.

But with conditions at home and abroad changing by the minute, and rarely for the better, the best bank or banker could stumble, as tidings from Philadelphia, Chicago and points between demonstrated. In the cause of averting major and minor mishaps, Thatcher was putting in longer-than-usual hours in his sixth-floor suite. He himself regarded this as simple prudence but he did not regret the sense of urgency it conveyed through the ranks. Infusions of adrenaline never hurt.

He did, however, discourage heroics. "No, McAdoo, now is not the time to revise the formula," he said. "We'll

10

set the prime the usual way this Friday. Just leave those papers for me, will you? Yes, Miss Corsa, what is it now?"

His secretary, arriving in time to speed McAdoo on his way, was peerless as a bearer of tidings, good or bad. Miss Corsa was accurate, efficient and completely detached. Should enemy bombs ever fall on Alabama, Thatcher hoped the news would come through her. She could reduce Armageddon to manageable proportions.

"This just came. I knew you would want to see it immediately, Mr. Thatcher."

After that touch of drama, the document she handed him was an anticlimax. At first glance it seemed to be routine.

"By order of the U.S. District Court," Thatcher read aloud, skimming down the text. When he had grasped the gist, he looked up at the waiting Miss Corsa. "This is only a court order freezing the account of Vandam Nursery & Seed Company," he said.

She nodded vigorously. "Yes, it arrived this morning. Naturally, I noticed it on the list at once."

Bank accounts are sitting ducks. Death, taxes, divorce, litigation—or any combination thereof—focus attention on assets. An institution like the Sloan required a special desk in Commercial Deposits to accept legal paper, oversee compliance and circularize internal staff.

Solely because Miss Corsa expected it, Thatcher delved deeper. "This order is in connection with the lawsuit by . . . let's see . . . someone called Wisconsin Seedsmen, Inc. Against the Vandam Nursery & Seed Company. The basis of the suit . . ."

She did not regard the specifics as her province, as she informed him. "The minute I saw it was Vandam's, I brought it right in to you."

Thatcher digested this. Miss Corsa, unmoved by municipal default from Cleveland to Waco, indifferent to a total shutdown of the Board of Trade, assumed that anything happening to the Vandam Company deserved Mr. Thatcher's attention. Why?

Walter Bowman, fitly enough, supplied the answer. Bouncing in again, he said, "They're still sweating it out over at Manny Hanover, John. Meanwhile, the Fed will get revisions out after close of business. Boy, there'll be hell to pay in the bond market tomorrow." Then, having said what he had come to say, he impenitently added, "Sorry, am I interrupting anything important?"

"No," said Thatcher, incurring a reproachful look from his secretary. "Or rather, Miss Corsa and I were just discussing a court order we've received freezing an account of the Vandam Company."

Bowman more than compensated for Thatcher's deficiencies. "Vandam's?" he said alertly. "I was thinking about them just last weekend. Now that Christmas is over, the Vandam catalog should come any day. This year, I'm going into vegetables in a big way."

Some circles maintained that Bowman did everything in a big way.

"Last season," said Miss Corsa with modest pride, "we canned a dozen quarts of string beans."

"Should I try Vandam *Verdipod?*" Walter asked humbly.

Miss Corsa's grandfather, she replied, swore by Vandam *Sugarina*.

Thatcher, who resided in a Manhattan apartment-hotel, did not beguile his sleet-sodden Januarys with dreams of spring planting. This, he could see, might be the minority position.

"What's happening to Vandam's?" Bowman inquired after Miss Corsa withdrew.

"Nothing cataclysmic," said Thatcher. "After all, we're not Vandam's main bank. They're somewhere in Illinois, aren't they? I assume they keep a small account with us for import-export dealings."

Bowman had been thinking, and not about green beans. "You're not forgetting that Standard Foods took them over last year, are you, John?"

"I believe I was," Thatcher said, stirring some mental embers. Standard Foods, already a giant in food processing from soup to nuts, had recently launched a whirlwind of acquisitions—Mother Stella's Fish Cakes, Old Homestead Pizza Pies, Pretty Pussy Cat Food and, yes indeed, the Vandam Nursery & Seed Company.

And Standard Foods was a large and valued Sloan client.

"Which," Thatcher was the first to admit, "puts another complexion on Miss Corsa's eagle eye, doesn't it?"

The Sloan habitually informed depositors when the law stepped between them and their bank accounts. Nine times out of ten, this was empty courtesy, since frozen assets tend to come after, not before, other troubles.

But a customer as profitable to the Sloan as Standard Foods called for more than pro forma notification. Personal attention is one of the indubitable advantages of multimillion-dollar status and not simply, as politicians insist on reiterating, because life is unfair. It was very possible that Standard Foods knew nothing about this wrinkle; with countless operating divisions, and God knew how many bank accounts, *Wisconsin Seedsmen v. Vandam* could easily have slipped through the cracks. So SF was going to hear directly from its friend at the Sloan.

The decision made itself and, despite other calls on his time, Thatcher did not regret it. However, he still needed more data.

"Exactly whom should I contact at SF, Walter?" he asked.

"Let me think," said Bowman.

Going straight to the top is a stratagem best left to amateurs. The president and the chairman of the board of Standard Foods resembled the Joint Chiefs of Staff—too wise, too farseeing and too remote for the nuts-and-bolts working of their complex apparatus.

Walter Bowman saw the problem and made short work of it. "Earl Sanders is the man you want," he said. "I know he handled the Vandam takeover. And SF's acquisitions department has a New York office."

"Better and better," said Thatcher, buzzing Miss Corsa.

"I'll get right to it, Mr. Thatcher," she said, sinking whole clutches of his crowded docket.

He was sure she would.

Events, or at least Earl Sanders, conspired to help her surpass herself. Two hours later, she was ushering the man himself into Thatcher's office.

Sanders, a small dapper man, was by choice, if not by nature, a smiler. His entrance, his recognition of Walter Bowman, his introduction to John Thatcher, were all a genuine pleasure to judge from his mouth. His eyes were not quite so guileless.

"No, no," he assured them. "No trouble at all to drop by the Sloan, although I was surprised to hear from you. Vandam's is headquartered in downstate Illinois, and they've always banked at Midwestern Trust, you know. When we took over, we didn't alter those arrangements."

Handing Sanders the court order, Thatcher said, "I assumed as much, which is why I expect this is no more than a nuisance suit of some sort. I'm not familiar with the seed or nursery business, but I suppose they're just as bedeviled as everybody else."

"I guess so," said Sanders vaguely. Then, on a gust of genial frankness, he confided, "To tell you the truth, I don't know the ins and outs of running a big seed and nursery business myself."

"You knew enough about Vandam's to snap them up for SF," Bowman chimed in.

This could have been, and was, interpreted as a compliment by Earl Sanders. Not so by Thatcher, who knew Walter too well. Quite apart from warmth about Vandam's—or about the Vandam spring catalog—there was the man's beaver nature. When Walter advised the Sloan to buy anything, he had to be forcibly prevented from sharing every minute detail. The whole Investment Division had reeled under nautical gear when he recommended Acadia Marine.

But Sanders was still preening himself on the acumen he had shown. "Yes," he said, with the broadest smile yet. "Vandam's is going to be one of our sensational acquisitions. Of course, the financials were all right, too."

Walter's nose all but twitched. In general, financial statements are not an afterthought with sensational buys. Even a non-zealot like Thatcher felt some curiosity.

"When you bought it out, Vandam's was a family firm, wasn't it?" he asked, unashamedly fishing.

"Oh boy, was it!" Sanders chortled. "They're a family firm and an American institution, too."

"The catalog—" Bowman began.

Sanders laughed aloud. "To hear the Vandams, their catalog ranks just next to the Bible."

"Did the family want to sell, or have to sell?" Thatcher asked.

"It depends on which Vandam you're talking to," said Sanders. But, as Thatcher had anticipated, he could not resist the temptation to unburden himself and, stripped of editorial asides, a coherent and familiar saga emerged.

The founder, Cornelius Vandam, had begun with a farm-supply outfit in Rowe, Illinois (since renamed Vandamia). His firm prospered, and within his lifetime Vandam Nursery & Seed Company became a mail-order business. Cornelius' son, Hendrik, expanded into bulbs and nursery stock, with production fields stretching from California to Pennsylvania. Year in and year out, sales skyrocketed and the catalog grew glossier and glossier.

"But the trouble started with the third generation," Sanders said.

"It frequently does," said Thatcher encouragingly.

Hendrik Vandam II inherited the largest mail-order nursery business in the world, and a mountain of headaches. Both the company and the family had changed since Cornelius' days. Vandam's had become a huge enterprise, too diversified for the modest administrative talents that Cornelius' many descendants had inherited. Furthermore, unbroken affluence had changed the Vandams, who no longer regarded flowers, vegetables and seeds as their immutable destiny. With the Vandam money behind them, heirs wanted to go into publishing, heiresses married college instructors, and one great-granddaughter was a professional basketball player.

"So, Hendrik the Second decided to sell out?" Thatcher hazarded.

"No," Sanders told him. "He simply retired. The Vandam who was running the show and who decided to accept our offer was Hendrik's son, Richard. He has a good fat management contract from us—and so do too many other Vandams, I don't mind telling you."

Sanders' sketch of this lesser American dynasty was new to Thatcher, although the outlines were predictable. He had long since suspended disbelief at what the descendants of Pittsburgh steel, Detroit cars, and Texas oil chose to do with their wealth. The Vandams sticking with the firm were more down his alley.

Bowman had not been attending closely. He probably knew more about the Vandams than Earl Sanders did. But he had not let an opportunity to inform himself pass. While

Sanders expounded, Walter plucked the court order from his hand and began leafing through it. As usual, he hit pay dirt.

". . . to insure compliance with the court decree enjoining commercial exploitation of the tomato herein referred to as *Numero Uno,* it is . . ."

Sanders stiffened. "What was that?" he barked. "Did you say *Numero Uno?* My God, here—let me see that!"

He grabbed the court order from Bowman and excitedly began scanning it. "It can't be *Numero Uno,*" he muttered to himself. "But if it is . . . where the hell . . . oh, here it is. Wisconsin Seedsmen . . . contesting patent application . . . oh, my God!"

The distress, which reduced Sanders to unintelligible gabbling, told Thatcher a lot—about the Sloan, as well as Standard Foods. The standard operating procedure that had induced him to call Sanders had just paid off. Standard Foods had not known. And, as Sanders' anxious scowl demonstrated, Standard Foods was deeply concerned.

This, in turn, might explain why SF had bought Vandam's in the first place. All the enthusiasm so conspicuously lacking in Sanders' account of the firm, its history, its market position, and its management, seemed concentrated on this one product.

"The *Numero Uno* tomato?" Walter prompted. "What's so special about it?"

Sanders, immersed in the court order, looked up. *"Numero Uno,"* he said reverently, "is the tomato of the century."

Before anybody could comment, less lofty sentiments overcame him. "Good God, it can't really be threatened, can it?"

With sheepdog neatness, Bowman bustled in to separate hard information from all this agitation.

"Exactly how is it the tomato of the century?" he demanded sternly.

Sanders was still distracted. "It's a hardy biennial," he said. "And the second year it bears like a tiger for a full six months in most places."

Bowman's expectations had been much lower. "Six months!" he said, awed. "That's a genetic miracle."

John Thatcher had his own hobbies. "It's more than that," he observed. "It's an economic revolution, isn't it, Sanders?"

Startling discoveries about life forms, genes, microbes, and cells were giving the country a true scientific breakthrough. Thatcher was prepared to take the fundamentals on faith. But many of these incredible findings had been flowing across his desk since science had become a growth industry.

"A super tomato," he mused, contemplating the most obvious implications. Millions of dollars worth of tomatoes were bought by the big canners, like Standard Foods, for soup, juice, pizza and no doubt other ends mercifully hidden from Thatcher. There were the farmers planting tomatoes each spring, the outfits manufacturing mechanized tomato pickers, there were home gardeners, suburban nurseries, seed companies . . .

Every single one of them would be affected by a tomato that could be planted, wintered over, then harvested. Costs, risks, profits—the whole commercial landscape would explode, then re-form. Tomatoes being a cash crop with a vengeance, *Numero Uno* was an immensely valuable property.

Sanders was momentarily soothed by their response. "Yes indeedy," he purred. "As soon as we got wind of Vandam's results, we swung into action. *Numero Uno* is going to shake up the whole food processing year, and we wanted to be on top of it." Words failed him as he looked back with pride. Then the unpleasant present overwhelmed him. "But this! . . ."

He glared at the offending document as if it were a cutworm.

"Now, don't leap to any conclusions," Bowman comforted him. "With a discovery as valuable as this, it stands to reason that every nut in the country is going to try to claim credit."

"I suppose so," said Sanders, not noticeably convinced.

"And remember, Vandam's has a great track record in developing new and better vegetables and flowers," Bowman continued.

"Sure," said Sanders, dismissing All-America beets, carrots and hydrangeas without a qualm. "I just wonder why they didn't bring this court case to our attention. Well, I don't want to take up any more of your time, Thatcher. Thanks for bringing this up. I'm sure it's only a nuisance suit, but we want to keep tabs on it."

He was itching to get away and Thatcher made no effort to detain him.

"Where would you guess he's headed, Walter?"

Bowman quite rightly treated this as rhetorical. Standard Foods was not taking any chances with this wonder tomato of theirs. So Vandam's was about to learn that, no matter what the terms of the merger agreement, there are no such things as family-owned-and-operated subsidiaries.

"*Numero Uno* is going to be worth millions to SF," he murmured, rising. "Well, I'd better get back to the money supply—and see if AT&T has cut the dividend."

His pleasantry was spoiled by the entrance of Miss Corsa, announcing that there were endless high-priority calls backing up on Mr. Thatcher's line.

Thatcher, fully appreciative of her Horatio-at-the-bridge endeavors. delayed reaching for the phone.

"Oh, Miss Corsa," he said, catching her at the door. "At a guess, the Vandam situation is nothing to worry about. They may be having difficulty adjusting to their new role in Standard Foods, but that's about all."

"I'm very glad to hear that," she said.

Unfortunately, neither of them had read the fine print.

2 GOING TO SEED

CONTRARY to some opinions at Exchange Place, the Sloan Guaranty Trust was only one small portion of the civilized world. There were places where frozen bank accounts were a matter of complete indifference. In a significant number of these benighted areas, it was another aspect of *Wisconsin Seedsmen, Inc. v. Vandam Nursery & Seed Company* that was the kicker.

The federal judge had issued a restraining order, enjoining Vandam's from attempting to exploit *Numero Uno*. He had then agreed to attach a bank account in order to ensure compliance. The assets tied up at the Sloan were a minor inconvenience compared to the real blockbuster. The Vandam spring catalog was printed, stacked and ready. Now, under penalty of law, it could not be mailed.

This hit the non-Sloan sphere with devastating force. Each January the Vandam catalog found its way to over twenty million addresses. It traveled to business offices, to suburban homes, to remote RFD routes, and to far-flung APO boxes. It formed the basis of commercial projections, park planning, landscape designs, backyard gardens and, most of all, hopes and dreams. New homeowners, looking out on the wasteland left by bulldozers, could see leafy shade trees and lilacs in full bloom. Organic gardeners deposited one symbolic load on a virgin compost pile and already, in their mind's eye, had a year's supply of vegetables. An infant fruit tree ordered from Vandam's was the promise of branches bowed down with ripe peaches.

The first shock waves were felt at the printers, now charged with restructuring the catalog so as to delete all reference to the new discovery.

"My God, did they have to brag about the damned tomato on every single page?" the layout man asked bitterly.

He was overstating the case, but not by much. *Numero Uno* not only graced the cover and the tomato section, it was also central to the dicussion of an ideal small vegetable plot, it led the recommendations for short-season areas, it ran rampant through gardening aids.

"Seventeen pages, I make it," he finally concluded.

"Oh, Christ!" groaned his superior.

But when push comes to shove, businessmen—so the *Wall Street Journal* claims—roll with the punches. John Q. Public, on the other hand, is a fretful baby, demanding instant gratification of his every whim. This theory received a good deal of support when the Sunday newspapers hit the streets. Traditionally, at this time of year, every home-and-garden page in the country carried the same advertisement. As a harbinger of spring it showed a clump of daffodils tossing in the breeze together with a cheerful offer by picturesque old Hendrik Vandam II to send his catalog free on request. For the first time in over a century those daffodils were missing. In their place was the stark announcement, in bold black type, that mailing of the Vandam catalog would be delayed until further notice.

Even television realized that this was a heaven-sent human interest feature. Accordingly on the Wednesday night news, after the usual dismal review of inflation, OPEC and Soviet military might, the scene shifted to a living room in the small town of Shelburne, Vermont.

"Here in her home five miles west of Killington, Mrs.

Elissa Tyrone has just learned that she will not be receiving her Vandam catalog at the usual time," ran the introduction.

Mrs. Tyrone, a spry sixty-year-old sitting in front of a wood stove, then took up the tale.

"We have big winters here in Vermont," she began, then paused while the camera zoomed through the window to pan over a landscape of unrelieved white. "And they can seem mighty long sometimes."

Christmas, she went on to say, was a bright spot. But after that, it was hard, very hard.

"I just don't know what I'm going to do this year."

Gravely the newscaster tried to reassure her. Nobody would be planting anything for at least twelve weeks.

But Mrs. Tyrone was inconsolable. "You don't understand. It's as if that catalog is the only thing that can convince me spring really will come."

In theory a human interest story is universally acceptable. Not so with this one. Growers south of the Mason-Dixon line were incensed.

"Those goddamned dummies! They think New York is the whole goddamned country!" raved a substantial tomato farmer in Texas. "Twelve weeks! We've got to plant in three."

His partner had an irritating habit of looking on the bright side. "We don't need the catalog. Why don't we just phone in last year's order?"

The look he got should have incinerated him.

"What the hell do you think I've been trying to do? The Vandam switchboard has been jammed for three solid days."

He was not the only one who had tried using the phone as a substitute for the catalog. And two-star generals are less accustomed to being balked than most men.

"What do you mean you can't get through to them? Use

your head. Send Vandam's a telegram telling them to call us."

"I did," the aide reported unhappily. "Two days ago."

"Look, Sweeney," the general growled, leaning forward with menace in every muscle, "I said that airport would be operational in February and it will be. But we have to have the poplars as a windbreak."

"Yes, sir. But nobody else can fill the order."

"These goddamned defense contractors," said the general, casting Vandam's in a whole new light. "So they think they've got me by the short hairs. Sweeney, you get on the first plane to Illinois and put the fear of God into those nits. Tell them they'll never get another order from DOD!"

"Yes, sir."

"Tell them I'll go to Japan for those poplars!"

Neither telephone nor airplane extravaganzas occurred to the owners of McQuaid's Nursery in Tarrytown, New York. They had been saying the same thing to each other for hours.

"Jerry's a good boy," Alexander McQuaid repeated.

"I know he is," Jerry's mother said indignantly. "But he's only been back from college for two years. We can't leave this in his lap. It wouldn't be fair to him." She hesitated for a moment, then folded her lips.

The fond father was willing to go further. "And he could put us in the red." Before his wife could explode, he added hastily, "Through no fault of his own."

Appeased, his wife leaned forward to clasp his hand. "Oh, Mac, what a time for this to happen."

"Well, what other time of year could it happen?" Mac asked reasonably.

From early spring right through the holiday season the McQuaids labored unceasingly. But experience had taught them it was the decisions made during the first two weeks of January that spelled the difference between profit and loss. Unlike most readers of the Vandam catalog, they studied it with an eye to its effect, not on themselves, but on their customers. Over the years Vicky McQuaid had developed an uncanny knack for predicting the desires of the yeomen of Westchester. She would look at forty-three different petunias, narrow her eyes, commune with her soul, then point a finger.

"That's the one they'll go for."

And three months later, long after the plants had been raised, she would be rewarded when couple after couple would enter, flapping the catalog and pointing to the same place.

"There! That's the petunia we want."

It was unthinkable that the ordering should be left in Jerry's willing but untried hands.

"I guess we scrub the trip, huh?" Mac asked heavily.

Invariably, after the order had been dispatched, the elder McQuaids took off for the Caribbean.

"I guess so," Vicky agreed sadly.

There was one household where the laments occasioned by the absence of the Vandam catalog had nothing to do with the wares it offered.

"But it was going to have my picture in it," Mrs. Mary Larrabee reminded her husband.

"I know, I know."

"Do you think, if they do another catalog, they'll take my picture out?" she asked anxiously. "I've told so many people about it."

Pete Larrabee had done some boasting himself, but nothing in the world would have made him admit it. "What difference does it make, Mary? You won the contest. You're going to get the award in Chicago. That's the important thing."

"I promised a copy to Mother."

"She's already got plenty of pictures of you."

Mary sniffed. "It's not the same. And I promised one to Susie and Tom."

Pete Larrabee was a genuinely affectionate husband but Mary came from a large, close-knit family to all of whom she had promised copies of the catalog.

"Look, honey. Chicago's only two weeks away, and there's bound to be an army of photographers there."

Mary had a very sound notion of the difference in distribution between the seed catalog and some publicity shots. "After all, the contest has been running for over eight years. They've been looking for the right sweet pea all that time. You'd think they'd want to commemorate the occasion," she said wistfully.

Pete was tempted to ask if a ten-thousand-dollar check didn't represent commemoration, but he was a man who valued domestic harmony.

"You sure would, honey," he said.

But hardest hit by the great catalog dislocation was the Vandam Nursery & Seed Company itself.

The switchboard at Vandam's neo-Colonial headquarters, the showplace of Vandamia, Illinois, was for all practical purposes out of action for the duration. While this communications washout certainly aggravated the situation, it was not without its advantages. Headquarters, to put it bluntly, was in no shape to talk to anyone.

Consumer Relations, for example, was in shock. So was its director, David Vandam Maynard. Not since the days of the founder had it occurred to anybody in the company that marketing could be pursued actively, not passively. D.V. Maynard and his large staff sat in their gracious quarters, surrounded by the finest equipment in the world, trying to assimilate what was happening to them. In their particular firmament, the catalog was divinely ordained. As surely as the earth turned, the catalog went out, orders trickled back in January, then swelled to flood tides in March and April. Throughout this natural progression computers hummed, D.V. bustled in and out, and another Vandam season passed.

But no catalog, no orders. D.V. could have been elbow-deep in radical ways to meet this emergency. He could have been organizing a Vandam first—radio and television spots. Instead, he sat dull-eyed with incredulity. His secretary, who had been with him for years, was so unnerved that she forgot to water the rare potted plants in his window.

All the sprigs, shoots and collaterals of the family flourishing in the extensive compound were equally demoralized.

And, as so often happens when catastrophe strikes, the leadership was out of town.

3 STORM DAMAGE

THE chairman of the board was in Japan, judging chrysanthemums. But Hendrik Vandam II's twinkling smile and homey admonitions, familiar to millions of Vandam's contented customers, were not much missed during these dark days. For as long as most people could remember, Hendrik's contribution to the firm had been strictly photogenic. The man-in-charge was Hendrik's son Richard, and he was not propping up morale on the home front because he was fully occupied in New York, meeting the enemy head-on.

The battle, the site and the ground rules were not of his own choosing.

For this, he had no one but himself to blame. Dick Vandam had made the decision to sell out to Standard Foods; he had forced it through the family; he had hammered out all the details, held out for a whopping price and wangled fat employment contracts for most of the Vandams still active in the company. Since his victory, Vandam honestly believed that he had contrived to improve on perfection. The last three days had opened his eyes.

Hour after hour with the lawyers was an exercise in frustration. Far from following his orders to get that damned injunction lifted, they were treating it as a mere footnote to the underlying patent action.

Now, Standard Foods was rubbing it in.

"Forget your precious catalog, Dick," Sanders advised. "When I saw that bank attachment, I was afraid you were having trouble with the Patent Office. Maybe the examiners didn't think *Numero Uno* was patentable yet. But it turns out that somebody else claims the patent should be awarded to him. And that, I don't have to tell you, is a lot more serious than all the flower catalogs in the world."

Hot words, and plenty of them, trembled on the tip of Vandam's tongue. But for the first time in his life, he was not dealing with a captive audience.

Furthermore, this skirmish was taking place before a neutral observer.

John Thatcher, who had a fair notion of Vandam's feelings, avoided any show of sympathy, or even comprehension. When visitors to his office were at obvious cross-purposes, he liked to stay on the sidelines.

"The Sloan is delighted to cooperate with Midwestern Trust in facilitating the shift so that your foreign payments and receipts aren't prejudiced," he said, recalling them to the ostensible reason for this conference.

But one minor bank account, even if frozen, was not the trouble.

"Although," said Sanders, "this injunction proves that the situation is more serious than Dick seems to realize. If there's the slightest possibility that this patent interference will stick . . ."

"I repeat," said Vandam forcefully, "that patent is as good as in our hands."

Sanders showed no inclination to accept this ringing declaration. With a pained smile he said, "I only wish our lawyers were equally convinced."

He had hit another sore spot.

"I have explained it all to our lawyers," Vandam growled. "And, at your request, I have repeated it to SF's lawyers. Frankly, I think the whole bunch of them are part of the problem, not part of the solution. And that judge must have been crazy! To think, the Vandam catalog held up, God knows how many hours and dollars wasted! Simply because some god-damned kook—"

"You keep calling him that!" Earl Sanders could not help saying.

Stung, Vandam forgot himself. "Well, how was I to know?"

Thatcher sighed. Had he been less experienced, he might have wished he had never heard of *Numero Uno*. But where others regaled themselves with lush seed catalogs, Thatcher's reading included lines of credit, commitment letters and balance sheets. Like Standard Foods, the Sloan had a bundle riding on Vandam's *Numero Uno*. That tomato had as valid a claim on Thatcher's attention as Chrysler Corporation.

So following its fortunes was compulsory. The awkwardness was introduced by the organization chart. Working with Standard Foods would have raised no difficulties, but Standard Foods had to work through Vandam's. Worse still, SF and the Sloan had to assume that Vandam's knew what it was doing.

Dick Vandam did not make this easy.

Puffing out rosy cheeks, he spoke as one peer to another. "I still maintain that someone"—he looked darkly at Sanders—"is making a mountain out of a molehill."

At issue, Thatcher knew, was more than the vaunted *Numero Uno*. A subsidiary does not necessarily inform its parent company of every nuisance suit—or shakedown artist—to come its way. *Wisconsin Seedsmen, Inc. v. Vandam Nursery & Seed Company* fell into one of these two categories, or so Dick Vandam had chosen to believe until far too late.

But the injunction that was playing havoc with the catalog had escalated matters out of Vandam hands. What the lawyers had already unearthed was not what anybody in Thatcher's office wanted to hear.

On paper, Wisconsin Seedsmen, Inc., could have been

designed for the sole purpose of preying on Vandam's. In business for only five or six years (the Vandam centennial catalog had been mailed a decade ago), Wisconsin Seedsmen sold modest amounts of seed and supplies on a strictly local basis. They also, or so they claimed, pursued advanced research.

Moreover, as if to confirm the collective Vandam suspicion, Wisconsin Seedsmen was undeniably small. What kind of legitimacy could a two-man operation have? Dick Vandam still felt this way.

"All right, they're not a couple of guys named Joe," he snapped. "That still doesn't mean they're not cheap, two-bit crooks who think they're going to cut themselves in."

As *The New York Times*, the *Washington Post* and the *Farm Bureau Monthly* had discovered, Wisconsin Seedsmen's two principals came equipped with disturbing respectability. Edward L. (Ned) Ackerman had put in twenty years at the Department of Agriculture, retired, then gone back home to Wisconsin to start this second career.

Vandam had no trouble pegging *him*. The real threat came, as everybody kept insisting, with the other one.

The other one was Scott Wenzel. He had a Ph.D. in plant genetics and had published regularly in scholarly journals. It particularly galled Dick Vandam that, while the newspapers described him and his relatives as prominent businessmen, Scott Wenzel emerged as a brilliant young scientist.

"It isn't just that Wenzel himself sounds pretty high-powered," said Sanders, studying Vandam intently. "It's the lawyer he's got—"

Paul Jackson, Thatcher knew, was about as high-powered as you could get.

"—who seems to believe that Wenzel really did develop a tomato. What's got our legal department worried, Dick, is the tons of evidence Wenzel is submitting—lab notes, test records, the whole bag."

"Impossible," Vandam snorted, more magisterially than before.

To his indignation, he found his audience regarding him with open speculation.

"Look here," he argued, "do you have any idea of the research effort that went into *Numero Uno?* The laboratory work was monumental, then there were field tests, which means hand pollinating, tabulating results, and studying whole generations of seedlings. This has been a major project, and a very costly one. There is no way Wenzel could have replicated what Vandam's has done. Either he has falsified the whole thing or else . . ."

Too late, he broke off.

"Or else?" Sanders pounced. "Tell me, what kind of security does Vandam's enforce?"

Before Vandam could get on his high horse again, Thatcher intervened to soften the charge. "Yes, I wish you would explain the process to us. Presumably you cannot keep an undertaking like this secret?"

"No indeed," Vandam told him. "When you've got acres filled with ripe red tomatoes and there's still snow on the ground, people all over the county notice."

"Then what's to keep a competitor from stealing some of your plants, starting a crash program of his own tests, and beating you to the finish line?"

Thatcher's inquiry soothed Vandam's ruffled feathers. He expanded visibly as he brandished expertise: "Time," he said tersely. "You can't rush nature when you're in the field. Any thief would be at least a season behind us, even if he could finance the kind of effort required to propagate these plants. Very few of them can, and certainly not this Wisconsin Seedsmen!"

Sanders saw another possibility. "Okay," he conceded. "But what about somebody getting an early pipeline into the Vandam labs—so he could track you every step of the way?"

"I suppose it's just barely possible," said Vandam unwillingly. "Almost any project involves dead ends. There were some with *Numero Uno*. Nothing out of the ordinary, mind you, but enough so that someone with access to our records could have avoided our errors and caught up with us."

"Christ!" said Sanders savagely. "That brings us right back to your security."

"Vandam's maintains the strictest possible security," Vandam said stiffly. "As do all our subcontractors—"

"What?" said Thatcher, fastening on the word.

"The people who do research for us on a contract basis," Vandam explained, as if a vice-president of the Sloan Guaranty Trust might not be familiar with the concept. Then, still defending the Vandam way of doing things, he said, "As it happens, *Numero Uno* was not developed in-house. Of course, we reviewed the basic research and did all the field testing ourselves, but we had commissioned an independent geneticist—"

"Independent? This is the first I've heard of any independent geneticist," Earl Sanders sputtered. "Have you mentioned this to the lawyers?"

He was wasting his sarcasm.

"Of course," said Vandam, rising. "And that's what they want to explore in greater depth. I'm running late as it is, so I think I'd better be going. Unless we get relief from that injunction, we may be heading for serious difficulties. I'll keep you informed, Sanders."

Sanders did not let him escape unscathed. "Do that!" he shot back.

Vandam treated this like any closing civility, removing himself from Thatcher's office with bland aplomb.

"Well," Sanders demanded the minute the door closed, "what do you think?"

Thatcher understood that Sanders wanted odds, not character analysis.

"I don't have enough information to make an educated guess," he said, keeping to himself reflections about Paul Jackson and the successful clients he represented.

"I suppose not," said Sanders, who liked to talk, not listen. "But if Dick Vandam thinks he can get away without leveling, he's got another think coming. How did you like that wild pitch he casually tossed? All of a sudden, we're talking about subcontractors and independent geneticists."

In the interests of fairness, Thatcher pointed out that Vandam had, by his own testimony, seen fit to mention this to his lawyers.

"To hell with the lawyers," said Sanders recklessly. "He should have informed Standard Foods. Does he think we're going to play games with him—about *Numero Uno?* Like hell we are! I'm contacting this independent right away. . . ."

"Which is no doubt why Vandam was careful not to give you his name or address," Thatcher said gently.

Sanders was thunderstruck.

Dick Vandam, meanwhile, was battling against an icy wind, heading two blocks south of the Sloan. He was more troubled in mind than he had been in years. There were too many balls in the air and he was assailed by a premonition that, just this once, he might not be able to juggle them.

He plowed ahead, lost in unpalatable thoughts. Even so, Vandam was every inch an important man with important things to do. With his slicked-back hair, starched collar and conservative tailoring, he could have been a portly model for the Midwestern mogul. So, when he finally reached the elevator that would lead him to more lawyers, he took scant notice of his fellow passengers. The modishly casual young man in a stadium coat sported the latest look in curling black hair. The young woman at his side was attired with more propriety but Vandam could tell she was only a secretary.

He was taken aback when the young man suddenly said, "Talk about a small world! You're Vandam, aren't you? Richard Vandam?"

In Vandamia, Dick Vandam was a great man. Everybody in town might not work for him, but they all knew who he was and, frequently, pointed him out to the tourists visiting the Test Farms or the Gardens. So he saw nothing unusual in the question.

"Yes, I am," he said with a brief smile and a courteous nod. While he did not want to encourage conversation, he knew what was required of a public figure.

"I'm Scott Wenzel," said the stranger. "You can call me Dr. Wenzel."

"Oh, Scotty," the girl murmured.

"And this," Wenzel continued with high good humor, "this is my associate, Mrs. Gunn."

Embarrassed, she tried to disappear into the corner of the elevator. Since this was impossible, she smiled apologetically at Vandam.

"I'm going up to see my lawyer," said Wenzel conversationally. "Maybe you've heard of him, Paul Jackson? We could have got somebody who cost less, but I said nothing but the best was good enough when you're taking on Vandam's. Didn't I, Barbara?"

By now, she was past response, so Wenzel continued his performance solo. "Jackson wants to go over all our lab notes and affidavits and provide summaries that everybody can understand. It sounds like a waste of time to me—but then, he says, there's got to be no question about any of the steps I took while I was developing the VR–117."

Vandam was still astonished at the encounter.

"You're the one who's claiming that Vandam's did not

produce the *Numero Uno,*" he said, as if there could be any doubt.

Wenzel dropped his affectations. "That's me," he said arrogantly, "and I'm the one who's done the developing. You can forget about this *Numero Uno* of yours. There ain't no such animal, friend. Vandam's isn't calling the shots on this one—no matter what you had in mind."

Dick Vandam recognized personal hostility when he heard it. Therefore, with a restraint that might have surprised some of his relatives and acquaintances, he asked, "Have we ever met before?"

"No," said Wenzel, flushing slightly. Then, with studied indifference, he amplified. "No, I tried to get Vandam's to fund my research but the big brains in your R&D offered me a job instead. Washing lab equipment, or something like that. I never got as far as the president's office."

"This is the first I've heard of it," said Vandam.

"Yeah," Wenzel drawled.

For once, Vandam ignored the manners and style, both of which he detested. Instead he concentrated on the germ of an idea. If Wenzel was nursing a grudge, or settling an old score, maybe the lawyers were on the wrong track. Maybe the whole thing could be resolved here and now, just the two of them in an elevator in a downtown Manhattan building.

Clearing his throat, he said, "Of course, it's always hard when you scientists have to scratch around for research funds. Perhaps Vandam's could make some contribution—"

"WHO . . . THE . . . HELL . . . DO . . . YOU . . . THINK . . . YOU . . . ARE?"

Wenzel's intensity was as violent as a slap in the face. Vandam froze, not noticing the elevator doors had opened.

"Scotty!" the girl pleaded, clasping Wenzel's arm and tugging. "We've got a plane to Madison to catch. Let's dump this stuff in Mr. Jackson's office."

Wenzel was more interested in Dick Vandam than in planes or anything else. He stepped out of the elevator, but then he halted, waiting for his antagonist to join him.

"Vandam's," he said, ignoring the traffic around them, "is about to get the lesson of its life."

Then, with a cavalier salute, he swaggered off.

"Excuse *me*," said an enraged secretary, straggling in late from a coffee break.

Somehow Vandam removed himself from her path. Almost dazed, he moved down the hall, not knowing if he was even on the right floor. If he had been troubled before, now he was truly appalled.

Scott Wenzel was out for blood.

4 IN FULL SUNSHINE

DITCHDIGGERS enjoy less prestige, and less take-home pay, than brain surgeons. Asking why, economists have come up with more explanations than you can shake a stick at. All of them are wrong. The differential exists because mankind esteems what it does not understand. As history proves, incomprehension always informs the prevailing standard of value. Keepers of the people's secrets—Zulu indunas, kings imbued with Divine Right, Mahdis who saw what others did not—were yesterday's top dogs. Today we have scientists.

So long as they are the only ones who see precisely why E equals mc², scientists have us where they want us.

But contrary to widespread superstition, they are not all Albert Einsteins. They are actually a representative cross section of the general population, with the important reservation that whatever they are doing is totally baffling to the rest of us.

Until of course, it cures us, blows us up, or lands us on the moon.

In short, these modern mandarins come in many shapes and forms. Howard Pendleton, for example, was a towering figure in the world of plant genetics. His first, path-breaking paper on the hybridization of winter wheat, written back when he was a brand-new Ph.D., had stirred Moscow and Peking, as well as Fargo and Washington. Since then his contributions had been legion: a brilliant stint in the Luther

Burbank Chair at the University of Wisconsin, important findings in high-yield soybeans and mosaic-resistant tobacco, experiments and papers in an unending flow.

But, although he was an authentic hero of the Green Revolution, Pendleton bore no resemblance to a mad genius. He did not even look like an absent-minded professor. Tall, rangy, with humorous eyes and hair that had once been fiery red, he looked like a man who knew how to get things done.

This impression was accurate. Pendleton did not pursue his researches in a backyard laboratory, but in the large well-equipped Institute of Plant Research in Aleman, Puerto Rico. IPR had three separate buildings, five acres of test gardens, an electron microscope, and a staff of twenty-six professionals. It was one of the largest independent plant research facilities in the Western world and, by any standard, a very considerable enterprise. Pendleton, who had founded it, presided over this empire with efficiency and success.

In return, IPR made him dean of an increasingly common breed, the scientist-entrepreneur. Devising new life forms for profit has only recently made the headlines, but Pendleton had been doing it for decades. Since new strains of petunias, spring onions, and sorghum are less ominous than recombinant DNA, the media had barely noticed.

Plenty of other people had, including the United States Department of Agriculture, the Food and Agriculture Organization of the UN, and Burpee's, Parke's, Kelly's—and Vandam's. IPR not only developed new fruit and vegetable strains on its own initiative, it did research for others at cost plus a handsome fee. In the beginning, Pendleton's reputation and the caliber of work he demanded from IPR had made the difference between profit and loss. Now, with established patent rights, Pendleton was, to his mild surprise, growing rich. Since his personal tastes were modest, the practical consequences of this windfall could be seen in

IPR equipment. Always excellent, in recent years it had become superb.

Most people, including his wife, would have sworn that nothing could shake Howard Pendleton's self-possession.

"Are you there?" the phone barked.

"Yes, of course I'm here," Pendleton drawled, trying to curb his impatience. "You're not making much sense to me, Dick. You say something's cropped up about *Numero Uno*—"

"I did not say something's cropped up," said Vandam sharply. "I said we've got a helluva mess brewing."

"What exactly does that mean?" Pendleton said uncompromisingly.

Dick Vandam forced himself to slow down. He found Pendleton as trying as Pendleton found him. Still, much had to be forgiven the man who had single-handedly developed *Numero Uno*. Modulating into a more conciliatory tone, he said, "Look here, Howard, you didn't have any trouble with *Numero Uno*, did you?"

"Why don't you tell me what you called for?" Pendleton ordered. "I don't know what you're talking about. Trouble? You've got complete copies of all my findings, my lab notes—everything."

With the best will in the world, he could not help sounding possessive. Vandam's might own rights to *Numero Uno*, they might go on to market it. But it was still Howard Pendleton's baby, the fitting crown to a distinguished career.

Vandam, who should have welcomed that proprietary note, bristled. "All right, I'll tell you. Someone's contesting our patent application. He says that *he's* developed a biennial tomato."

After a long pause, Pendleton said, "Say that again."

With perverse relish, Vandam repeated himself.

"Nonsense!" Pendleton snapped.

"Of course, of course," said Vandam hurriedly. "That's

what I've told . . . but Howard, I think it would be wise for you to come up. We all know how vital . . ."

It took ten minutes for Pendleton to extract a coherent account from Vandam. Once he did, his patience was exhausted. "All right, I'll call back this evening," he said, unceremoniously downing the receiver midway through one of Vandam's sentences.

For a few moments he sat tapping a pencil against his teeth, oblivious to his surroundings. The office he occupied when he was wearing his manager's hat was as lifelessly correct as an interior decorator could make it. But despite the executive carpets and paneling, it was not completely removed from the real work of IPR. The door behind Pendleton did not lead to a sumptuous bathroom, but to the data center where the punch of a button could summon reams of IPR results, abstracts from all over the world or simply lightning-swift computations. His windows looked out on one of the test plots where just now a sweating crew was measuring the seedlings set out in arrow-straight rows.

Pendleton, deep in his thoughts, saw none of this. He sat reviewing what Dick Vandam had said, and not said. Then, when he had come to certain conclusions of his own, he set forth in search of his wife.

He relied on her more than he realized. When they had first married, Fran was a graduate student and he already a professor; the twenty years that yawned between them shaped the marriage. But Fran had become a mother and a grandmother and, somewhere along the line, those twenty years had evaporated. Now the roles were reversed. Fran provided the ballast in their partnership.

When he went seeking her, he headed for a greenhouse, not a kitchen.

"Fran!" he bawled into the humid emptiness, over the benches containing thousands of rose plants, in all stages of development. The only reply was silence, broken by the rhythmic gurgle of the automatic watering apparatus that fed droplets of water into the tubes snaking down the center gutter. "Fran!"

"Wait a minute!"

"Where are you?" he demanded.

"I'm fixing this damn filter again," said the unseen voice. "If I've told Ramon once, I've told him a zillion times to keep the switch off when we're running the humidifiers. He's jammed it again, and he's going to keep on jamming it."

To this accompaniment, Fran backed out from under a table halfway down the greenhouse. Since she was nearly bursting out of disreputable jeans, this was not a posture that showed her to advantage. Neither did the greasy hands she rubbed on her shirt as she rose.

"I'm going to kill Ramon," she said, ruffling her short, wiry hair.

"You could always fire him," said Howard gravely.

"Oh, well," she shrugged. Some of the grease from her hands and jeans now adorned her forehead.

"Did you get it fixed?" he asked with real interest.

"I certainly hope so," she said. "Otherwise, I could lose every last one of those Chinese crosses."

Fran Pendleton was a well-known geneticist in her own right, a world authority on roses, and an extremely capable woman. As everyone at IPR knew, she could no more fire Ramon than she could fly.

"Fran," he said, "I've got to talk to you."

Communication between them was so good that he did not have to add that her greenhouse would not do. Fran's research assistants, the maintenance men, even the wretched Ramon, could wander in at any moment.

Involuntarily, she cast a look of regret at her Chinese crossbreds. Floribunda roses were dear to Fran's heart. Howard, of course, came first—but only by a hair.

42

"Wait until I wash my hands," she said from the sink.

The concession was to hygiene, not vanity. Almost despite herself, Fran was still an attractive woman. Her gold hair was streaked with grey, and blight-resistant floribunda engrossed her more than manicures or weight watching. But she was happy and contented, which beats all the blue eye shadow in the world.

"They haven't changed the program again, have they?" she said following him into his office, possibly the only place where privacy could be guaranteed. At IPR, the atmosphere was informal. Horticulturists chatted in greenhouses, chemists brewed coffee in the labs, entomologists flitted in and out like moths. Howard's office was not out of bounds, but it was usually empty.

"What program?" he asked, at a loss.

"What pro . . . Howard, what on earth is the matter?" she cried. The annual meeting of the American Society of Plant Sciences, due to open in Chicago in a week, was an important fixture on the Pendleton calendar.

"I think," he said, regarding her steadily, "there is some sort of controversy shaping about *Numero Uno.*"

"Oh, is that all?" she exclaimed, relieved that he was not breaking really bad news, like death, accident, illness. There was a fractional click between them, compounded of his disappointment and her awareness of it. Hastening to make amends, she said, "What kind of controversy can there possibly be?"

In theory, Fran knew all about Howard's epochal experimentation to perfect a biennial tomato and shared his pride in the triumphant results. Actually, as they both recognized, she was as single-minded as he. While he had concentrated on tomatoes, Fran had been knee-deep in roses. And since roses, particularly her improved strains, made their own handsome contributions to IPR's coffers, Howard could scarcely resent the rivalry. To his credit, even on a purely personal level, this had never occurred to him. When it came to work, he and Fran went their separate ways.

"The controversy, Fran," he said with a hint of his old classroom manner, "comes in the form of a lawsuit against Vandam's."

Fran left the business side to her husband but Vandam's had funded too much IPR work for her to overlook their importance. Even so, it took her a moment to make the connection. "I thought you said this was about *Numero Uno,*" she started before braking to a halt. "Oh, Howard, you don't mean somebody's disputing the patent award?"

"I mean just that. And you'll never guess who it is."

Fran was already running down the list of notable research competitors. "I never heard a whisper about any of the big outfits trying for a biennial tomato," she decided with wrinkled brow. "It isn't those Germans, is it? The ones who did the squash?"

"It isn't a big outfit," said Howard, putting an end to the suspense. "It's Wisconsin Seed."

"Scotty?" she cried. "You mean Scotty's been working on the tomato, too?"

Howard Pendleton's mouth tightened. "So he claims."

Scott Wenzel had worked at IPR for two years before going off to set up a laboratory of his own. He had been a familiar figure to both of them during that period and a casual acquaintance ever since. Fran's whole face was contorted with concentration as she agonized over some arithmetic calculations. Finally she heaved a sigh of relief.

"Well, that's all right. I've just figured it out. Scott was gone from here before you ever began on *Numero Uno*. So there's no question of hanky-panky," she announced. "Not that Scotty would ever do anything like that."

"I was not implying anything of the sort," Howard said stiffly.

Fran shook her head at him. "If that wasn't it, what were you implying?"

"I don't know," he confessed. "This business about a lawsuit has rattled me. But there's another thing about that call that got to me. Apparently Vandam's has been sitting on this for weeks without breathing a word to me. And when they do get around to telling me, suddenly it's Dick I'm talking to instead of the head of Research and Development. Why didn't Jason Ingersoll get hold of me as soon as they knew?"

"Maybe they didn't think it was worth bothering you with," Fran suggested.

Pendleton smiled bleakly. "That's what Vandam claimed. A nuisance suit, that's what they thought. But Fran, that doesn't ring true—not one bit. In the first place, *Numero Uno* is probably the most important product Vandam's has ever handled, commercially speaking. And I happen to know it was crucial in their merger with Standard Foods. Talking about nuisance suits is utter nonsense. Which leaves the question, why put off calling me until the last possible minute? It's as if they were hoping I wouldn't find out."

His last suggestion was so outlandish Fran dismissed it with a wave of her hand. "Vandam's didn't want to remind the world that you developed *Numero Uno* and they didn't," she said with down-to-earth shrewdness. "Depend on it, that's the explanation."

"Leaving us to take the cash and let the credit go?" he said with a rueful smile. "Not even Dick Vandam is such a fool as to think he can do that. Every geneticist in the world would notice that little footnote in the catalog."

But she was thinking of something else. "It's funny when you come to think of it, that we never realized Scott was working on a biennial tomato, too. We've seen him lots of times since he left here and he never mentioned it."

Pendleton chuckled. "Be fair, Fran. I'll bet I never mentioned to him that *I* was working on it. None of us takes possible competitors into our confidence. I've noticed you can be pretty closemouthed when you're around other rose developers."

Fran had the grace to blush. "I suppose that's so. Well, anyway, it shows what an idiot Dick Vandam is, trying to handle this on his own. You and Scotty can clear this up in five minutes after you've seen each other's lab books. It's clear enough what happened. You and Scotty started to work on the same thing and you got there first. It'll be interesting to see how far he reached and if he followed the same line you did. I always said he was a bright boy."

"You think it's going to be that cut and dried?" he asked, looking at her quizzically. "Somehow I can't believe Vandam would be in such a flap if it were that simple."

Fran's eyes widened. "For heaven's sake, Howard, you're not seriously worried about a dead heat or anything, are you? Even if Scott started working the same day you did, he doesn't have anything like IPR's resources. Barbara told me she had to fight for an electric typewriter. He has to be at least two or three seasons behind you."

"If he's that far from a patent application himself, what in the world makes him think he can block me? That's what I don't understand."

At IPR research assistants came and went in a steady flow. Howard knew their qualifications inside out when they came, and their professional competence when they left. It was Fran, even in the midst of her roses, who managed to catch the human flavor, the personality quirks.

"He isn't trying to block you," she announced with sudden decision. "He's trying to block Vandam's. Scotty's hated them since the day they turned down his independent research project. You remember the way he used to carry on about the corporate establishment and the power it had to decide which projects would go forward. To hear him, you'd think Vandam's was manufacturing napalm. He'd go wild if he spent four or five years on research and then Vandam's scooped the pot. He's probably ready to claim they've burglarized his safe or bribed his field hands."

Howard was nodding appreciatively. "That hadn't occurred to me. Of course he doesn't know yet that I did the development."

"And as soon as he finds out, he'll calm down," Fran predicted. "Naturally it will be a disappointment, but he'll just have to swallow it."

It would be a bitter pill, she admitted to herself, particularly for a young man like Scotty. Just as sure of himself as Howard, and determined to make it on his own. Smart, difficult, cocky, ambitious . . .

Suddenly she remembered another research assistant with some of these same traits.

"Eric!" she exclaimed.

Pendleton had been writing a list of things to say to Dick Vandam. Looking up, he said, "Eric Most? What about him?"

"Oh, Howard, he'll explode when he hears," she said with maternal exasperation. "You'd better break this to him as gently as you can. And if you have to go up to Vandamia to straighten things out, you'd better take him along with you."

He considered this. Then, thoughtfully, he replied, "You know, Fran, that might not be a bad idea."

Eric Most was Pendleton's current research assistant. This enviable position had been a springboard for many of his predecessors, there being no better qualification in plant genetics than an internship at IPR. But it was not enough for Most. He persisted in regarding himself as Pendleton's colleague.

". . . so I said to Howard that I thought it was worth a

try. The second generation of the Siberians was what really did it . . ."

"Uh-huh," said the biometrician. "Look, Eric, I promised Steve these photographs this afternoon."

Obligingly he slid down the counter, leaving her camera accessible. He did not leave.

The biometrician, a pretty brunette as well as a highly skilled technician, sighed. Eric's deep resonant baritone should have tipped her off. He might look like a golden-haired All-American but, as one interminable evening with him in Old San Juan had proved, Eric was a dried-up stick before his time.

". . . my name on the paper, together with Howard's," said Most, trying to sound blasé. "You know, Alice, I never expected to be a celebrity at the meetings."

"Uh-huh," she said again. The paper, it went without saying, was on *Numero Uno*. No one at IPR doubted the achievement. Opinion about Eric Most's contribution was considerably less unanimous.

"As I was telling Howard this morning—"

Fortunately for Alice's temper and Steve's pictures, the house phone buzzed.

"Yes? . . . Oh yes, Dr. Pendleton. . . . Yes, he's here. . . . I'll tell him right away."

Downing the phone, she turned to Eric Most. "It's Howard," she said with honeyed mockery. "He wants to see you right now, Eric."

"Thanks," he said casually.

But, as she did not fail to note, the eyes gave him away. That outstandingly promising young geneticist, Dr. Eric Most, was scared to death.

Farther north, another touchy interview was already taking place.

"What did Pendleton have to say about this guy Wenzel?" Jason Vandam Ingersoll demanded.

Looking him straight in the eye, Dick Vandam said, "Nothing."

Ingersoll could not keep from frowning. But, swallowing hard, he said, "That just proves I was right. You should have let me talk to Pendleton. He's used to me and, after all, I was the one who first saw possibilities in *Numero Uno*. Besides, R&D has been dealing with Pendleton all along—"

His argument was brushed aside.

"The circumstances have changed," said Vandam weightily.

With any other subordinate, this would have been enough. But, as they both knew, Jason was not any other subordinate. Like his uncle Richard, he was a Vandam heir as well as a working executive.

"Exactly what circumstances do you mean, Dick?" he persisted. "Standard Foods or the lawsuit? Either way, we've got to defend *Numero Uno* with everything we've got. I've said so all along."

Jason Ingersoll saw himself as the new wave at Vandam's. It was not a view calculated to make him a universal favorite.

"We agreed not to bring Pendleton into the picture unless we had to," Vandam reminded him. "Now it's necessary and we'll have to play it by ear."

"If it's not already too late," said Ingersoll, accepting the dismissal and rising to leave. Ignoring it would disrupt the pretense of harmonious working relations that both men maintained. "Meanwhile I'd better get back and see what D.V.'s doing—if anything."

"Yes," said Vandam absently.

Jason closed the door with extreme care. But he gave no

sign of internal churning until he reached his own office down the hall. There, his self-control got one test too many.

"What the hell are you doing here?" he exploded to an unexpected visitor.

Milton Vandam was a relic of the bad old days. His fussy devotion to Vandam's was equaled only by his incompetence. Cousin Milton had been a thorn in everybody's side for decades. Only the Standard Foods merger, and a good deal of dissension, had eased him into early retirement.

Unfortunately, before SF stepped in, Jason and Milton had been called upon to work together. Even more unfortunately, the bone over which they had snarled and bickered was Research and Development—in other words, *Numero Uno*.

"During a crisis of these proportions," Milton said sanctimoniously, "it is my plain and simple duty to be here, with whatever aid, support and experience I can offer."

Jason glared. "Look, Milton, we're all busy."

"I should hope so. Do you realize that this is the first time since grandfather died that the Vandam catalog has been delayed?"

Jason willed himself to silence.

Milton was not that easily deflected. "Is Dick back from New York?" he inquired.

"He got in an hour ago."

"How did things go?"

Since Ingersoll did not really know, this exacerbated his already simmering irritation. Milton, who was shrewder than his detractors admitted, recognized this and exploited it.

"Sometimes Dick's self-confidence can be a liability. He should keep the rest of us fully informed—family as well as company. After all, we do have a stake in what happens, don't we?"

These sentiments were too close to Jason's for comfort.

"How does Dick see things?" Milton continued smoothly.

Before he could stop himself, Jason said, "He's got every confidence—"

"Yes indeed," said Milton, scoring the point before moving ahead. "Of course, there can be no merit to the claim that anybody but Vandam's developed and owns *Numero Uno*."

Remembered grievances swept over Jason. "Vandam's owns it, but we didn't develop it. We funded Howard Pendleton, remember?"

"It amounts to the same thing," said Milton, a past master at glossing over. "But since you raise the matter, what does Pendleton feel about this suit?"

He had put a pudgy finger on another sensitive area.

"He's coming up to discuss it," said Ingersoll. Then, goaded, he continued, "Dick just got off the phone to Puerto Rico. Pendleton says that the other side doesn't have a leg to stand on."

Once again, he had underestimated Cousin Milton.

"Dick himself called?" he mused aloud. "Well then, we don't really know, do we?"

"What are you talking about?"

"Why, whether that's what Pendleton thinks, or what Dick wants him to think."

5   POOR MAN'S
MULCH

WISCONSIN Seedsmen, Inc., outside of Madison, Wisconsin, was miles apart from the Institute of Plant Research in more ways than one. From the greenhouse to the front office, where the entire staff was currently assembled, the whole operation was makeshift, and looked it.

Despite these shortcomings the celebration, fueled by New York State champagne in Styrofoam cups, was going strong. Even Ned Ackerman was letting himself feel euphoric.

"What did Vandam say then?" he demanded, enjoying the answer before he heard it.

"I didn't wait to see," said Scott Wenzel with a grin of such pawky mischief that Ackerman laughed aloud. "But I'll tell you one thing, Ned—he's beginning to realize what he's in for. He looked sick, didn't he, Barb?"

The partners of Wisconsin Seedsmen were united in many things, but not all. Wenzel, assisted by the crew of high school kids now congregated in the corner, took care of the technical side. Ackerman shouldered the burden of keeping them all afloat. For years he had raised money they could not afford to lose, borrowed when necessary, and stretched payments to the limit in order to finance Wenzel's research. Now, with a payoff in sight, even warm champagne did not blur his levelheaded realism.

"It was the injunction against the catalog that got through their thick hides, Scotty," he observed.

Scott Wenzel had unbounded confidence in his own powers. But since linking up with Ackerman he had begun to appreciate other, less exotic, talents. Sketching a toast to the older man, he said, "That, I'll hand you, Ned. You called it absolutely right."

At any other time, this handsome concession would have tickled Ackerman, representing as it did a new plateau in the maturation of Scott Wenzel. Working with a young genius had not been the least of Ackerman's difficulties.

"Me," Ackerman said wryly, "and Paul Jackson."

Expensive Wall Street lawyers made a dent in Wisconsin Seedsmen's budget. Although Ackerman was convinced that the risk was worth taking, the outlay made him wince. "But we've got Vandam's just where we want them, and Standard Foods, too. Listen, Scotty, you didn't give Vandam any hint—?"

"Hint?" Barbara Gunn broke in indignantly. "Scotty went after him like a wild man. You know him, Ned. When would Scotty hint?"

Her intervention forestalled any more serious conversation between the two men.

"I nearly died of mortification in that elevator," she said, trying to make a joke of it.

Her performance was good enough for Wenzel. "Oh, come on, Barb," he said indulgently. "You have to admit he had it coming. After all, I may have lousy manners—"

"*May?*" she said ironically.

Ignoring her, he swept on. "—but Richard Vandam and all his relatives are a bunch of goddamn thieves."

"He's right, you know," Ackerman told her more gently.

Ned was always unsure of the two others. When Wenzel turned up five years earlier with his business proposition, Wisconsin Seedsmen had taken an unexpected and, to Ackerman, exciting leap into the big time. Mrs. Gunn had arrived two months later—an appealing little thing with soft brown hair and a trusting mouth. She had, Ackerman was told, worked at IPR for Scotty and, without consulting anybody, Wenzel had hired her again. At the time, Ackerman thought he understood why a widow with a small baby had made the long trip from Puerto Rico. But the woman who had moved into Scotty's apartment was named Hilary, not Barbara.

A sudden uproar from the corner claimed his attention.

"Who gave you kids champagne?" he demanded with jovial ferocity. "You're all underage. Besides, we're not paying you to hang around here boozing. Beat it!"

Dutifully the part-time help began filing back to the greenhouse, halting only for an earnest declaration from their leader.

"We want to say congratulations, Dr. Wenzel," he said, quavering from bass to tenor. "All the way!"

Then, overcome by embarrassment, he fled.

"Next stop—the Nobel Prize," said Wenzel flippantly. "I suppose I'd better get back to work, too. Barb, will you type up those notes I gave you? Ned, Jackson gave me a list as long as your arm for the stuff he wants."

Wisconsin Seedsmen's long-distance charges were ballooning, too. "I talked to Jackson this morning," Ackerman said. "Don't worry, I've got everything pretty much under control."

"Fine," said Wenzel, trudging off to the greenhouse.

Shaking her head, Barbara looked after him. "And he'll be there until midnight," she said, going over to her own desk. "I understood why he was working day and night until he finished VR–117. But what's he doing now?"

Wenzel wasn't the only one who wore blinkers, Ackerman reflected. Barbara Gunn typed the lab notes and listened in on most of their conferences. But all the time she was thinking her own private thoughts, and they did not revolve around plant genetics. Whether they centered on Scott was an open question.

"I expect he's studying catalogs of equipment," said Ackerman. "Once we start marketing VR–117, you won't recognize this place. Scotty's tired of making do with chicken wire and high school kids. And I don't blame the guy. He deserves better facilities to work with."

"Just my luck," she said. "You'll get a decent bathroom in this dump the day after I leave."

To his relief, she did not sound sentimental. Because, if Scott Wenzel had big plans, Barbara Gunn had small ones. Next fall, when her daughter, Tracy, was old enough to go to school, Barbara was going back to college herself.

Ackerman sometimes wondered if the fact that Scott's Hilary was a lawyer had influenced this decision.

"I don't know how we'll get along without you," he said with more kindness than accuracy. Part of the upgrading at Wisconsin Seedsmen was going to involve office staff.

"Maybe I'll get a Ph.D. . . . and come back."

She busied herself with her typewriter for a moment. Then, in a burst of confidentiality, she said, "You know, you really should have come to New York, too."

"Two fares was enough," he grunted.

"It really was an eye-opener," she said. "Until we were sitting in Mr. Jackson's office—well, I guess I never really took VR–117 seriously enough."

"Yup," he said, "hard as it is to believe, VR–117 is going to be every bit as important as Scotty said all along."

Usually she was easily diverted by this sort of avuncular badinage. But not today.

"Ned, what's going to happen now?" she asked.

Perhaps because of the champagne, he slipped back into the private thoughts that he too had. "Now we start throwing everything but the kitchen sink at Vandam's. They're going to be so busy ducking, they won't have time to think about anything else. And by the time they do manage to lift their heads, we'll have whipped Vandam's—and we'll have whipped them good."

Barbara was dismayed. "But Scott didn't say anything about all this. He acted as if getting that injunction was what mattered."

Still in a half-reverie, Ackerman spoke in little more than a whisper. "Scott doesn't know all the details yet."

"Well, don't you think it's time he found out?"

With a jerk he returned to the world around him. "He doesn't have to," he said cheerfully. "That's the beauty of it. Scott does his part of the job and I do mine."

For a moment Barbara stared at her keyboard in dissatisfaction.

"I don't know what's gotten into both of you," she complained. "It's bad enough when Scotty starts ranting and raving, but at least it usually doesn't last very long. Now you've caught the bug, and, if you ask me, you're deliberately keeping him stirred up with all your talk about hitting them where they hurt and getting them where you want them. Why don't you leave Scotty alone so that he'll calm down and go back to work? That's what he'd do if he had half a chance."

At Wisconsin Seedsmen the three very different personalities sharing the office tended to mesh neatly rather than to rasp against each other. Ned Ackerman wanted to keep it that way.

"Look, Barbie," he said kindly, "this isn't your ordinary disagreement. Somebody's trying to steal our results."

"What makes you so sure they're stealing?" she persisted. "Every time there's a new discovery, it turns out that people on different sides of the globe were working on the same project. It happens all the time."

Ned sighed. So long as Barbara did her work conscientiously, it was her business if she drifted around the office without knowing what was going on. But that certainly gave her no right to question his judgment calls.

"Yes, it can happen that way," he said, making a final effort. "But not with exactly the same tests on exactly the same timetable."

Barbara liked to think the best of everyone. Her frown told Ackerman how distasteful she found his black-and-white analysis. For once, however, she was trying to understand the issues involved.

"But if everything is identical, then nobody can tell who really invented the VR–117 and you'll have to compromise somehow, won't you?" she asked at last.

"Now don't you worry about that," Ackerman said hearteningly. "Scott isn't sitting still for highway robbery, and neither am I. We'll get our rights."

Barbara Gunn had little taste for slug fests and none at all for uneven odds. "Vandam's is awfully big, isn't it? I've known about them all my life."

"In some ways that makes them more vulnerable. They couldn't keep the catalog injunction from becoming big news. And as soon as they get over that shock, we'll hit them with something else. That's why we'll be taking your deposition next week."

"My deposition! What does it have to do with me?" Barbara squawked, horrified.

Ackerman leaned down to pat her shoulder. "Whoa, there, Barbie! There's nothing to get excited about. All the field hands will be doing it, too."

She was far from reassured. "But I don't know anything," she protested. "And I can't stand the idea of a lot of people watching while someone barks at me and tries to trip me up."

"You've been watching too much television," Ned said tolerantly. "This is no big deal. You'll be sitting in an office telling a lawyer about your filing system, that's all. Now you can do that, can't you?"

"You're sure that's all there is to it?"

"Absolutely!" he trumpeted, inwardly cursing himself for alarming her. He had intended to be as offhand as possible, but Barbara was such a frightened mouse that it had been a mistake to link her deposition to the general escalation in hostilities.

As she continued to wilt before his eyes, Ackerman cast around for supporting arguments.

"Nobody knows better than you how hard Scott has worked for this moment," he said, shamelessly appealing to her emotions. "The credit for this discovery will make him the recognized authority in his field. Now it's only fair that he gets what he's worked for, isn't it?"

"I suppose so," she said reluctantly.

Ackerman's tone hardened. "I'll spell out some other things, too. This tomato has taken most of our assets and time for five years. It was a long shot and, now that it's paid off, we certainly aren't going to let it slip away. We've pinched pennies around here long enough."

6 NEEDS PROTECTION

PINCHING pennies has always been relative. It was true that Ned Ackerman had performed miracles of credit manipulation to make the last five years possible. On the other hand, he was going home that Friday night to a substantial suburban house to enjoy a meal cooked by his wife and to share with her a letter from their married son in Oregon.

None of these material or emotional comforts awaited Barbara Gunn at the end of the work week. Her whole life consisted of a frantic juggling act in which the claims of breadwinning, maternity, housecleaning, laundry, and shopping had to be constantly maintained in fragile equipoise. At five o'clock she did not sign off duty; she merely raced from one set of chores to another. Her first stop was always the neighbor who took care of several local children.

Like almost everyone else, Marge Kemper unconsciously softened her style when she was dealing with Barbara.

"It's only quarter to six," she said soothingly as she opened the door and caught sight of Barbara's anxious face. "You're nowhere near late."

"Oh, I know. It's only I was hoping to catch Phyllis but I guess she's already been."

"Thank God!" Marge breathed enthusiastically.

There was never any doubt as to whether Phyllis' twin boys were rampaging around the premises.

"I guess they are a handful," Barbara said in duty bound, but the response was sheer reflex. She was surprised herself at her crushing disappointment. Phyllis, whose husband was a sports addict, frequently asked other mothers to bring their children over during the weekend. These sessions were almost as meaningless to Barbara as they were to Phyllis . . . usually. But this Friday some worm of discontent had impelled Barbara to rush through traffic in order to dispel the specter of two completely empty days.

"Is there anything wrong, Barbara?" asked Marge.

Barbara pulled herself together. "Nothing, nothing at all," she stammered. "It's this damned winter. I get so sick of all this snow."

Marge, trying to strike a positive note, remembered that one of the rare breaks in Barbara's treadmill existence was on the horizon.

"Well, you'll be going to Chicago soon. It will make a nice change and give you some time with your family. Do you know whether you'll be taking Tracy yet?"

"Yes, I heard from my parents. She'll stay with them."

The annual convention of plant geneticists usually required Marge to act as surrogate mother.

"Wonderful! And I just gave Tracy some milk and crackers because I know you have late supper on Fridays."

During Barbara's endless parade up and down the supermarket aisles, she had plenty of time to come to grips with her dissatisfaction. New York, she decided, had unsettled her. It was the sight of those bustling throngs everywhere, all taking part in a splendid exciting world from which she was forever debarred. There must be more to life, she thought mutinously, than a daily round confined to a young man who never noticed anybody else's existence (*except Hilary's, except Hilary's,* said an inner voice that should have been stilled years ago), an old man ready for retirement, and a six-year-old child.

Her depression continued through the trip home and was not lightened by the discovery that, after paying Marge, the supermarket and the landlord, she had barely enough left for Tracy's new snowsuit.

What's wrong with you? she asked herself. Life isn't one country club dance after another. Lots of people have to work hard. Look at Scotty—he'll be at the lab all weekend without a break and you don't see him complaining. Why can't you be the same?

But certain emotions are like runaway horses. Once they get the bit between their teeth, there is no stopping them until exhaustion takes its toll. Tonight, everything Barbara touched turned sour. The chicken was overdone, Tracy balked at bedtime, the fluorescent fixture in the kitchen began to blink ominously.

It's only for one more winter, she told herself grimly. By this time next year you'll be back in college making a new life for yourself. And God knows you've earned a change, you've paid for it in sweat and blood. So look on the bright side! If you've held out this long, you've got it made.

Like most exhortations to look on the bright side, this one was accompanied by steadily falling spirits, as the iron ritual of Friday night unfolded. Barbara shampooed her hair, Tracy emerged for her last glass of water, the light in the kitchen expired. By the time that Barbara, in a decrepit old robe, was curled up on the sofa with the television set blaring the late news, she was feeling suicidal. A long look at herself in the bathroom mirror had been the final straw. Her face had looked plucked and naked with the fine colorless hair hanging in long wet strings.

"Oh, God," she thought longingly, "what I want is a body permanent, a new peignoir and a tan."

* * *

Barbara, devoured by her own troubles, had oversimplified her notions of other people. Ned Ackerman was not an old man sinking into a comfortable rut. He was planning changes in his life style almost as thoroughgoing as Barbara's. Most of the weekend he spent planning a golden new future with his wife.

"It's damn near in the bag," he promised her. "And we're not plowing everything back into the company either. What do you say to a house in the Caribbean for the winters?"

On the subject of Scott Wenzel, Barbara was even further afield. Her conception of the dedicated scientist came straight from late-night movies, and her own stillborn romantic hopes did not help. It was true that Wenzel put in long hours, but his existence was by no means as monotonic as Barbara believed. On Friday night, for instance, his labors were interrupted about eight o'clock when a car pulled into the lot and Hilary Davis emerged, carrying a bucket of chicken and two bottles of beer. She, too, had been working late, at her law office.

For forty-five minutes the two of them picnicked together while Scott brought her up to date on the New York trip. She laughed outright at his description of the elevator encounter.

Nonetheless she shook her head at his analysis. "You may have given him a hard time for a couple of minutes, but that won't be what's worrying him," she declared.

"If he isn't worried by now, he's more of a fool than I think," Scott retorted.

"Of course, of course," she said impatiently. "But what's got him going is that Paul Jackson is representing you. Even if Vandam doesn't know what that means, his attorneys will have clued him in. He knows he's got big trouble."

Hilary had only a passing interest in the *Numero Uno* lawsuit, which lay miles away from her own specialty, but it was she who had steered Wisconsin Seedsmen into the arms of the right trial lawyer.

And Hilary was never unduly modest about her achievements.

Scott shrugged. "So we've got a wonderful lawyer," he said negligently. "We've also got the most irrefutable laboratory results you've ever seen."

Hilary Davis had long since satisfied herself that Scott Wenzel was a first-class scientist. Otherwise she would not have been living with him. There was no room in Hilary's life for bush league efforts of any description. So she felt no qualms about abandoning their discussion at this point.

"Well, you should know," she agreed, rising and neatly sweeping her debris—but not one particle more—into a trash basket. "And don't forget that we're running for Environmental Clean-Up tomorrow morning. I'll probably go to bed early."

Thanks to her training, Scott's first response was to dispose of his own chicken bones. "I'll remember but, if I work late, I may not make it," he warned her.

This was nothing more than a declaration of his formal right to refuse, and they both knew it. The reality was that at six o'clock the next morning he would automatically join Hilary in donning winter gear and running ten miles to promote a worthy cause. Even so, his participation on a freezing Saturday morning was regarded, by himself at least, as doing Hilary a favor. Fortunately Hilary was always willing to settle for substance as she went about the onerous process of socializing Scott Wenzel.

How far she had come along that road became clear to her when the triumphant runners were digging into blueberry pancakes.

"Hilary's got all that stuff about high-carbohydrate preparation for a marathon," he was saying casually to the man on his other side. "I'll bring it to Sally and Ed's tomorrow if you want to take a look at it."

Scott was not only planning to attend a cocktail party voluntarily, he was also using it as an occasion for a mild interaction with someone else. Four years ago she had to haul him, kicking and screaming, to any function that was not heavily larded with plant geneticists.

But by the time they were driving home from Sally and Ed's, she realized that there were forces at work far beyond her own tuition. For Scott to listen to a twenty-minute lecture on the bond market was downright unnatural. The tide of well-being she had sensed in him on Friday night had been swelling steadily all weekend. And every increment was the result of a session at the laboratory.

"Have a good time?" she began, as neutrally as possible.

"Great!"

This was so uncharacteristic that Hilary began to be worried. "Then it's a good thing we made it. You were so late getting back from the lab, I thought you might have decided to give the party a miss."

"Hell, no. I just forgot the time while I was planning the new greenhouses. You wouldn't believe the amount of computerization we can introduce."

Euphoria was all very well and good but, at the rate that Scott's was running, it threatened to break the dam.

"Don't you think you'd better win your case before you start spending the royalties?" she advised.

Scott swung the car into the parking lot with a joyful swerve. "I'm just going to be in a posture of intelligent anticipation when all that money starts rolling in."

Hilary sighed. In some ways Scott was an innocent. He seemed to regard a law court as a medieval tourney where the champion of right and purity automatically prevailed. She had been in practice long enough to know better.

"Look, Scott, the Vandams have been in this business a

long time. They're not going to show up at the hearing with empty hands. I know you've got wonderful lab records. Has it ever occurred to you that they do, too?"

Scott had already swung open his door and clambered out. As he turned back to her, his face was under the dome light and she could see that his eyes were dancing.

"It doesn't make any difference what records they've got. We're still going to wipe them out."

In their own ways, both of the women close to Scott Wenzel had tried to urge compromise. Both had been rebuffed. There the similarity ended. When Monday morning rolled around, Hilary Davis was engulfed by different concerns but Barbara Gunn returned to Wisconsin Seedsmen.

As she hung up her coat, she saw that Wenzel's parka and boots were dry enough to indicate that he had been at work for over an hour. The pile of dictation cassettes in her basket, the result of his weekend labors, seemed to confirm her view of his monastic regimen.

By the time Ned Ackerman arrived she was well launched into the first cassette and receiving confirmation of other opinions as well.

"I was right," she announced as soon as they had exchanged their usual greetings.

Still bundled up, Ackerman had headed straight for the coffee pot. Now he came to her side, his cheeks still rosy with cold, his hands cradling the cup so that his fingers could share its warmth.

"About what?" he asked.

"About Scott," she retorted as if it were the only subject possible. "You said the VR–117 was the most important thing in the world to him. But he's spent the whole weekend working on this new thing of his, the MF–23 or whatever it is. That's what he's excited about now. I can hear it in his voice as he dictates. Another month and it will be all he thinks of. *Then,* he'll be too busy for this lawsuit. So why don't you make him stop being pigheaded now?"

Ackerman smiled. "Scott would die if he didn't have some project going in the lab, that's what keeps him alive. And he's bound to get enthusiastic about whatever's on the fire. That doesn't mean he's forgotten VR–117. Not when it could mean so much to his career."

"Oh."

He laughed outright at her disappointment. "But you've got the real corporation mind, Barbara," he congratulated her. "That's the way big companies think. If you were a betting woman, I'd offer you five to one that we'll still hear talk about compromise. But from them, not us."

The possibility had never occurred to her.

"From Vandam's?" she gasped, awestruck.

"That's right!" he said buoyantly. "I can smell it in the air."

7 MEATY PODS

WITHIN twenty-four hours, other noses were twitching as well. John Thatcher's first whiff came from his luncheon guest.

Paul Jackson was all affability as he strolled up to Thatcher's table at the Banker's Club. But the wolfish gleam in his dark eyes was more pronounced than usual and it was he, not Thatcher, who took the plunge.

"When Ackerman and Wenzel came to me about going after Vandam's, I knew that meant Standard Foods. But I must have been asleep at the switch. I didn't plug the Sloan in until a few days ago."

Thatcher had more sense than to rise to this bait. He waited courteously.

Jackson was not perturbed. "Tell me, how much is losing *Numero Uno* going to cost SF, John?" he asked.

On Wall Street, information is paid for in kind. According to Vandam's and SF, the *Numero Uno* case was open-and-shut. But, as the injunction against the Vandam spring catalog demonstrated, there was another side represented by Paul Jackson. Within the limits of propriety, Thatcher wanted to round out his picture. To do so, he had to be willing to trade.

"Standard Foods is solid as a rock," he said, submerging thoughts about their most recently acquired subsidiary. "They can get along very nicely without *Numero Uno*. But you know better than I do that *Numero Uno* will be worth millions to whoever controls it. Standard Foods will fight tooth and nail to keep that right."

Usually the prospect of battle exhilarated Jackson. But now he said only, "Don't be too sure of that. This morning we got the nibble I've been expecting."

"The nibble being . . . ?"

"An offer to compromise," said Jackson. "Oh, that's not how they put it, but that's what it amounts to. They want to talk."

So much for Dick Vandam's defiance! Thatcher's reflection was interrupted when Jackson went on to say, "In many ways I suppose it's the only sensible solution."

Thatcher cocked his head thoughtfully. Jackson, in spite of his joy in combat, was far too able a counselor not to employ sweet reason when it was desirable. There might have been grounds for Paul Jackson to sound disappointed, but why the tone of wry detachment?

Jackson grinned. "It doesn't make any difference what I suppose," he confessed. "There is no way anybody can make my boys budge an inch. Even me."

"They're confident they have a strong case?" Thatcher suggested.

He was talking to a man who made strong cases out of straw. "They're confident—period. Even if it means going to the Supreme Court," said Jackson with approval. "When they finally agreed at least to attend this confab, I was willing to fly out and sit in. You know what Ackerman told me? He said not to bother, he and Scotty could handle this one themselves. They're saving me for courtroom work, and they want to keep costs to a minimum."

Thatcher was suitably impressed. "I thought, when you took a case, you were the one who called the tune."

Jackson shook his head in mock despair. "It's a hell of a note when the clients know more than the lawyers about what's going on. But this plant genetics business has been an eye-opener for me. And it sure as hell isn't a subject you bone up on overnight."

They had now reached the point Thatcher was interested in. "I admit that until recently I thought of plant protection as something that covered a few roses and shade trees. Then Bowman filled me in on the new legislation, and I realized it was much bigger than that."

"The Plant Variety Protection Act of 1970," Jackson said glibly. "Did you know that tomatoes were originally excluded from its coverage? Standard Foods damn near split a gut lobbying to keep them out—and a few other things like celery and carrots. They were scared to death that they'd end up paying through the nose for the vegetables they use the most. But the act resulted in so many new varieties that nobody could justify continued exclusion of tomatoes. So there was an amendment and the boys in the back room got busy. Anyway, at least one boy got busy."

"And Standard Foods decided to guarantee itself low-cost tomatoes by getting its hands on the tomato patent," Thatcher continued. "That's why they bought Vandam's."

"If you can't do it one way, you do it another," Jackson said cheerfully. "But I wasn't talking about legislation. It's the experimentation itself that's surprised me. You do realize that you can get patent protection only for propagation by asexual reproduction?"

"I don't like the sound of that," Thatcher observed.

"Who would?" replied Jackson. "But it means propagating by seed is out. It's got to be a lot more basic than that. And the media boys have distracted us with all their hype. They've scared us to death with talk about creating new forms of animal life, cloning human beings, unleashing deadly viruses by accident. And while we've been bird-dogging the zoologists, it's the botanists who've been having a field day, juggling one phylum with another. We're probably all going to be killed by a man-eating petunia."

Thatcher was prepared to defer his anxieties about homicidal flower beds. Instead he reminded Jackson of the statistics about high-yield rice and high-yield wheat. "In the meantime the world gets a better supply of food, as you well know. But I suppose what you're really complaining about is that you don't feel you're on top of this patent suit."

"You've got to let the scientists call the shots. They're the only ones who know what's going on. In an infringement suit, you just have to prove that the defendant has been poaching. That means everyone's gotten into manufacture. But, with an interference hearing, you're still in the laboratory stage. When Wenzel tells me that there's no way on earth his experiments could have been duplicated by accident, I take his word for it. What else can I do?"

On examination Thatcher decided this statement of faith was not as broad as it might be. "You take his word that there's been stealing," he murmured. "Do you also take his word on who's doing it?"

"How the hell can I tell a crooked plant geneticist from a straight one? I've never seen one before," Jackson grumbled irritably before passing to one small blessing. "But what the hell! I'm a lot better off than poor Art Bixby, who's representing Vandam's. *His* mad scientist is down in Puerto Rico and hasn't even been consulted."

"It sounds to me as if they should get him up here."

"They should have done it months ago. I've had the benefit of talking with the guy who's in on the ground floor. Art's been getting everything filtered through Dick Vandam. The only reason Pendleton's attending the conference is that he was coming to the States anyway for the meetings."

Thatcher frowned. Paul Jackson's gusto occasionally made him incomprehensible. The conference was clearly the first attempt at negotiating a compromise. "Then what are the meetings?"

"The plant geneticists are having their annual powwow in Chicago next week," Jackson explained.

"Ah! A professional convention. That should make for an interesting coming together of the principals. From what you say, it's the one arena with a lot of people competent to judge some of these claims."

"More interesting than you think. Vandam's had been planning to stage a big demonstration of their tomato, hard on the heels of their catalog publicity. Now there's a court order squelching that program." Jackson grinned complacently. "That's the peg on which they plan to hang these discussions with my clients."

The self-confidence obtaining at Wisconsin Seed must be infectious, Thatcher decided. Even if Scott Wenzel were one of those rare scientists who were not for an age but for all time, what did he know about the kind of business conference where an opening gambit could win the entire game?

Paul Jackson answered his unspoken question. "Wenzel may be God's gift in the laboratory, but Ackerman's pretty useful outside it. He wasn't satisfied with the tempo of the Patent Office. It was his bright idea to get an injunction, and really shake things up."

"Yes, but that's only temporary," Thatcher pointed out. "At some time the new catalog will be released and normalcy will return."

"Don't you believe it." Jackson was full of admiration for his client. "Now that Vandam's is off-balance, Ackerman wants to keep them that way. His latest dodge has been to step up the schedule for depositions. He's got a nice feeling for tactics, does Ackerman. Half the time I think he should be sitting in my chair. I can tell you a lot of people at Vandamia are in for a real experience."

"Vandamia?"

"Vandam's headquarters in downstate Illinois. That's where they plan to do their bargaining. Between you and me, that's another one of their mistakes. They think that, on their own turf, they can overawe Ackerman and Wenzel. Take it from a man who's tried. It can't be done."

Thatcher was beginning to be curious about the guiding lights at Wisconsin Seed.

"I hope to meet this pair someday," he said incautiously.

Fate obliged him sooner than he expected.

Earl Sanders caught him ten minutes after he got back from lunch. Sanders' version of coming attractions differed markedly from Paul Jackson's. In the first place, the word compromise was not mentioned.

". . . getting together both sides and exploring the situation," he said earnestly. "After all, *Numero Uno* is a complex issue, and we don't want to get hung up on disagreements that may not go to the heart of the matter."

Thatcher, while accustomed to clients lulled by the sound of their own meaningless words, did not have unlimited patience. "Do the Vandams agree with you?"

In a rapid descent from the stratosphere, Sanders said, "Like hell they do! We had to twist their arm—hard."

With Paul Jackson's confidences about Wisconsin Seed fresh in his mind, Thatcher did not comment, as he might have, that the outlook for rapprochement was dim.

"But . . . well, we're hoping that everybody will see reason," Sanders continued heartily. "Now, Thatcher, I'm calling because . . ."

Thatcher had seen this one coming. He understood, none better, why Standard Foods wanted the Sloan by its side. A show of big guns—or, in this case, big bucks—never hurts. The Sloan accommodated a select few of its customers this way, and Standard Foods was as select as they came.

". . . since you yourself have become so familiar with the *Numero Uno* controversy," Sanders was saying persuasively.

Not even Standard Foods rated Thatcher himself. But

the scales had been tipped in their favor. Five minutes earlier Thatcher's second-in-command had reported from Chicago where he was overseeing the collapse of Wenonah industries, Incorporated.

"So far, I've been talking to stone walls," Charlie Trinkam had said. "These guys aren't in the mood to listen to sense. I may have to use a club."

Roughly translated, this meant that Charlie could use reinforcements. Thatcher, who had been thinking of which subordinate to dispatch, now saw his duty clear. When you can kill two birds with one stone, a trip to the heartland is small price to pay.

"Yes," he said to Sanders, meanwhile buzzing for Miss Corsa, "I will be able to join you. . . . Fine. . . . Miss Corsa, I'm going to have to fly out to Chicago tomorrow."

Seeing protest forming, he added, "So that I can be in Vandamia for a morning conference—about your precious Vandam catalog."

This rearrangement of the truth distracted her from appointments that must be canceled and meetings that must be rescheduled. "Vandamia," she said wistfully, with all the warmth lacking in her references to London, Paris and Rome.

"I expect to be gone a day or two . . . at most. On the way back I'll look in on Trinkam and see if I can help get the Wenonah talks moving."

But, even while he outlined an optimistic itinerary, he was congratulating himself. Joining Trinkam in Chicago would repay time and effort but Vandamia, he suspected, was going to be a total loss—except for Miss Corsa.

Whether she knew it or not, there was an all-expenses-paid tour of the world-famous Vandam gardens in her future.

8   RESISTANT TO HEAT

MISS Corsa would be visiting Vandamia in June, July or August, Thatcher reminded himself the following morning. Then, no doubt, it would be roses, roses, all the way. On this icy Wednesday in January, Vandamia consisted of miles of snow-covered fields under a menacing grey sky.

The town proper was little more than a general straggle of nondescript buildings surrounding the one-block Main Street with the usual rural landmarks: two gas stations, a drugstore selling souvenirs and, behind a curtained front window, Estelle's Home Cooking.

Two miles south things began looking up. First came a strip with motels offering swimming pools for the tourist and Lotus Lounges for the businessman. Beyond that was open country, with distant views of residences far too substantial to be mistaken for farmhouses.

Finally, under an arch still reading *Vandam Nursery & Seed Company,* appeared the home office, its architecture suspiciously similar to the mansions past which Thatcher and Sanders had been sweeping.

Vandamia, in sum, was a Grand Duchy set down in the corn and soybean belt of southern Illinois. The reigning Grand Duke had no time for pomp or circumstance.

"Thank God you finally got here," said Dick Vandam,

74

meeting Sanders and Thatcher at the reception desk. "They're upstairs already."

The list of participants in this ill-omened summit, as furnished by Sanders on the flight from Chicago, was lengthy. But Thatcher knew who *they* must be and, once they reached Vandam's spacious office, had no difficulty identifying Paul Jackson's clients. The Vandam lawyers wore the tight expression of their kind. Both Ned Ackerman and Scott Wenzel were completely at ease.

In fact, himself apart, they were the only ones present of whom this could be said. Dick Vandam was holding himself in check by maintaining a rigid silence that spoke louder than words. Sanders' edginess took an even more unfortunate form.

"You mean you didn't bring your lawyer along with you?" he said solicitously. "Of course, it's your decision, but I'm not sure it's wise. We certainly don't want you thinking we've taken advantage of you."

This impersonation of guide, philosopher and friend got the reception it deserved.

"You won't," Scott Wenzel told him coolly.

If the opening was inauspicious, what followed was worse. Sanders, ignoring Wenzel's remark and a sardonic glance from Dick Vandam, persisted with soft talk. "When we lay everything out, I'm sure we'll find that we all want the same thing. And that is an orderly and profitable exploitation of *Numero Uno*. Now, unfortunately, it is true that Vandam's and Wisconsin Seedsmen have this disagreement about patent rights, but that really doesn't affect the basic issues."

This time it was Ackerman who humored him. "It doesn't?" he asked politely.

"Certainly not," Sanders plowed on. "Let's take a look at the fundamentals. Now, we all know this tomato is going to revolutionize American agriculture—and gardening and food processing. You'll have to agree that the only way to handle it is with a major sales and distribution operation. Vandam's has just that. So, it makes good sense to go ahead as planned, put the revenues into an escrow account, then let the courts decide how to divvy the pot. That way, we all get the advantages of—"

"No."

Thatcher was beginning to think that Wenzel was a man of few, if pithy, words when the young geneticist continued, "Look, you're wasting time and effort. There's no way anybody is going to distribute my VR–117, anybody but Wisconsin Seedsmen. And that's that."

"Vandam's," Dick Vandam promptly countered, "will market *Numero Uno,* which was developed under Vandam auspices and is solely owned by Vandam's—as the Patent Office will certainly judge and, if not them, the appeals court."

Deadlock, and in record time, Thatcher reflected. Naturally Earl Sanders and the assorted legal talent were not similarly impressed. For a full hour they argued, cajoled and threatened—to no avail. Wenzel and Ackerman treated most of the suggestions that came their way as a joke. Dick Vandam was also adamant, though giving no indication of suppressed amusement.

As Thatcher had foreseen, the shadowboxing finally embroiled him. Vandam's lawyer, Arthur Bixby, repeated his main point. "Look, Wisconsin Seedsmen is simply not equipped for the *Numero Uno* avalanche. You won't be able to handle the orders because you haven't got the capacity, and you won't be able to develop it. You don't have sufficient financial backing."

"Hold it," said Ned Ackerman placidly. "We might as well clear that up right away. I've been talking to money sources in Madison, and in Chicago too. As soon as we get clear title, they'll be standing in line. You're the ones who brought a banker along. Ask him."

He delivered this advice with a friendly nod in Thatcher's direction.

There was only one thing any representative of the Sloan Guaranty Trust could say. "I agree that undisputed legal ownership of the patent would make Wisconsin Seedsmen attractive to many financial institutions," Thatcher said judiciously.

For a brief moment, it looked to him as if Dick Vandam and Earl Sanders intended to quarrel with this temperate description of how the real world works.

Art Bixby, however, was determined to finish his argument. "All a patent does is buy you lead time over the competition. Now, we're all reasonable men," he said winningly. "We all know *Numero Uno* will be displaced by something better within five years. Two years wasted in court—and whoever ends up with the patent has lost forty percent of its value."

Percentages did not frighten Ackerman either.

"I guess we'll just have to grin and bear it," he said unmoved.

Before his underlying assumption could be challenged, there was an interruption that enlarged the cast of characters.

Jason Ingersoll led the way. "I don't know how many of you already know Dr. Pendleton, and Mrs. Pendleton," he said smoothly, presenting his companions. "They're from the Institute of Plant Research in Puerto Rico. And Dr. Eric Most, here, is Dr. Pendleton's assistant."

As he spoke, there was a balletic regrouping, with the lawyers drawing back and the newcomers taking front and center. All was courtesy until Scott Wenzel bestirred himself.

"Jesus!" he exploded. "Are they sucking you into this fast one of theirs, Howard?"

Sputtering protests arose from every corner. Howard Pendleton had no trouble quelling them. "Hold it, Dick," he said calmly. "All right, Jason, I can handle this. Scotty, nobody's sucking me into anything." He paused to emphasize his next words. "IPR developed the *Numero Uno* tomato for Vandam's."

Eric Most almost stepped on his line. "And," he said heatedly, "we've got all the lab notes to prove it, and Vandam's field test records too."

Wenzel, staring at Pendleton, ignored Most. It was plain that this was the first he had heard of IPR's role in *Numero Uno* but, to Thatcher at least, he looked more puzzled than troubled.

Ned Ackerman, however, scented danger. "You think it's going to help your case?" he said, addressing the Vandams impartially. "Claiming that it was IPR, not Vandam's? Take it from me, it's not going to do you one damn bit of good."

Now he sounded as placid as a baited bear.

"Look here, Ackerman," Vandam began forcefully.

Jason Ingersoll spoke right over his uncle. "I don't care for that implication, Ackerman. After discussions about the feasibility of a biennial tomato, R&D agreed to fund Dr. Pendleton's research. It was a perfectly standard procedure, and you know it. I seem to remember Wenzel himself begging for funding from Vandam's once upon a time."

His final sentence was a mistake.

"Sure, it's standard," Wenzel said unpleasantly. "But Howard, you should have been leery of dealing with an outfit like Vandam's. Did they say the stuff they passed on to you was the product of their own research, or did they just gloss over everything? I suppose even this bunch would hesitate to admit that they stole my work outright."

"Oh, dear," said a voice in Thatcher's ear. Mrs. Pendleton, seated next to him, was watching Wenzel and Ingersoll snarl at each other. "This is no time for Scotty to lose his temper. He's going to get wilder and wilder—and drive everybody else wild, too."

"You have to admit that Ingersoll set him off," said Thatcher.

"Ye-es," she said.

Her husband took a more dispassionate stance. "Talking nonsense isn't going to help any of us," he said firmly. Then, with a deprecating smile, he added, "Your trouble has always been jumping to conclusions, Scott. Why don't we wait until we have some facts—"

"I've got all the facts I need, Howard," said Wenzel, still glaring at Ingersoll. "Do you?"

Pendleton shook his head in resignation. "You don't change, Scott."

"They don't look as if they're coming to blows," Thatcher remarked to Mrs. Pendleton.

"You mean Howard and Scotty?" she asked. "Oh, Howard may think Scotty's too brash and Scotty thinks Howard is old hat, but they get along. It's not Howard I'm worried about. It's the rest of them. They're not used to Scotty." After a pause, she added fair-mindedly, "And Scotty's not used to them."

It was an idiosyncratic view, but Thatcher saw what she meant. Pendleton and Scott Wenzel could spar without bitterness. It was the seconds who were out for blood.

Taking advantage of a lull in the hostilities, one of the lawyers tried to retrieve the irretrievable. "What we seem to have here is a situation where two laboratories, following similar lines of research, have approximated the same results. The best approach is to let the courts decide that issue. But in the meantime, we could concentrate on some practical details."

"What practical details did you have in mind?" asked Ned Ackerman with swift suspicion.

At issue was the unveiling of *Numero Uno* at the meetings

of the American Society of Plant Sciences, in Chicago. Could it be shown, and under what name? Vexed and knotty though this problem was, it was of no interest to John Thatcher. So, while the negotiations proceeded, he withdrew his immediate attention from the substance of the drama to its players.

Contrasts abounded. In the younger generation, a cursory glance would seem to pit Jason Ingersoll against Scott Wenzel. Style and status obviously informed their open antagonism. But, Thatcher could not help noticing, Wenzel was even more hostile to Eric Most. His remarks to Ingersoll were deliberately insolent, those to Most were contemptuous.

Their elders also constituted an instructive study. Dick Vandam was perhaps the easiest to read. He remained what he was, determined to take on all comers—including, Thatcher guessed, members of his own family. Ackerman and Dr. Pendleton, on the other hand, were more complex. Superficially, the two were affable and open-minded. Underneath, Thatcher suspected, they were both iron.

Odd man out, in more ways than one, was Mrs. Pendleton. She was not only outspoken but, as Thatcher learned in the course of conversation, a distinguished plant geneticist in her own right.

"No, I haven't done any work on tomatoes, thank God," she said, watching the roiling controversy. "My field has always been flowers. I'm just along for moral support, not that Howard needs it. The one who did the bottle washing for him was Eric." She sighed as a particularly sharp remark by Wenzel set off a buzz of response. "Honestly, my heart sinks when I think of Chicago."

"You mean, this difficulty about displaying *Numero Uno?*"

"That," she said frankly, "is the tip of the iceberg. Once

word gets around that Scotty is suing Vandam's—well, I only wish that—"

Whatever she wished remained unspoken, for some sort of limited consensus had been reached in the main ring.

"Okay," said Ackerman, stubbing out his cigar. "We all agree to waive any public claims for the duration of the convention."

Eric Most set his prominent jaw. "I still think that's a mistake."

"Who cares?" said Wenzel.

Nobody paid Most the slightest attention.

Still, the meeting of minds was too insubstantial to satisfy Earl Sanders. "We'd hoped we could do better than this," he said fretfully. "It looks as if we brought you down here for nothing."

Ackerman saw an advantage, and took it. "Oh, it wasn't for nothing," he told Sanders. "We've met each other now, and I figure that Standard Foods and Wisconsin Seed are going to be doing a lot of business with each other. In the not-too-distant future."

On this valedictory, he detached Scott Wenzel from his private conversation with the Pendletons and sailed out.

Ingersoll shed some of his suavity the minute the door shut. "That cocky son of a bitch," he said venomously. "They're riding for a big fall, aren't they, Howard? Once you get all your expert witnesses lined up, and they get a crack at this stuff of yours versus Wenzel's—hell, it's going to prove without a shadow of a doubt who developed *Numero Uno*, isn't it?"

It was Eric Most who answered him.

"It certainly will," he promised. "I've got fourteen notebooks containing hourly readings of growth rates and root structure. In addition, I've kept tapes—taken at the time—of all the observations on pigmentation and leafage. That's over and above the daily records."

His spate of technical information, which had a self-serving tinge, brought a quizzical smile to Howard Pendleton's face.

"Nobody's denying that you did a lot of hard work, Eric," he said mildly.

"No, no," said Dick Vandam. "We have every confidence in your work, Howard, and . . . er, Dr. Most."

Instead of the gratitude he might have expected, he was assailed by a blast of common sense from Fran Pendleton.

"Well, I don't know that it's right to have too much confidence," she said bluntly, startling everybody except her husband. "Now that we've had a chance to compare Scotty's lab books with IPR's, things are a lot worse than we thought. The expert witnesses will say that the two sets are identical. Either you believe in astronomical coincidences or . . ."

Breaking off suddenly, she looked at her husband. He finished the sentence for her. "Or," he said, "somehow or other Scotty got hold of our results."

"You mean stole them," Eric Most corrected indignantly. "It's as plain as the nose on your face."

Pendleton was unwilling to go that far. "I'd just as soon let the experts characterize it."

"I must say I don't understand your attitude toward Wenzel, Howard," Dick Vandam said angrily. "He's a thief, pure and simple. Furthermore, he's out to destroy you if he can. That's absolutely clear. We are not talking about cheating on an exam, you know, or plagiarizing."

If Pendleton had been overly tolerant, he made up for it now. Rising to his full height, he said, "I know you don't understand my attitude. You seem to think tantrums will advance our cause. Well, they won't. Whether or not he's a thief, Scott Wenzel cannot destroy me. But, as Mr. Sanders' presence here proves, what he can destroy is Vandam's. Fran, I think it's time for us to be getting along."

To Thatcher's way of thinking, when it came to parting shots, honors between Ned Ackerman and Howard Pendleton were equally divided.

9 FINE FOR FREEZING

IN a strictly physical sense, John Thatcher was transported from Vandamia to Chicago in great comfort. There was nothing utilitarian about the Vandam Cessna that was winging him and Earl Sanders to O'Hare Field. Ten more passengers could have been accommodated in style. There was a solicitous steward. Thatcher occupied an ample easy chair, and he had every confidence that his luggage was being cosseted with velour, too.

Spiritually, the atmosphere left much to be desired.

"The Vandams treat themselves to nothing but the best," said Sanders, sourly looking around what was now Standard Foods' property. "Yes, I will have another Scotch and water."

Whatever enthusiasm Sanders and Standard Foods had brought to their acquisition of Vandam's had been pegged to *Numero Uno*. This morning's debacle gave Ned Ackerman's final thrust some muscle. If *Numero Uno*—or VR–117—belonged to Wisconsin Seedsmen, then Vandam's and the assorted Vandams were out in the cold, leaving their Cessna behind.

"And frankly I don't give a damn whether they were lunatic enough to steal *Numero Uno*—or feebleminded enough to lose it," said Sanders, following this thought all the way.

"Surely there's another possibility," Thatcher suggested.

"Pendleton may have been the one who did the losing. I'm surprised Dick Vandam hasn't pressed that alternative."

Sanders' teeth glinted briefly. "He'd like to. Unfortunately, Ingersoll did his homework, and it's on record that IPR is a pretty secure setup. So it boils down to the old story—somebody pays a file clerk to siphon off the experimental results as soon as they're put on paper. And if there wasn't so much money involved, I could almost see it as a spite job. Did you notice the hostility between Wenzel and that Eric Most?"

"I could scarcely avoid noticing it," Thatcher said, then closed his mouth firmly.

In fact the antagonism had seemed overdone to him, almost as if it were being rammed down his throat. Why should Wenzel be so contemptuous of a man whose credentials were presumably very close to his own, if they had landed him the same job? Why should Most automatically distrust a researcher who had not previously been in competition with him? Of course it would not be the first time two people had fallen prey to an instinctive aversion. But it would also not be the first time two young schemers had conspired to rob a successful employer.

Then there was the third young man, the one who did his homework so carefully.

"Is Jason Ingersoll the only Vandam besides Dick who's in top management?" Thatcher inquired.

"The whole place is infested with them," Sanders grunted. "There are dozens of them on the payroll, and not at starting-level salaries, either. But yes, now that old Milton's been tossed to the wolves, it's Jason and Dick who are running the show, if you can call it that."

Disregarding hyperbole and disparagement alike, Thatcher asked exactly who Ingersoll was.

Sanders shrugged. "All I know is that his mother is the Vandam who's had six husbands."

"And presumably a healthy chunk of company stock," said Thatcher, disregarding inessentials.

"Yes," said Sanders. "But, to tell you the truth, Ingersoll is the best of a pretty bad lot. He was the one who bulldozed the *Numero Uno* project through, in the teeth of all sorts of opposition. Once it paid off—if it has paid off—everybody climbed aboard, including Dick. But it was Jason who realized that Vandam's had to do something big, or else sink beneath its own weight. He was surprised when Dick came up with our merger offer, but he saw the possibilities right off."

"Yes," said Thatcher. "He struck me as an ambitious young man."

"He sure is," said Sanders shortly. "Ingersoll plans to be president of Standard Foods some day. Let me tell you, if anything, anything at all, happens to *Numero Uno*, he's out on his can, just like the rest of them. Oh, waiter, do you want to top this up for me?"

O'Hare, Hogarthian nightmare though it was, came as a decided relief. Thatcher shook hands with his traveling companion, who was heading out to Oakbrook.

"You're staying downtown at the Hyatt, aren't you?" Sanders said. "After I've touched base with headquarters, I'll get in contact."

"Splendid," said Thatcher heartily, with every intention of putting tomatoes behind him as soon as possible. Hard goods, not soft goods, were next on his agenda. Unfortunately, in the current economic climate, this did not constitute a marked improvement.

Charlie Trinkam brought this home to Thatcher when he strolled into the Sloan suite an hour later.

"First of all, the price of gas is killing Wenonah. Then, there are mortgage rates. Now, OSHA is suing them because of dangerous levels of asbestos particulates. On top of that, the union wants a twenty-two percent across-the-board increase, and a roof has just collapsed at their plant in Benton Harbor. How were things downstate, John?"

"Standard Foods is no doubt facing a major problem," said Thatcher. Now that he had taken his own reading of Wisconsin Seedsmen, he could add, "It may be more serious than they realize. As for Vandam's, my impression is that the outlook is not bright, no matter what happens."

Trinkam was not one of the Sloan's passionate gardeners. "Tough," he said indifferently. "Wenonah, I don't have to tell you, is dead in the water."

Wenonah Industries, producer of recreational vehicles, had been a star performer until the heavens fell. Now, despite the best efforts of a highly touted management, the end was in sight.

"No hope at all?" Thatcher asked.

Trinkam had been in Chicago for over a week, taking a last hard look.

"They're beginning to talk about getting a government guarantee for their bank loans," said Charlie sadly.

Doctors are not the only ones faced by the agonizing question of whether or not to pull the plug. Terminating a major credit line is never a pleasure either. With Wenonah Industries it was not even easy. Thatcher's arrival, which Wenonah should have recognized as the last rites, simply sparked them into prodigies of misdirected effort.

Two tedious days passed and Charlie Trinkam's capacity for enjoyment began to wilt. "No," he said wearily when Thatcher inquired about any after-dinner plans, "I'll just turn in early tonight."

He could have been in Peoria.

He and Thatcher had just survived a marketing session designed to prove that, come April, the American buying public would stampede into showrooms filled with forty-thousand-dollar vehicles getting five miles to the gallon.

"And I know what they'll come up with tomorrow," said

Charlie bleakly. "They'll be full of plans to convert to defense production. It's enough to make you want to bomb a business school."

Thatcher had a more effective way to deal with lost causes. "Don't they have a note falling due at Midwestern Trust? I think we should find out what Midwestern proposes to do. God knows, we've made the Sloan position clear. One way or another, I'm returning to New York. If, by any chance, Midwestern wants to prolong the agony, you may have to stay on for a day or two."

"I'll take my chances," said Charlie with a grin. Midwestern Trust was a byword among bankers.

Thus, the following morning saw them heading for LaSalle Street, a far more congenial milieu than Wenonah Industries. Even Edgar Brown, the presiding genius and resident terror at Midwestern, made a nice change. No one had ever classed him with the nation's dynamic executives.

"Bad business, John," he grunted after Charlie and his local equivalents disappeared to hammer out Wenonah's fate.

"In every sense," Thatcher agreed.

"I told them they were expanding too fast. That kind of boom never lasts. What goes up has to come down."

Brown and this philosophy had been at Midwestern Trust as long as anybody could remember. He had no private personality to speak of, having assumed the coloration of his institution. Brown and his bank believed in self-liquidating loans, God, and the Republican Party.

"Did you come to Chicago to keep an eye on what Trinkam's doing?" he asked.

Employees at Midwestern Trust were spectacularly downtrodden, and Thatcher hastened to dispel any such view of Charlie. "As a matter of fact, I just happened to be passing through."

"Passing through from Vandamia?" said Brown craftily.

"That's right," Thatcher reminded himself. "You're Vandam's bank, aren't you?"

"We sure are," answered Brown, "and we have been since the old man started out."

"Which old man?" asked Thatcher, who knew Brown.

"Cornelius Vandam," said Brown, savoring every syllable. "He was a giant, John, a real giant. This crowd couldn't even begin to fill his shoes. Still, it's too bad to see them swallowed up by Standard Foods."

Cynics would claim that Edgar and Midwestern Trust had cause to regret any move jeopardizing such a substantial account.

"And I'm damned if I think it was necessary, or desirable," Brown continued irascibly. "Vandam's had a nice, stable business, year in and year out. With a very fine cash flow, no matter what those damned Arabs were doing with the price of oil. To tell you the truth, John, I nearly bust a gut advising them to reject Standard Foods' offer. But it didn't do any good."

"It rarely does," said Thatcher, as one banker to another.

"The trouble is that there are too many Vandams," Brown said. "Most of them care more about money than about tradition. A shame."

Thatcher observed a moment of silent respect for this sentiment, then asked about the Vandams still active in the firm. "From what I saw of them," he commented, "they seem to be reasonably commercial-minded."

"Oh, Dick's got his head screwed on right," said Brown promptly. "Milton was pretty sensible too. I'm not so sure about young Jason. He's got a lot of ideas."

"Yes," said Thatcher, who was not unalterably opposed to ideas. "Jason impressed me that way too. But I don't think I met Milton."

Tact prevented his asking outright if Brown was evoking

more shades from the heroic past. But Milton, it turned out, was alive and kicking.

"You didn't meet him because they threw him out," said Brown. "Helluva way to treat him after all the years he put in. Caused quite a rumpus at the time. From what I hear, Jason was behind that too."

"At least Standard Foods wasn't the villain," said Thatcher.

"Standard Foods never has been the villain," Edgar Brown said roundly. "If they'd all pulled together, instead of playing one faction against the other, Vandam's would never have had to sell out. You know about this new tomato of theirs? Hell, if they'd waited, they could have bought out Standard Foods."

Ned Ackerman, Thatcher reflected, was probably thinking along just those lines.

"Too bad, too bad," Brown mourned. "And, on top of everything, it's the first time in God-knows-how-many years that the Vandam catalog hasn't been in the mail by January first. You know, you look at what's happened to Vandam's, and you wonder where the country's headed."

It took twenty minutes for Thatcher and Charlie to taxi from Midwestern Trust back to the Hyatt. During that interval nothing significant happened to Japanese imports, the inflation rate, or U.S. housing starts. Nevertheless, according to Edgar Brown's admittedly peculiar lights, the Union was safe. The Vandam spring catalog was being distributed to the waiting world.

Thatcher discovered this happy circumstance in the boldly chromed lobby of the Hyatt where Dick Vandam had stationed himself. Vandam could have been the father of the bride, radiating pleasure, pride and unfocused cordiality. Near him, their arms filled with the precious catalogs, were four young men and behind them stood three dollies, piled high with cardboard cartons.

Thatcher and Charlie found themselves caught up in the cavalcade.

"Good to see you, good to see you," Vandam was saying with a relentless smile. "It's going to be a great meeting, and Vandam's wants to be sure you've got your copy of the catalog."

He and his minions were working the crowd like politicians. "Good to see you here, yes indeed, a great day— oh, it's you, Thatcher."

Charlie was critically studying the one hundred fifty pages that had been thrust upon him. From his expression, he was not the man for the sweet pea that adorned the cover.

"Hello, Vandam," said Thatcher, conscious of a line forming behind him. "What exactly is going on?"

"Phil, take over for a minute, will you?" said Vandam, stepping out of the receiving line and joining Thatcher. "Well, I suppose you'll find it hard to believe after that farce the other day in Vandamia. But there is some progress, thank God. As you see, we have finally got the catalog off the presses."

Since this niche of the Hyatt resembled a paperback store, Thatcher could indeed see that the catalog was out. Furthermore, he knew without looking that all reference to *Numero Uno* had been deleted. It was the rest of the hoopla that eluded him and he said so.

"Why, it's the Plant Society meetings. That's what all these people are checking in for," said Vandam, pointing to the crowd at the desk. "Isn't that why you're here?"

"No," said Thatcher, "I'm in Chicago on other business. I recall your talk about the convention, of course. But I don't see that the Sloan has anything to gain by attending."

For one telling moment, Vandam's mask of joviality slipped. "I don't mind saying I think you're wrong. You mark my words, by the time these meetings are over, we're going to have this entire *Numero Uno* situation signed, sealed and delivered."

"I hope you're right," said Thatcher, preparing to detach himself.

"I know I'm right," said Vandam, with a resurgence of his old style. "There's a limit to how long situations like this can hang fire, you know. Sooner or later, somebody has to do something."

10 ATTRACTS PESTS

THE annual conventions of learned societies are not simple forums for the dissemination of knowledge. Each convention is a beehive buzzing with activity. There are people reporting on research, there are members intriguing for committee appointments, there are publishers' reps in search of authors—and there is even commerce. Every discipline uses something that somebody else is selling. Suppliers of laboratory equipment, computers, microfiches all rent hospitality suites in which to woo new customers.

With all these interests converging on even the simplest meeting, it is not surprising that many of them attract satellite functions. For example, when the plant geneticists sat down in McCormick Place, the annual trade show for nursery equipment occupied the mall level of that giant complex, while the Illinois Flower Show was ensconced on the lobby level. The helicopter pad just outside, the taxi ranks to the east, the shuttle buses running from every major hotel in Chicago, were all delivering hordes of people to one or another of these events. Heedless of the icy temperatures reigning outdoors, heedless of Lake Michigan stretching in crystalline splendor under an arctic blue sky, they hurried indoors to the promise of lush, abundant fertility.

And, in the finest traditions of horticulture, there was a good deal of cross-pollination. Flower growers inspected new sprinklers, greenhouse manufacturers buttonholed passing botanists, and geneticists stole a few moments to take in the new lilies. But even under the pressure of this triangular traffic, it was surprising how many persons found time to add to the swelling rumors about *Wisconsin Seedsmen v. Vandam's*.

Partly this was the result of simple physical circumstance. The flower enthusiasts and the nurserymen were provided with acres and acres of exhibit space. On those floors it was normal for crowds to amble from one booth to another, listening to sales pitches, watching live demonstrations of new equipment, accepting glossy brochures, and even gently inhaling the fragrance of exotic blooms. The plant geneticists, however, were made of sterner stuff. Their activities were conducted in a series of conference rooms, ranging from small cubbyholes to vast amphitheaters. In this antiseptic atmosphere, the only exhibit in evidence was like a splash of primary color in a sea of grey.

Everyone entering the meetings had to stop at the registration desk and then pass through double doors leading to their section of the convention center. In the foyer area directly before the doors *Numero Uno* stood on a pedestal in solitary splendor. A placard listed the virtues of the plant, but the only reference to origin was the chaste legend: *Patent Applied For*. The pedestal was flanked by two employees of the Society of Plant Sciences, ostensibly there to provide additional technical information, actually to ensure that Vandam's and Scott Wenzel abided by their agreement to avoid proprietary claims. There was a constant crowd surrounding the pedestal, continually reinforced by newcomers, and the air rang with their comments, surmises and appreciation.

In fact, Barbara Gunn was halted in her tracks by the display. It was an eye-opener even for someone who had spent five years on the job.

"Have you heard about the patent suit?" one spectator called to another. "I wondered why they were washing their dirty linen in public before I saw what's at stake. But, God, this baby is going to be worth millions. No wonder they're willing to slug it out."

"I hear they're ready to commit murder over at Standard Foods," came the reply, so cheerfully given that the speaker had to be a competitor. "They had it all sewed up, and now there's a good chance it will slip away. They'll pull every trick in the book to hang on."

This invigorating prophecy encouraged more speculation.

"It'd be like losing the patent on Polaroid," someone offered. "What do a few warm bodies matter?"

Barbara was accustomed to Scott Wenzel and Ned Ackerman. This was her first exposure to public opinion.

"I don't understand," she said cautiously to the man who had just apologized for jostling her. "They bring out new tomatoes every year, don't they? Why should this one be so much more important?"

He was delighted to explain to a young, pretty girl.

"All the others have been variations on the same old theme—hybrids that are disease resistant or more productive. But, from an overall point of view, this one is a revolution. Just as an example, canners will be able to operate year-round. And scientifically speaking, it's a real breakthrough in methods of propagation."

"Yes," she said quickly. "I can see that, but why are you so sure that there's going to be a big fight about it? Maybe they'll get together and share it."

She remembered saying something like this to Ned Ackerman. This time her listener laughed aloud.

"Share it!" he hooted. "Good God, would Newton have shared the theory of gravity, would Darwin have shared the origin of species! This is a once-in-a-lifetime kind of thing. If it were mine . . ." Words failed him as he searched for the right metaphor. Finally: "Would a mother share her newborn baby?"

His flow of eloquence was more impressive than he realized. Little by little, the bits were falling into place for Barbara. She had started by assuming that genetics was something of no interest to ordinary human beings. When the fireworks began, she attributed them to Scotty's prickly personality. But here in McCormick Place it was finally coming home to her how much money and prestige was riding on that bush. And for the first time, she made a vital connection. She, Barbara Gunn, was going to be in the thick of it.

When the lawyers had scheduled her deposition for immediately after the meetings, Ned Ackerman had made light of her apprehension. Why should she be more nervous than a pack of teen-agers?

How alike men were, she thought bitterly. They soothed you and cajoled you, they appealed to loyalty and friendship, while they were playing on your ignorance and misinformation.

She might not understand genetics, but she did understand office procedures at Wisconsin Seed. Who else could swear to the day on which Scotty dictated certain lab notes? Who else was going to have to say under oath that there had been no alteration in certain shorthand books? Who else knew the order in which certain charts had been filed?

She was not going to be lost in the crowd; her ordeal was not going to be confined to giving a deposition.

"I'm going to be the star witness at the trial," she thought with a lurching stomach. "Oh, damn them all! They might have told me the truth!"

The commercial value of *Numero Uno* came as no surprise to Howard Pendleton. Nor did the rapacious interest of his colleagues. In his experience, the more elevated the academic status, the firmer the attachment to things of this world. But although he was prepared for what he found, he still did not like it. All morning his progress through McCormick Place had brought him face to face with animated knots of gossipers. He had been safe for the last hour and a half, during which period he had been moderating a panel. The furlough was about to end.

"If there are no further questions from the floor?" he asked, his practiced ear having noted the faltering tempo of the last exchange.

"Well then, I think we can declare this meeting adjourned, pausing only to express our gratitude to the distinguished panelists who have given us the benefit of their research work in this area. And of course our special thanks go to Professor Christian Helsgrod for bringing us up to date on the research in Stockholm."

There was a polite patter of applause, most of the assembly scrambled for the doors, and one beady-eyed man headed straight for the chairman.

"Well, Howard, it's a relief you were able to make it. And I can't thank you enough for going on with the panel."

Pendleton pretended to misunderstand. "I agreed to be moderator last August, Stuart," he said.

"Yes, I know, but you've got so much on your hands these days, Howard, we all would have understood if you'd withdrawn."

Pendleton had learned to control himself in public a long time ago. He agreed that he was busy, very busy.

"I can't remember when we've had so many simultaneous projects at IPR. We may have bitten off more than we can chew. But one thing's certain, we're going to have to take on a few more assistants. That's why I have to start interviewing. Otherwise I'd love to have a bite with you."

Stuart Downing and Pendleton had been competitors since their student days. Downing had always been consumed with envy. Pendleton had achieved prominence early in his career. Pendleton was head of his own institute. Above all, Pendleton's salary was not dictated by a state legislature. If he was now heading for a fall, it was only fair. Some of the rumors—and downright slander—suggested this might be the case, and Downing hungered for signs of confirmation.

But none was forthcoming. Howard was not nervous, Howard was not embarrassed, Howard was not even using his schedule as an excuse to avoid conversation. On the contrary, he was his normal cordial self, busy but never too busy for a few words with a friend. "I expect we'll be running into each other at the interviews," he continued.

"Not the way research funds have been drying up," Stuart muttered, automatically falling back on a stock complaint.

"Ah, yes, I'd forgotten. These are lean days at the state universities," Pendleton said with a kindly air of detachment.

Pricked, Downing moved to the offensive. "Actually I thought you'd be so busy with this big lawsuit of yours, you might not show up at all."

"Good Lord, no. Vandam's is taking care of all that," Pendleton replied negligently. "Of course, they've asked us to recommend some expert witnesses to review the scientific exhibits."

The gleam of anticipation in Downing's eye was not wasted on Pendleton.

"I've told them you can overdo that sort of thing," he went on, calculating every word. "Far better to concentrate on quality than have an army of nonentities trooping to the stand and boring everybody to death. I advised them to be satisfied with three experts, so long as they were three of the top men. It's not so easy to find them, though."

Downing was almost licking his lips by now. But the next sentences he heard were not those he expected.

"Whittingsley and Santanelli go without saying, naturally," said Dr. Pendleton judiciously. "But where in the world am I supposed to find a third man of that caliber?"

For a moment his glance appraised his companion. Then he passed on to a new subject.

"By the way, Stuart, as you won't be doing any hiring yourself, you don't know a bright youngster we could use, do you? Fran is looking for an assistant on her floribunda work and she really needs someone who has . . ."

Late that evening Dr. Pendleton described the outcome to his wife.

"That S.O.B. really thought I was going to beg him to be a witness, so he could have the pleasure of refusing. By the time I was done with him, it was the other way around. There's nothing he wouldn't do to be linked with Whittingsley and Santanelli. I haven't known Stuart Downing for thirty years without learning what'll make him go down on his knees."

"You're so good at handling people, Howard," Fran murmured without lifting her eyes from the paper she was delivering the next day.

Dick Vandam could have used lessons in this all-important subject. By now he was convinced that the Pendletons had been unnecessarily pessimistic about the amount of support to be wrung from their witnesses. After all, Vandam's had certain levers unavailable to most defendants. As he advanced on his prey, Dick forgot that, in order to use a lever, you first need a place to stand.

"Dr. Santanelli! What a coincidence running into you!"

He had been tracking the man down for an hour.

"Mr. Vandam! I didn't expect to see you until the banquet tomorrow night."

Mrs. Mary Larrabee was receiving her check for ten thousand dollars at the annual dinner of the American Sweet

Pea Society and, consequently, Vandam's had adopted a possessive attitude toward the occasion.

"I'm glad you're going to be there. We expect it to be a great evening. Mrs. Larrabee's *Firecracker* will be in gardens all over the country next year. And we do like to encourage amateur enterprise of that sort, although we realize it cannot compare to the work being done with modern technical facilities."

Dr. Santanelli did not disappoint him.

"Such as in our new laboratory."

"I've been meaning to ask about that. I hope it's working out as well in practice as the architect promised."

Vandam's did not confine its benefactions to contests for the general public. Most major universities had a Vandam Graduate Fellowship. Dr. Santanelli's own particular bailiwick now boasted a Vandam Laboratory of Plant Science.

The professor waxed enthusiastic. "A beautiful building! And the equipment is everything we could ask for. The temperature-control rooms, the humidity system, the computer terminals."

"I'm pleased to hear it." Vandam smiled modestly before tossing in a negligent addendum. "By the way, you may not know about our lawsuit. I wanted to ask you—"

Beaming, Dr. Santanelli did not let him go further. "Howard Pendleton has already asked me to be an expert witness for you. I agreed at once. From what he tells me of the evidence, there is no possibility of independent research and I will so tell the court."

"Fine! And we'd like to emphasize the different caliber of the two research teams. Naturally everybody knows the kind of effort we put into our development program, but it won't hurt to make sure the judge gets a realistic view of the probabilities."

Santanelli stiffened. "I could not possibly pretend to evaluate the comparative competence of Dr. Pendleton and Dr. Wenzel."

"But you've known Howard Pendleton for—"

"An expert witness is only asked for his judgment of factual evidence. I can look at two sets of laboratory notes and say that, in my opinion, one set has been copied from the other. But as to which is genuine and which is fake . . ." Here both palms turned upward. "For that you want a crime expert, not a botanical expert."

Vandam reddened angrily. That's gratitude for you, he thought to himself. Fifteen million dollars for that building and all we get in exchange is a lecture. Well, that's the last penny Dr. Joseph Santanelli ever sees from us. He's going to find out he's offended the biggest force in contemporary horticulture.

Dick Vandam should have known better. His company was not the biggest force in horticulture and never had been. In America that honor rests with the U.S. Department of Agriculture.

And their two representatives were having lunch with Ned Ackerman.

McCormick Place has taken every possible precaution to ensure that its visitors are adequately nourished at a price they can afford. Leaving aside the stand-up sandwich bars intended for transient spectators, there were basically three types of eatery available. Corporate executives and the high panjandrums of academia instinctively found their way to the dining room restaurant where they could lunch in splendor looking out over the lake. Earl Sanders had never considered any other locale for his tête-à-tête with Milton Vandam over expense-account veal piccata. Flower exhibitors, graduate students, and secretaries just as instinctively headed below to the cafeteria, where Barbara Gunn and Eric Most had the misfortune to find themselves elbow to elbow with overcrowded trays, a stalled checkout line, and no possibility of ignoring each other. But the separation into have's and have-not's is by no means this absolute. Right in the middle of the bustling lobby there is a cheerful sidewalk café, and it was here that Ned Ackerman and his old friends were having a substantial meal in solid second-class comfort.

"I hear you're beating the bushes for expert witnesses, Ned. How come you're not asking any of us?"

"Listen, Steve, the last thing I want right now is anybody from USDA testifying," Ackerman replied amiably. "Scotty can round up a couple of big shots for the witness stand."

The third man, a gaunt skeletal figure who required immense amounts of food, pushed away an empty plate and, with the serious work of the noon break taken care of, entered the conversation.

"That's a wonderful way to find out who's entitled to a patent," he jeered in friendly fashion. "You've got experts, they've got experts, and in the meantime the ones who could blow the whole thing apart are kept a long way from the courtroom."

Ackerman was not visibly troubled by this criticism. "Being on your own is a lot different than working for the Department, Gus," he replied. "They play by different rules out here."

Gus rubbed his nose thoughtfully. "Sure, but how long do you think you can sit on this thing?"

"Just as long as we have to. You boys know the kind of capital I have. Wisconsin Seed has got just one chance at the big time, and we're not blowing it!"

Steve was not convinced. "There's such a thing as playing your cards too close to your chest, Ned. You can get burned that way."

A grin split Ackerman's face. "It depends on the odds. There are capers you can pull off in a small outfit that wouldn't stand a chance in a big one. This time the advantage is on our side. Nobody in the world knows a goddamned thing except Scotty and me."

Downstairs in the cafeteria Barbara Gunn threw a despairing glance at the bottleneck by the cashier's desk. Would she never be able to end this encounter?

"No, Eric, I'm not going to discuss it anymore," she said through trembling lips. "I've already told you too much."

11 ORGANIC MATERIAL

THOUSANDS of out-of-towners were swirling around McCormick Place, working or pretending to work. Other thousands were not even pretending. The sedentary were hailing a cocktail waitress, then settling in for a good talk, frequently about *Numero Uno*. The more energetic were touring the Art Institute, shopping at Marshall Field's or exploring Rush Street. In pre-ERA days these extracurricular delights (minus Rush Street) had been laid on for the wives. Now, with everybody's consciousness raised, the frills offered for spouses were scrupulously non-sexist.

Nevertheless, most of the Entertainment Committee's clients were still wives, not husbands. It was through this Ladies Entrance that John Thatcher was inexorably sucked into the festivities.

The lady in question was Mrs. Mary Larrabee, recipient-to-be of Vandam's ten-thousand-dollar prize for the perfect sweet pea. Wishing to do the right thing by their heroine, Vandam's had consulted the Entertainment Committee. None of their proposed outings impressed Vandam's. Finally someone had the daring notion of asking Mrs. Larrabee what *she* would like to do or see in Chicago.

Mrs. Larrabee wanted to visit the stockyards. She had wanted to see the stockyards since she was a small child.

But her mother and father had refused to take her and, as for Pete . . .

The stockyards, the Entertainment Committee retorted, had left town.

Pete Larrabee heaved a sigh of relief while Mary thought deeply. "Then I'd like to tour the market," she said firmly.

"You mean the Board of Trade?"

"No, the wholesale produce market. Where stores buy their fruits and vegetables."

The Entertainment Committee, which prided itself on a lengthy roster of tourist attractions, huffily told Vandam's that no one had ever before turned down the Oriental Institute and Sears Tower in favor of the market. As a matter of fact, the Entertainment Committee was not at all sure it could make the arrangements.

Vandam's in turn told Standard Foods, and Standard Foods told John Thatcher.

"It shouldn't be insuperably difficult," he said rashly. "Find someone who goes to the market, and get him to take Mrs. Larrabee along."

With those unconsidered words, he established himself as an authority on the subject and considerably delayed his return to the Sloan.

"Find someone who goes to the market?" Earl Sanders asked helplessly. "Who goes to the market?"

"A good many of Standard Foods' customers," replied Thatcher, knowing full well that Sanders thought of SF customers as permanently glued to their expensive desks. "What you want is someone who drives a truck."

Leaving Sanders completely flummoxed, Thatcher departed for the Midwestern Trust where Edgar Brown took this harmless anecdote and ran with it. First he delivered a pithy sermon about hands-on experience as an essential step on the corporate ladder. Then he initiated several phone calls.

"Oh thanks, but—" Thatcher protested.

"Easiest damn thing in the world," Brown assured him.

Willy-nilly, Thatcher found himself cast as tour leader. Mr. Bernard Gordon, owner of the Gordon Markets that spangled Cook County, was delighted to oblige any friend of Edgar Brown's. It would take him no more than an hour, he promised, to set things up.

"Thank you very much," said Thatcher, now resigned to further involvement.

It began when he got back to the Hyatt. Just as he was preparing to join Charlie Trinkam for dinner, the phone rang.

"Mr. Thatcher." It was an accusation, not a question, and when Thatcher admitted as much, the caller said throatily, "Vince Mancuso."

"Oh yes," said Thatcher, putting two and two together. No one at Wenonah Industries sounded remotely like Vince Mancuso. Possibly this was part of their problem. "Mr. Gordon said someone would be calling—"

Mancuso fell on the name. "He told me to call you," he said, disavowing personal responsibility. "He says you want to go to South Water Street tonight. And he says you want to take some lady along."

Without giving Thatcher a chance to comment, he added, "And Mr. Gordon says that means I don't take the truck."

"I see," said Thatcher, beginning to fear that Gordon had used the stick, not the carrot.

But Mancuso only wanted to spell out his instructions. "It's okay by me, if that's what you want," he said generously. "Here's what we'll do . . ."

His subsequent words banished other concerns from Thatcher's mind.

"Say what you will about Wenonah Industries," he said to Charlie with some heat, "they've never asked me to get up in the middle of the night."

"Of course not," said Charlie, absorbed in his own problems, "even in broad daylight, they're not wide awake."

Chicago has its beauty spots. Nineteenth Street, between Racine and Morgan, is not one of them. At three o'clock in the morning on a frigid Tuesday in January it resembled an outpost of hell. The unearthly glow of sodium lights illuminated a vast, terrible wasteland.

The streets were almost deserted except for an occasional truck, a disquieting number of police cruisers and, courtesy of Bernard Gordon and Gordon Markets, a magnificently inappropriate Cadillac complete with uniformed chauffeur.

The passengers were pretty incongruous too. Mrs. Larrabee, the only one who had boarded with marked enthusiasm, was alternately shocked and fascinated by what she saw. Jason Ingersoll, escorting her on behalf of Vandam's, was noticeably subdued. The other two members of the expedition were Vince Mancuso and John Thatcher, and Thatcher always let experts hold the floor.

Mancuso, initially constrained by surroundings and company, got along with Mary Larrabee like a house afire.

"Oh, my!" she exclaimed as they glided past a particularly desolate intersection.

"Used to be real nice here," he said, breathing heavily.

Fortunately, before they could delve further into urban blight, the limousine turned into a short roadway and they rolled into the South Water Street Market.

"Oh, my!" said Mrs. Larrabee once more.

"Yes, indeed," said Thatcher, following her out of the car.

It was an astonishing sight—long city blocks lined with brightly lit loading platforms piled high with crates and mounds of potatoes, lettuce, onions, cabbages, mushrooms, bananas and celery. Trucks ranging from huge six wheelers to battered pickups jockeyed through the street between the cliffs of produce, while aproned men and boys swore and grunted as they heaved heavy burdens into the trucks. And, all the time, there was the ceaseless chant of market-making:

"How much?"

"Two dollars a bushel."

"Too much."

"Six bushels for eleven-fifty."

"Five for nine."

"Okay, Louis."

It was not the leisurely haggling of the bazaar but the electric current of split-second decisions that crackled in the pre-dawn air.

"You people want to come this way?" said Mancuso, gaining authority by the minute. Without waiting, he clambered up the ladder to the first platform, then turned into a darkened stairway that led to a second-floor room.

Sensible woman that she was, Mary Larrabee had come prepared in boots, slacks and a woolly cap. For following Mancuso, she was more suitably garbed than either Ingersoll or John Thatcher. Even so, she attracted all the attention. Business suits and overcoats might be uncommon at South Water; women were a rarity.

Upstairs, they discovered that Mancuso was starting the tour with hospitality. He gestured toward a battered coffee urn on an even more battered table before turning to the sole occupant of the room. "Hi, Bruno."

Bruno was large, heavily sweatered, and bemused. Impassively he nodded a reply, studied Mancuso's charges, gulped his coffee and lumbered off. Thatcher had a sudden vivid image of these two men meeting over this urn night after night.

"How far does your friend Bruno drive?" he asked, stirring his coffee.

"Wisconsin," Vince replied briefly, without realizing that he and Bruno were living confirmation of Adam Smith.

"That's a long way from here, isn't it?" Mary Larrabee marveled.

Indulgently, Mancuso formulated a maxim for her. "You want fresh fruit, you got to go a long way."

There was a respectful silence. Finally, tossing his cup into a refuse barrel, Mancuso said, "Whenever you're ready."

Obediently they all followed suit, then trooped downstairs where the first stop was an area big enough to berth a destroyer. It was filled with bags, bins, crates and bushels of potatoes. Vince left them standing (in everybody's way, it developed) and approached a tall man with clipboard, pencil and eyes that watched everything and everyone. After a minute's talk, Vince nodded and disappeared to the back of the floor where Thatcher saw a cashier. Mr. Gordon, he appreciated, was your true businessman. Vince was not giving them a guided tour; they were accompanying Vince on his regular rounds.

Another aspect struck Mary Larrabee as she was nipped from the path of an oncoming dolly. "You mean you bought all the potatoes for your chain of stores, just like that?" she asked.

A hunching of shoulders, a turning out of palms, was her answer. Why else would he be here?

"How many?" she wanted to know.

When she learned that Mancuso had just purchased five hundred crates of potatoes for Gordon Markets, she was impressed but still practical.

"Where are you going to put them?"

Gordon Market trucks were out there, shadowing Vince. The Cadillac was a nosegay for Mary Larrabee.

From what he had seen of her, Thatcher suspected she might have preferred to ride shotgun.

Certainly she enjoyed every moment of their progress from potatoes to onions, from spinach to grapefruit and on — past more potatoes and more onions. The provisioning of a great city thrilled her. Thatcher himself was no stranger to this link in the distribution chain. Middlemen, as well as consumers and producers, were solid Sloan clients. The artichoke king of Manhattan, for example, was solider than most. Nevertheless, the spectacle remained engrossing. Stripped of trucks and pocket calculators, South Water could have served Rome or Constantinople. In essence, they were viewing the bedrock on which the whole intricate system of capitalism rested. Without earlier Vince Mancusos, there would have been no Sloan Guaranty Trust.

Even Jason Ingersoll began waking up as they waited for Mancuso to buy strawberries or reject beets. In Ingersoll's case, it was not man and economics. It was produce. Totally aloof from the bargaining around him, he picked up a green pepper, then critically sniffed.

"Can you recognize a Vandam product when you see one?" asked Thatcher, noting out of the corner of his eye that the proprietor of the stall was gallantly presenting Mrs. Larrabee with a grapefruit.

Ingersoll grinned. "Some of the old-timers claim they can. Not me. But I can still tell you that this pepper is probably Vandam's." He tapped one of the crates piled high before him. *"The Vallejo Valley, Mexico,"* he read from the label. "Just about seventy percent of the Valley peppers are Vandam's *Peppino*. They've been switching more and more every year. The Vandam peppers are smaller, but they're uniform. That saves a whale of a lot in transport and processing costs."

"You can say that again," said a nearby voice. The owner of the pepper display, having finished with Vince, had a minute to spare. Like everybody else who had watched them, he was curious. "You know peppers?" he asked Jason mistrustfully.

"I should," Ingersoll responded. "I'm with Vandam's."

"How about that!" said the pepper merchant, turning alertly as a potential customer materialized from the rear.

After peppers, the character of their exploration of South Water Street changed. Vince Mancuso went on buying or not buying. Mary Larrabee watched with undiminished fascination, while collecting an avocado, two cucumbers and other tribute. But Thatcher and Ingersoll did not trail unnoticed in their wake. Ingersoll's connection with Vandam's sped ahead of them, by means unknown and unseen, producing widespread cordiality. In one stall—radishes—it flushed the proprietor, who emerged from a desk near the cashier to join his floor man. They were surrounded by carrots as well as radishes but, Mr. Mavroulis explained, root crops were winter only. In season he handled peas and beans.

". . . and those *Sugarinas* of yours. I could sell twice as many as I get."

"Well, you're going to be getting more," said Ingersoll, shaking hands vigorously. "Orders for *Sugarina* are really taking off. Just like our *Calico* corn."

"Good, good," said Mavroulis.

As they continued on, Thatcher told himself he was seeing a new and improved Ingersoll. He was friendly, open and, in view of the flattering attention, modest. Scott Wenzel would not recognize him. For that matter, neither would Dick Vandam.

The acid test lay just ahead. They had finished one long flank of the market. Mancuso climbed down to street level and was making for the opposite side when Mrs. Larrabee grabbed his arm.

"What about that?" she demanded, pointing across a pathway to an extension of the long row of buildings they had just traversed. To Thatcher's naked eye, it looked like more of the same, but then so did Mancuso's destination.

Mrs. Larrabee, however, was determined not to miss anything.

Mancuso had his standards. "That?" he said scornfully. "That's not the market."

"What do you mean, that's not the market?" she asked, her suspicions roused.

"I'll tell you," he riposted with gusto.

But reasoned explanation was not Mancuso's strong suit. Fortunately Thatcher grasped enough of the argument to interpret.

"That, Mrs. Larrabee, is where the independent truckers—those who service stores too small to come to market themselves—buy their supplies. They load up there, then make their own rounds. The sales volume is much smaller and, Mr. Mancuso feels, the quality is lower too."

"But small grocery stores always have better produce than supermarkets!"

"They have higher prices and, perhaps, better displays," he replied gently. Seeing the light of battle in her eye, he added hastily, "But possibly Mr. Mancuso is prejudiced."

Prejudiced or not, Mancuso left them no time to debate consumer sovereignty. Reaching the second side of the market, Thatcher discovered a more immediate topic of dispute. Tomatoes, tons of tomatoes, all large, unblemished, waxy and about as tempting as dyed baseballs—those tomatoes in fact that add color and nothing else to January salads and BLT's in the northern tier.

"From Mexico?" he asked Ingersoll.

"And a lot farther than Mexico," Ingersoll replied, examining the nearest specimen. "Picked weeks ago when it was green, treated chemically to bring up this pink tinge, which has nothing to do with ripening."

He had lowered his voice, but not enough.

"Hey!" said a pained Vince Mancuso, who had just bought three hundred cases of these pitiful objects.

Behind him, the vendor was less restrained. "Look, people want tomatoes, right? These are the only tomatoes we can sell them. You show me where I can get—"

"Next year, you'll be selling tomatoes from the Carolinas," said Ingersoll. "They'll be the next best thing to vine-ripened, and they'll be available year-round."

The tomato specialist favored him with a long hard look, then shrugged. "I'll believe it when I see it."

Ingersoll took this cyncism in good part. "When you see it, it'll be called Vandam's *Numero Uno,*" he said lightly, preparing to move on.

But he had struck a chord. Handing over clipboard and customers to an assistant, the wholesaler followed him. "I've heard something about that," he said. "There have been a lot of crazy rumors about some new tomato."

"They're not crazy," Ingersoll told him.

Again he was treated to suspicious scrutiny. "You have anything to do with it?"

Ingersoll explained his connection with Vandam's, inviting a comprehensive cross-examination on the availability, taste and probable wholesale cost of *Numero Uno.* As Thatcher looked on, incredulity warred with cupidity.

"If half what you say is true, I can triple my volume," said the dealer finally.

"At least," Ingersoll agreed.

Some variant of this exchange was repeated in each of the next twelve tomato stalls. By the time they reached the end of Vince Mancuso's circuit, Thatcher said, "In Chicago alone, *Numero Uno* is going to pay for its development."

"That's why . . ." Ingersoll broke off and started again. "In Chicago or New York or any other major market in the country."

That broken sentence, Thatcher knew in his bones, had to have something to do with Scott Wenzel.

By now a pallid dawn was lightening the sky. Trucks

were pulling out of the South Water Street Market, not into it, and the lights no longer stood out against the eerie, inky blackness. Beyond the grinding of gears and the cries of porters were other sounds—the throb of traffic on nearby streets. At four-thirty in the morning, the city was coming to life.

Mr. Mancuso was unable to accompany them back to the Hyatt. As if apologizing for a social lapse, he explained that the Produce Manager of Gordon Markets still had work to do. All those crates and bushels would be on display by nine when the stores opened.

"Including tomatoes," he said, emboldened to make a small joke. "Well, it's been my pleasure."

A Gordon Market truck stood waiting for him. After a hurried leave-taking, with special reference to Mary Larrabee, to whom he presented three beautiful oranges, they parted.

She sank back into the luxury of the limousine with a sigh of satisfaction. "What a nice man! You know, Mr. Ingersoll, this may have been the high point of my trip to Chicago," she said.

But Ingersoll had relapsed into his earlier isolation. He murmured something to the effect that Vandam's was happy to oblige, and left it to Thatcher to ask the obvious.

"Better than your banquet tonight, and your ten-thousand-dollar check?" he asked as the car sailed onto the expressway.

Chicago was preparing for the cold hard light of day and so was Mrs. Larrabee. Gazing past her lapful of oranges, grapefruit and peppers, she said, "Well, no."

"Let's hope not," said Ingersoll.

His attempt at geniality rang false. Clearly his thoughts were far, far away—and they were giving him no pleasure.

"It's going to be a long day, isn't it?" Mary Larrabee said sympathetically.

12 A CHOICE VARIETY

PRE-DAWN trips to South Water Street were not the only way to make the day long and hard. Dick Vandam had managed it without losing any sleep at all. His ill-advised attempt at strong-arm tactics had failed with Professor Santanelli and alarmed Santanelli's colleagues. As a result, those with hopes of future Vandam largesse became unavailable.

By midmorning Eric Most was getting desperate. So, when he finally spotted Dr. Whittingsley chatting with a small group, he rushed into action.

"Dr. Whittingsley!" he cried triumphantly.

The recognition was not mutual.

"Er . . . er . . ." Whittingsley stalled as his nearsighted eyes tried to decipher the name tag.

It did not help that one of the men who swiveled at the newcomer's voice was Scott Wenzel.

"This is Dr. Eric Most from IPR," he said obligingly.

What made this commencement particularly galling was Most's conviction that he looked like a man of distinction. He had blond hair, blue eyes and a reasonable build. His passport statistics, however, were misleading. He also had washed-out coloring, mass-produced features and no individuality. It was not unusual for him to be introduced to people four and five times. But to encounter Scott Wenzel was to recognize him for life. A mobile ugly face, a wiry undersized body and a thrusting combativeness may not be universally admired, but they are memorable.

After a curt nod of acknowledgment to his adversary, Eric began his pitch. "You probably know about our lawsuit, Dr. Whittingsley, and so—"

Scott Wenzel was enjoying himself. "You're too late, Eric," he broke in. "Dr. Whittingsley has signed up with our team."

Now that he had insured himself, Whittingsley could afford to be gracious to all comers.

"Yes, and having seen the tomato, I'm really looking forward to the notebooks. A remarkable development, no matter whether the credit belongs to Wisconsin Seed or Vandam's."

"Vandam's had nothing to do with it. They just did the field testing. The basic research is ours," Eric corrected him.

"Yours?" Whittingsley frowned, once more trying to place Most.

Again Scott Wenzel filled in the details. "You remember, Dr. Whittingsley, I told you that Vandam's is now claiming the research was done down in Puerto Rico, at IPR."

"There's no claiming about it!" Most snapped. "My experimental data is every bit as convincing as yours."

"Well, if one set of data has been copied from the other, you'd expect them to look alike," Wenzel explained slowly. "So it really doesn't make any difference who gets Dr. Whittingsley. All he can say is that something funny's going on."

"Why don't we let him make up his mind about that?"

Unfortunately Dr. Whittingsley was lagging two exchanges behind. "Isn't Howard Pendleton still head of IPR?" he asked the world at large.

"Of course he is," Most said too eagerly. "We've been working together on *Numero Uno*."

Wenzel grinned. "I'll bet Howard doesn't describe it that way. Not unless he's changed a lot."

Most ignored this. He had convinced himself that whatever damage had been done to the cause could be repaired by his persuasiveness.

"Of course now that you've agreed to testify for Wisconsin Seedsmen, there's no more to be said," he began, "but I wish you'd waited until you'd reviewed the evidence. I'm not puffing my own performance, but I think you'll be impressed at the very thorough foundation that enabled us to avoid dead ends in the intermediate stages."

Eric Most's high opinion of his own persuasiveness was not shared by other people. If Scott Wenzel was disturbed at leaving the field unguarded, he did not show it. With a casual flap of the hand he departed, saying there was a paper he wanted to hear.

The victory that Most had won was short-lived. Even as he was preparing further fluent sentences, Dr. Whittingsley realized that he, too, could rush off to hear papers.

"I certainly don't want to miss Faulkner, Dr. . . . er . . . er." Abandoning any attempt to recall the name, he tried to make amends. "And I certainly look forward to comparing your notebooks with Scott's."

On the whole, it was not one of Eric's better mornings.

Dr. Whittingsley and Dr. Santanelli were the acknowledged great men of their profession. Vandam's efforts to secure their services had resulted in losing one and alienating the other.

Earl Sanders did not like the score and, above all, he did not like discussing it with Milton Vandam.

"Disgraceful!" Milton was sputtering. "I can't remember when Vandam's has been treated this way."

Sanders was already regretting his ill-timed luncheon

hospitality yesterday. In Milton's book, they were now intimates.

"You've never had a major patent suit before," he growled.

"These problems would never have arisen if you'd had an experienced man in charge of R&D. But that's what happens when you hand over the most important operation in the place to a boy who doesn't know the people or the conditions or the competition."

Sanders stared resentfully around the expansive hospitality suite laid on by Standard Foods. In another hour it would be jammed with enough freeloaders to insulate him from unwelcome encounters. But, at ten-thirty in the morning, the rooms were just as the cleaners had left them. The deep-piled carpet was still airy and buoyant. Virginal ashtrays adorned every horizontal surface. And, in the opposite corner, an array of bottles that could have stocked a retail establishment winked in the sunlight.

"It was Dick who put everybody's back up," he said bluntly. "And, God knows, he's had enough years in the business."

"He shouldn't have been in a position where he had to make the approach," Milton replied. "That never would have happened if I'd still been in charge."

Discontentedly chewing his third antacid tablet, Sanders realized he should not be surprised that it was Milton, easily the stupidest of the Vandams, who was dogging his steps. Milton had been tossed out on his ear as a result of the takeover. After an experience like that, even a dumbbell recognized who had the muscle. Milton wanted his old job back from the very source that had deprived him of it.

"Look how everything's gone downhill," he persisted. "Money absolutely poured into IPR. A lab so free and easy that the first comer can steal their results. Then a patent suit that destroys our catalog schedule and embarrasses us in public. You can't say anything like that took place in my time. No thefts, no suits, no catalog delays."

"No nothing," Sanders said sourly, recalling the record of inanition built up by R&D. But he was surprised at the sweeping nature of the indictment. Maybe he had under-estimated Milton's objective. Maybe it was Dick's job he was after. "You haven't forgotten that you were there when the *Numero Uno* deal was put together, have you? And for four years afterward?"

"And everything was fine then."

"What the hell do you mean by that? That was when the theft took place."

"There's no point looking to the past," Milton said airily. "We must look to the future."

But he had delayed his battle cry too long. Earl Sanders' wishes had been fulfilled and they were no longer alone. Shyly pushing open the door and thrusting in his head was that stock character of all conventions, the perambulating drunk. As he wavered on the threshold—red-eyed, unfocused, his convention badge askew—he would have been an unprepossessing figure to most people. But to Sanders he was a pearl of great price.

"Come in, come in!" he trumpeted.

His excessive cordiality almost backfired. The boozer, unused to enthusiastic welcomes, first shied nervously, then turned coquettish.

"Don't want to butt in. I can always go someplace else. You two may want to be private," he declared, waggling his head solemnly.

By now Sanders had his elbow in a firm clasp and was steering him to the bar.

"Standard Foods is always happy to see any visitor to the genetics meetings," he said. "Have a drink."

The drunk recognized power when it was in his hands. "Not that bottle." He pointed an unsteady finger. "This one."

Milton was forced to screw his head around and speak over his shoulder. "And what's being done to solve our problems? Nothing, that's what! I say it's time we put some pressure on Wisconsin Seed. And considering that we're faced with an emergency, I may be forced to take action myself."

Clink! Clink! Clink! went the ice cubes, drowning him out.

Actually, Milton's efforts had already begun. Later that morning Jason Ingersoll was telling Howard Pendleton about them.

"Honest to God, I don't know what Milton thinks he's doing. First he's bird-dogging Earl Sanders. Now he's trying to pump one of the girls from Wisconsin Seed."

"Are you sure? I didn't think Wenzel traveled with a lot of flunkies and . . ." Pendleton broke off. "You don't mean Barbara Gunn, do you?"

"Her name tag just said Wisconsin Seed."

"Timid-looking girl?" Pendleton pressed. "Very fair and slight?"

"That's her all right," Ingersoll confirmed. "Except when I saw her just now she wasn't looking timid, she looked scared to death. Milton had her backed up against a wall."

"I didn't think they knew each other. Is Milton running around threatening total strangers?"

Jason's posture was that he and Howard Pendleton had been fellow sufferers under Milton. "You remember what he's like. He probably saw the name of the company and went into action. But he wasn't threatening her. The one phrase I overheard was: *There could be a nice little present in this for you.* Maybe he was trying to find out how she's going to testify."

Having trailed his lure, Jason sat back and waited for the fish to bite.

Pendleton stared at him, transfixed. "That's even worse than I thought," he said. "Do you realize he may not just be pumping her? He may be crazy enough to suggest perjury. To Barbara Gunn, of all people! She'd be horrified."

"She looked as if she was going to run to the first person she trusted and burst into tears," Jason said bluntly.

"This is too much," declared Pendleton, who was now angrily striding back and forth across the room. "I didn't like it when I learned about the patent suit. I knew there were going to be plenty of unpleasant consequences. But at least I thought Vandam's was united with me in a rational defense of our property. Instead, what happens? I get the top man in the country to testify for us, and your uncle Dick messes things up so much that I'm going to have to waste hours soothing Santanelli. And your cousin is running around trying to suborn witnesses who don't know anything about genetics anyway. What's more, he's doing it where any passerby can overhear him. And God only knows what you've been up to."

Jason shifted uneasily.

"I tell you I'm sick of all this," Pendleton continued in more measured tones. "I've a good mind to go to Earl Sanders and tell him that unless Standard Foods takes over the defense, they can count me out."

This was not the script Jason had planned. Pendleton was supposed to complain about Milton to Dick Vandam. He was not supposed to go haring off to Standard Foods with a denunciation of the entire Vandam family. Doggedly Jason tried to get them back on track.

"I realize you have every right to be upset," he said earnestly. "Uncle Dick himself would be the first to regret having made things more awkward for you. But, if you'll just talk this over with him, I'm sure you'll find him helpful. He may even be able to muzzle Milton before any real damage is done. I'd give it a try myself, except that I'd probably just put Milton's back up. Now Uncle Dick, he can handle Milton—and hopefully, he can do it before Wenzel's lawyers start yelling about bribery. Because that's what we're all after, isn't it?"

Howard Pendleton's eyes narrowed appraisingly during this speech. When it was over he could not keep the contempt from his voice.

"Do you think I'm a fool? I know exactly what you're after."

Pendleton would have liked to warn his wife about the latest vagaries from Vandam's, but her schedule at the meetings was even busier than his own. He did not see her until a sudden need for notes sent him back to his room at the Blackstone Hotel. As he impatiently waited for the up elevator, Fran emerged from a down car.

"Good," he muttered, grabbing at her as she marched unseeingly past him. "Fran, we've got a real mess on our hands."

"Not now, Howard," she said tightly.

He recognized the symptoms. Fran was in the grip of her chronic speaker's paralysis. She was an indefatigable researcher with a list of papers a mile long, but she dreaded mounting a platform and delivering them viva voce.

"This is important," her husband insisted. "The Vandams are busy planting a lot of land mines that are going to explode in our faces."

His urgency penetrated Fran's fog. She blinked several times as she decompressed from a world of terrifyingly expectant listeners to a world of more variegated vistas and problems. Unfortunately her emergent vision espied something that did not help.

"Look, there's Barbara Gunn heading this way. Oh dear, I meant to call her as soon as we hit Chicago."

Pendleton cursed softly under his breath. The last person

he wanted to see at the moment was Barbara. Not without more information about Milton's doings.

Meanwhile Barbara, forging toward the elevator, and Fran, battling away from it, had come face to face.

"Oh, Barbara," Fran plunged ahead, "I've been hoping we can get together as soon as this wretched paper is out of the way. Of course the banquet is tonight, but tomorrow is an easy day. You could take a couple of hours off at lunchtime, couldn't you, Howard? . . . Where has he gone? Oh, some people have nabbed him. . . . Well, never mind about Howard, Barbara, let's make it certain for lunch."

But Barbara was shrinking nervously away. "Oh, I don't think so, Fran. I mean, Scott's so busy, I can't really make plans."

Fran's eyes widened. "He's always busy at meetings. That's never stopped you before."

"Well, this convention isn't like the others," Barbara burst out. "It's just awful the way everyone circles around you the minute they see the name tag, hoping for some inside dirt."

The scant time that Fran could spare from her own activities had been devoted to sympathizing with Howard.

"Oh, come on, Barbara," she scoffed. "Are you trying to tell me that Scotty is bothered by the notoriety he's stirring up? He's too thick-skinned for that."

"I'm not talking about Scotty. I'm talking about me!"

Fran had spent too many years as a mother not to recognize a childlike wail of distress when she heard one.

"But, Barbara, this is between the two companies. It doesn't have anything to do with you."

"Oh, doesn't it?" Barbara bit down on her underlip to control the perilous trembling of her mouth. It was a moment before she continued. "I have to give a deposition when the meetings are over. Then I'll have to be a witness at the trial. And no matter what I say, I'm going to make out either

Scotty or Howard to be a liar. Oh, Fran, I wish I could get away from it all."

"Well, you can't!" Fran had been startled enough by Barbara's forecast to snap her reply. She was instantly contrite. "I'm sorry, but honestly, I think you're refining on this too much. Of course it's awful for you to be caught in the middle when they're both your friends. But just forget about the implications and tell the truth. It's that simple."

"You wouldn't say that if you were the one testifying!"

"But, Barbara—"

"I'm sorry, Fran, I can't stay. I have to go."

With each phrase Barbara had been edging farther away. Now she turned and bolted for the front doors.

Fran, left standing with her mouth open, looked first at the elevators, then at the doors. Finally she reached a bewildering conclusion.

"Why, she was running away. From me!"

By five o'clock that afternoon many of the chores scheduled for the Chicago meetings had been successfully completed. Both Scott Wenzel and Fran Pendleton had delivered papers. Fran's had been a major contribution to the lore of floribunda, timed to remind the world that IPR had more than one iron in the fire. Scott's had been a very small paper on a very small subject, designed to prove that he was not only a brilliant creative scientist, but also the kind of steady reliable man who cleans up loose ends as he goes along. The Vandams knew that the banquet had become a sellout attraction, largely because of interest in Mrs. Larrabee's *Firecracker*. The roster of expert witnesses had been finalized without further incident.

But the parties to the *Numero Uno* controversy, instead of being soothed by a sense of achievement, now found themselves with sufficient leisure for internal bickering.

"So what, if everybody likes *Firecracker?*" Milton complained. "We're not selling it yet."

"We will be next year."

"If you had taken the trouble to visit the flower show, Dick, you would have seen for yourself that the big crowds are around *Old Nassau* marigold and *Aquarius* snapdragon," Milton continued nattering. "And they're on sale right now by Burpee's and Parke's—our competition!"

Milton could maintain a high tide of indignation longer than anyone else he knew, Dick reflected. He sometimes envied Milton's ex, who had left for the divorce court years ago.

"I'll get around to the flower show," he promised. "But it will still be here next week, and the equipment trade show won't."

He had simply provided fuel for the fire.

"At this crisis in the company's history," Milton said sternly, "I think you should be concentrating more on making money than on spending it."

When Howard Pendleton finally found an opportunity to relay Jason's information, Fran was more confused than ever.

"Of course I'm sorry that all this is landing on poor Barbara," she said. "But that doesn't explain why she should be frightened of me. I tell you, Howard, she lit out of there as if I were some kind of monster. She could barely bring herself to speak to me."

"I'm glad."

A dawning suspicion was confirmed for Fran.

"Why, Howard! You deliberately skipped out on me by the elevators," she charged.

"I did," he agreed forthrightly. "For God's sake, Fran, use your head. If Milton has been bribing opposition witnesses, I don't want to know about it."

"Oh dear." Then, ashamed of this inadequate response, Fran tried for a more helpful approach. "But you said Jason wasn't sure. Maybe Milton just wanted to know how she would testify."

Eric Most took up the task of convincing Fran there was no happy solution. "If Barbara Gunn has agreed to lie her head off for Wisconsin Seed, that's why she doesn't want to talk to anybody from our side."

"I can't believe it," Fran protested. "In the first place, it's just too terrible to contemplate. No matter what Scott himself may have done, it would be ten times worse if he involved Barbara in it."

"That just means you don't want to believe it," Most pointed out. "It's not proof Wenzel didn't do it."

Fran looked at her husband's assistant with dislike. "In the second place," she grated, "Scott is quite shrewd about people. I admit he could probably get Barbara to agree to anything, but what good would it do him? You'd have to be a fool not to realize she wouldn't last two minutes under cross-examination."

"Probably that's why she's falling apart," said Most with every evidence of satisfaction. "The lawyers will have a field day with her."

Fran glared at him. "That's what you'd like, isn't it? To have Scotty and Barbara torn apart in public?"

"They should have thought about that before they stole my research!"

Belligerence was yielding to distress. "There has to be some other explanation," Fran insisted. "But I'll tell you one thing. I'm beginning to think Barbara ran away because in another minute she would have broken down and told me everything."

"Oh, God," groaned Pendleton. "Stay away from her, Fran, I beg of you. Regardless of whether it's Milton or Scott or even that Ackerman who's bothering her, it's going to be a professional disaster if she makes us her confidants. Let her tell the lawyers or the judge or some other intermediary."

"You don't really think Scott's asking her to commit perjury, do you?" Fran asked wistfully.

She did not get the reassurance she hoped for.

"I don't know what to think," Pendleton said slowly.

As a matter of fact, almost everyone was bothering Barbara Gunn. Her first action on entering the Wisconsin Seed suite was to snatch off her name tag and hurl it into the wastebasket.

"I'm not wearing it anymore," she announced to her two employers. "All it does is make me a walking target for every creep at this convention."

Ned Ackerman was not surprised. "Look, Barbie, you've got to understand this is the most exciting thing that's ever happened at these meetings. It's only natural for some of them to want whatever tidbits they can pick up."

"I'm not interested in understanding them," she stormed. "I'm not going to put up with them."

Wenzel took a different tack. "Why should you? Just tell them to buzz off," he advised. "That's what I do."

"Oh, Scott!" she cried, suspended between rage at him and pity for herself. "It's different for you. At least you know who's who. I can't run around insulting people and then discover they're committee chairmen or corporation bigwigs."

"And which bigwig would that be?" Ackerman asked.

Barbara looked as if she regretted her outburst. "It was one of the Vandams," she said sullenly. "This one is called Milton. He came oiling up to me at the ticket table, and he was so filled with insinuations I couldn't make out what he meant half the time."

"Isn't that wonderful!" marveled Ackerman. "And Dick

Vandam just happened to bump into me at the equipment show. Went out of his way to be very, very polite."

Wenzel had lost interest in Barbara's plight. "Well, well," he said softly. "All we need is for the preppy one to offer me a drink and we've got three of a kind. It's plain enough what's happening. The high and mighty Vandams are disassociating themselves from the mess. You know their latest amendment claims that all basic laboratory work was done in Puerto Rico, and there never was any research at Vandamia. I wonder how much they're paying IPR to carry the can."

"I thought our theory was that Jason gave the data to IPR, claiming it was a Vandam work product," Ackerman reminded him.

"That's probably the way it really happened. But once they found themselves in a real fight with real dirt flying, Vandam's was willing to pay to get off the hook."

Barbara sounded stony. "People don't do everything just for money, Scott."

"I'm not saying they do," he replied. "And it wouldn't be that crass. I can see Jason giving Pendleton a pitch about doing a small favor for an old friend, one that wouldn't change the realities but would help the publicity. That's the kind of talk Howard understands—he goes in for it himself all the time, the old windbag."

"Maybe," Ackerman said dubiously. "But if there was hanky-panky four or five years back, it wasn't Jason. I've just remembered who Milton is. They eased him out of the company a while back, but he used to be in charge of R&D."

This was proof positive to Wenzel. "That's why he's chasing Barbara. Trying to find out how much we've got on him."

Ackerman rubbed his grizzled head thoughtfully. "I'll buy that one. But wouldn't it be easier to fake data in a labyrinth like Vandamia?"

"Oh, no. Too many people running around. IPR would be ideal."

They had come to the nub of Ackerman's resistance. "I don't know. That Mrs. Pendleton seemed like a nice lady to me."

Wenzel stared at him, then smiled broadly. "For God's sake, Fran is a sweetheart. But you could rob the U.S. Mint in front of her, in perfect safety."

This was too much for Barbara. "Oh, come on, Scott. You've said yourself she's a first-rate researcher. And God knows you don't say that often."

"That's the whole point. Basically Fran is interested in floribunda and her grandchildren and nothing else." He grinned challengingly at her. "Remember the housebreak?"

Barbara produced a wan smile. "Oh, well," she conceded.

Wenzel turned to Ackerman. "Howard and Fran were seeing some tulip growers in Holland, then Fran came back early because the grandson was sick. When Howard walked into the house, the first thing he did was ask when the burglary had happened. For three whole days Fran hadn't noticed somebody had walked off with the television, the hi-fi, the microwave oven and all the dining room silver."

"Okay. You've proved your point. She's not the noticing kind," Ackerman acknowledged.

"Howard could fake up anything the way Vandam's wanted it. For those purposes, Ned, he's running a one-man show." Wenzel was complacent. "Just the way I do at Wisconsin."

Ackerman opened his mouth, then thought better of what he was about to say. Instead he turned the subject. "Well, this should be a wonderful banquet. I assume we'll all be there, outdoing each other in friendliness."

He had touched a sore spot.

"Do I really have to go? Into the arena with all those lions?" Barbara asked fretfully.

"What's to be afraid of? We'll all stick together," Ned promised.

Barbara shifted her ground. "I was counting on some spare time. I haven't even been out to see my parents yet."

"Tomorrow night. And all day the day after," Wenzel added hastily. "But tonight you know we want to put on a big show and we've only got four warm bodies."

"Thank you very much!" Barbara snapped before her attention was caught. *"Four* warm bodies?"

Wenzel nodded. "Yes. I got Hilary to fly down to swell our ranks. She should be here in an hour. So why don't you go and get dressed, and take your time off tomorrow."

"Oh, all right," said Barbara, already on her way to the door.

"Well, she changed her mind damned fast," Scott remarked idly.

Ackerman was amused. "She's got a lot to do."

He had noticed years ago that Hilary roused a competitive feminine spark in Barbara. There would be a lot more care paid to hair and makeup tonight than Barbara had originally intended. Scott, of course, would go to his death without noticing.

"In any event, I'm glad she's coming," Wenzel said, confirming Ackerman's opinion. "Our whole future depends on how we handle things right now."

"My future depends on it. Your future depends on it. But Barbara's doesn't," Ackerman said slowly and distinctly. "In case you've forgotten, she's leaving her child with her parents when she goes back to college. She's got lots to do in Chicago besides think about Wisconsin Seed."

Wenzel had the grace to be shamefaced. "That's right, she did tell me and I forgot."

Say what you would about Scott, Ackerman thought, he

pursued his own interests and he expected other people to pursue theirs. You just had to remind him of their existence occasionally.

"And it doesn't help for her to be dogged by guys from Vandam's and have you suspecting her old friends of taking payoffs," he continued, on the principle of seizing the moment.

"They're my old friends too, if it comes to that."

"I doubt if you exchanged baby pictures with Mrs. Pendleton," Ackerman said impatiently. "Just lay off Barbara, will you, Scott?"

Wenzel might agree, but he was damned if he was going to feel guilty. "All right, all right. But you're making a mountain out of a molehill. I've known her longer than you have. And she wasn't putting up such a big defense for Howard Pendleton. Besides it was a perfectly logical suspicion."

"She may not be as big on logic as you are."

"Anyway, I grant you that she needs some time off. And with Hilary here for the next couple of days, this is a good time for her to take it."

"Good." Normally Ackerman could take Hilary or leave her. She was even stronger on logic than Scott. But her presence tonight would be a real plus, and she would give Scott heightened visibility during the remainder of the week. "That's going to work out perfectly. With Hilary at your side, everybody's going to notice you and think they know what Wisconsin Seed is up to. In the meantime I can slip quietly away and even Barbara doesn't have to know."

Wenzel shrugged. "No reason why she shouldn't," he said negligently.

"Why add to her troubles? The less she realizes she's sitting on a keg of dynamite, the happier she'll be."

"You're probably right. God knows your methods seem

to be paying off. What about your old buddies at USDA? They still have their pipeline to the Patent Office open?"

"Open and operating," Ackerman said smugly.

Wenzel shook his head in admiration. "You've really got it made, Ned. Everybody has me pegged for the trouble-making S.O.B., while you're just a quiet good-natured pencil pusher. Little do they know who's about to pull the rug out from under them."

"I didn't do it alone, boy." Ackerman stubbed out his cigar and heaved himself to his feet. "Now we'd better go get dressed, and let's make a production of it. Remember, Scott, tonight we turn out looking prosperous, assured and very, very respectable."

13 EASY TO CULTIVATE

AT the McCormick Inn the first witnesses to all this resplendence were John Thatcher and Charlie Trinkam. The deathwatch at Wenonah Industries had left Trinkam with a new tolerance for any alternative activity. When Earl Sanders proffered tickets, it was Charlie who accepted.

"Why not?" he had justified himself. "As nearly as I can make out, the American Sweet Pea Society isn't heading for bankruptcy. That's good enough for me."

For Charlie's sake, Thatcher was pleased to see life signs of institutional vigor during the cocktail hour. Everywhere people were discussing new contests, new charter tours, new committee memberships. And the party from Wisconsin Seed did nothing to detract from this robust atmosphere as they walked through the doorway into the arms of the Sloan Guaranty Trust.

Hilary Davis would have been noticed anywhere. She used makeup to emphasize her individuality so that her thick dark eyebrows and long jawline became hallmarks. Similarly, she dressed to accentuate her tall, lanky body, wearing very high heels and a straight brown velvet suit highlighted by a low white satin tie. Barbara Gunn was more conventional but, true to Ned Ackerman's prediction, she had resorted more freely to blue eye shadow and rouge than usual. As a result she was able to carry off the brilliant blue silk that usually made her look too pale. Their escorts did them full justice. Most of the men present were in business suits, but both Wenzel and Ackerman wore dinner jackets. Surprisingly, it was the younger, trendier Wenzel who looked badly fitted. Ackerman's garment had long since given up the fight and conformed to his general contours.

The explanation was forthcoming when Charlie twitted him on his finery.

"I don't put it on more than once a year these days, but when I was assigned to FAO in Rome, it was one formal dinner after another."

Thatcher was interested to learn that Ackerman, so quintessentially a Midwestern type, had logged enough years with the Food and Agriculture Organization of the United Nations to qualify as an expert on some aspects of international trade and investment.

"Of course most of the gut work is setting up programs in underdeveloped countries, but you'd be surprised at how much else you pick up," Ackerman concluded, after a well-informed discussion of world wheat movements.

He would have been happy to drop it there and let Scott Wenzel talk about the day's meetings. But Hilary Davis, seconded by Barbara Gunn, egged him on to become anecdotal.

The ladies, Thatcher decided, were exercising their superior social sense. He was all wrong as he discovered ten minutes later.

Ackerman had been regaling them with tales of a Swiss team of agronomists, all experts in high-altitude cultivation, who spent their lives circling the globe, pausing only at locations ten thousand feet above sea level. In consequence they had missed most of the major social developments of the post-war world.

"Nothing happens that high up. They hadn't even heard about the population explosion. But what the hell! I would have been just as bad, except that I was into hot, arid areas so I was a lot closer to the action."

There then followed one of those pauses that overtake ill-assorted groups. Charlie Trinkam, in an attempt at light conversation, turned to Barbara Gunn.

"They tell me this bash is really a song of triumph by Vandam's. Under the circumstances you're pretty good sports to join the cheering crowd."

Suddenly a grey pall descended on her. One moment she had been laughing about the Swiss, as pretty as any girl in the room. Now she looked ten years older.

"I don't know anything about that," she stammered with painful intensity. "Really I don't."

It was Ned Ackerman who rescued her.

"Oh, sweet peas are neutral territory," he said easily. "We'll let Vandam's keep them. Of course I'd like to see a little reciprocal generosity from them about tomatoes."

What had been intended as a pleasantry reminded Hilary Davis of a legal question.

"I've been meaning to talk to you about that. You know Scott told me what the Standard Foods lawyer said, about decreasing the useful life of the patent. Naturally he was using it as an argument for immediate production. But it does raise some interesting ramifications. Once you establish your claim to that patent, I see no reason why you shouldn't recover for that loss. Certainly if you can show criminal or malicious intent—"

"Whoa, Hilary!" Ned Ackerman backed off in mock alarm. "You're way ahead of me. Just give us undisputed possession of that patent, and I'll be satisfied. Making legal history may be fun for you lawyers, but it's an expensive hobby for the rest of us."

Wenzel was not sure he agreed. "I don't know about that, Ned. Every little bit helps."

Ackerman began unobtrusively semaphoring. His dislike

of this discussion was perfectly apparent to Thatcher and Charlie. It seemed, however, to be lost on the two who counted.

"Not just a little bit," Hilary corrected. "A great deal."

Wenzel was still talking to his partner. "Of course I'd want Paul Jackson's opinion. Hilary could be all wet. You don't learn much about patents doing pro bono work."

Thatcher could feel Charlie flinch. But a remark guaranteed to trigger warfare between most couples left Hilary Davis entirely unruffled.

"Go ahead and call Jackson. You'll find I'm right. Besides," she continued, "I'm not talking about patents, I'm talking about damages. And you learn plenty about them in pro bono work."

Thatcher, who felt they were still in dangerous territory, seized this opportunity to shift the conversation.

"I know a good many young lawyers who are going into your field these days," he remarked. "I suppose it has a sense of purpose lacking in more traditional areas."

"I regard ecology cases as the most important contribution I can make to society," she replied resoundingly. "We have an environment rapidly deteriorating past the point of no return, and other attempts to control the situation—scientific conferences, government watchdogs, committee reports—have been worse than useless. The only way you can force anyone into ecological responsibility is by making them pay through the nose for the consequences. That's why the litigation approach is so valuable. We're breaking new ground every day in extending traditional areas of liability. On a smaller scale, they did the same thing with manufacturers' warranties. Well, we're going to make it financially disastrous to have anything to do with pollution."

"That's fine if your targets are the Fortune 500," said Charlie, whose sufferings with Wenonah Industries had marked him. "But some of the worst delinquents are relatively small outfits. You get awarded really big damages and they just declare bankruptcy."

Hilary smiled menacingly. "I do not accept the thesis of judgment-proof defendants in this area. If the malefactor can't pay, then what about his banker?"

"His banker!" Charlie echoed in spite of himself.

"Certainly!" she said militantly. "As far as I'm concerned, you're financing the discharge of industrial contaminants. Why shouldn't you be responsible?"

Since Charlie was now speechless, Thatcher took over.

"We're providing the culprit with a service," he admitted. "But so is the taxpayer who provides highways, so is the federal government which provides military protection and, for that matter, so is every single consumer who purchases the end product. Morally, you could use the same argument to go after them."

"I'm not interested in moral justification, I'm interested in feasible points of attack," she said with more honesty than many of her fellows. "We'd lose public support if we went after consumers, and we'd get creamed if we went after the federal government. But stockholders and banks, they should be easy."

It was Thatcher's turn to smile.

"Don't be too sure of that," he counseled.

"That's some bunch they've got at Wisconsin Seed," Charlie commented half an hour later as they were joining the drift into the dining room.

"They're certainly not the normal foursome they appear," Thatcher agreed.

"And what the hell was the matter with the secretary? I addressed two simple sentences to her, and she froze and didn't utter one more word while we were there."

Some women have a light hand with pastry. Charlie

Trinkam prided himself on his light hand with the ladies. He was genuinely puzzled by his signal failure with Barbara Gunn.

"She was unnerved, there's no doubt about that, but I don't think you were the cause," Thatcher reassured him. "She can be happy as long as nobody is talking about the *Numero Uno* lawsuit. If they start, she goes into shock."

"Then she should look for another job!" Charlie retorted. "And what about the other two? They're playing house by some pretty strange rules. She shuts him up whenever he gets started on his specialty, but has no qualms about letting fly with her own. And he's ready to tell the world that her professional opinion isn't worth a hill of beans. He doesn't seem to think much of her competence as a lawyer."

But Thatcher had become thoughtful. "I can think of another reason why he'd want a second opinion."

Charlie, when not distracted by social failure, was capable of rational thought. "You mean because he hasn't told her everything?" he speculated. "The more you think of it, the more sense it makes. She realizes he's holding back, so she doesn't scratch his eyes out when he won't accept her advice. What's more, she discourages him from starting a line of talk that could lead to *Numero Uno*. And when we get there anyway, she flaps a lot of ecology at us."

"It's a coherent theory," Thatcher said cautiously.

"But it may be a lot of hogwash," Charlie grinned, completing the thought. "She may simply be the kind of woman who prefers the sound of her own voice to any other."

"They do exist. But the net result, for no matter what reason, is that Scott Wenzel and Hilary Davis flaunt their professional qualifications while Ned Ackerman lurks in the background."

"That Plain-Joe act of his is near perfect. I wonder how many people realize he's the brains of the outfit."

Thatcher reviewed what he had been told. "Not many.

I remember that at first Vandam's was inclined to dismiss this suit as a mere nuisance claim. It wouldn't surprise me if they still regard Wenzel and Ackerman as two petty con men. Sanders, however, is beginning to take Ackerman's measure."

"And I suppose this Pendleton has taken Wenzel's?"

"You can ask him yourself. The Pendletons are joining us at Earl Sanders' table."

Charlie's researches died aborning. This was partly due to Howard Pendleton's repressiveness. He had the knack of returning such discouraging monosyllables that even the most assiduous questioner flagged. Yes, he had known Scott Wenzel for years. No, he had never heard of Ackerman before the lawsuit. Yes, Barbara Gunn was a strange girl.

Even more of an obstacle, however, was Mrs. Earl Sanders, who had flown into town for the evening and was flanked by two luminaries of the Sweet Pea Society. Mrs. Sanders, it developed, was a slave to her flower garden, and when she discovered that Fran Pendleton had created the *Long John* delphinium, she was beside herself.

"But that's the one I planted! You know, Earl, the row on the west side of the garage. It's wonderful."

Fran blushed with pleasure. "I'm glad you like it. I do, too."

"Like it!" Mrs. Sanders felt this did scant justice to her feelings. *"Long John*'s ten times better than what I had before. And I wouldn't even have tried it except that it was an All-America winner. You plant breeders are a salvation for the rest of us."

"We're not the only ones coming up with results. Some of the work being done by amateurs is astonishing. Have you seen *Firecracker,* the sweet pea that's getting the award tonight? You really ought to try that."

But Fran's suggestion was not well received.

"Oh, sweet peas!" Mrs. Sanders cried tragically. "I really don't know what they want from me. I give them the right soil, the right trenching, the right feeding. And all they do is curl up and die!"

She was immediately buried under a hail of advice from her neighbors. To each well-intended instruction she made the same reply: "I tried that. You remember, Earl?"

And her husband would say wearily, "I remember, I remember."

By the time dessert was served, the luminaries had exhausted their stratagems but were still convinced that the fault must lie with Mrs. Sanders. In some way, shape, or form she was failing to provide a proper home for sweet peas.

"If you do the right thing by them," the elder insisted, "they'll do the right thing by you. I have never known it to fail."

Mrs. Sanders was frankly mutinous. "Well that's not much help if nobody knows what that thing is."

"All of which proves why any amateur accomplishment is so impressive," said Fran, spreading balm. "Any kind of fieldwork is subject to so many variables, like micro-climates, that we can control in the laboratory. Somebody like Mrs. Larrabee has really earned her prize check tonight."

The luminary was reminded of his obligations. "I only wish more seed companies realized that. Vandam's has provided a great incentive for all of us with their contest," he said with stately commendation.

Considering that Standard Foods and IPR were both linked to Vandam's, Thatcher was surprised at the lack of enthusiasm greeting this sentiment.

Sanders, after a sour glance at the head table that fairly bristled with Vandams, said, "They're certainly reminding everybody who's picking up the tab for *Firecracker*."

"And God knows what kind of payoff they expect," Pendleton muttered. "They like more than a tax deduction for their charitable contributions."

And even Fran could do no better than, "If they'd only stick to contests, it wouldn't be so bad. At least they know how to do that."

All three looked at each other with such fellow feeling that Thatcher knew only the presence of outsiders was preventing a general dissection of Vandam's.

"Makes Wisconsin Seed look good, doesn't it?" Charlie whispered to him.

"At least they're united," Thatcher began, only to be halted by the clatter of a spoon on glass.

The master of ceremonies was introducing the featured speaker of the evening.

"Neither Hendrik Vandam nor the illustrious company for which he is spokesman needs any introduction. They have both secured for themselves a firm place in our affections and respect by their untiring devotion to . . ."

14 WINTER KILL

WHATEVER the annual banquet of the American Sweet Pea Society represented to others, it was an unalloyed triumph for Mrs. Mary Larrabee. How much of a triumph she did not realize until later in the evening.

From the first rewriting of the Vandam catalog, Mary had been the unwitting beneficiary of the *Numero Uno* battle. Her *Firecracker* now adorned the cover, her success was now spread over the space originally intended for biennial tomatoes. And, although the Vandams might engage in other private activities, in public they behaved as if their main reason for being in Chicago was to beat the drums for Mary Larrabee. Then, when the time came for the official award, old Hendrik Vandam let himself go. Every courtly instinct, honed by years at flower shows, was called into play as he benignly hailed her achievement. His grandiloquent tribute demanded more from Mary than the simple acknowledgment she had planned. So, flustered and stammering, she proceeded to tell the world about her pleasure in gardening, her pride in past flower beds, her vision of future arbors.

When the banquet broke up, several commercial interests sitting at widely separated tables had come to the same conclusion. The president of Hogarth Equipment, Inc., was the first to accost Dick Vandam.

"You know, Dick," he said, "I think that little lady would be perfect promotion for our rototiller."

142

As the Vandam catalog accounted for fully a third of the sales of the Hogarth rototiller, he was not speaking to a disinterested observer.

"That's not a bad idea," Vandam agreed. "But we can't talk here. I'll tell you what. We'll bring the Larrabees up to your suite, and we'll see how they feel about it."

At first, the Vandams were filled with pride in the success of their protégé. Forming themselves into a phalanx, they escorted her upstairs to the Hogarth suite and prepared to radiate approval on the union between Mary and rototillers. But as word of her location spread and more and more supplicants appeared, it was one rude shock after another.

One of the judges of the sweet pea contest was the editor of a national gardening magazine. Seized with the idea of a monthly column by Mary, he was determined to speak to her. At the same time he had no intention of releasing his grip on Mrs. Pendleton, who was producing the most photogenic roses he had yet seen. A joint descent on Suite 1408 was what he had in mind.

Fran cast an apologetic glance at her husband. "I'm sorry," she whispered to him, "but it won't take long, and it will be good publicity for IPR."

She need not have worried. Manlike, Howard had only one ambition after those long speeches. "They serve drinks, don't they?" he grunted.

Their arrival was the first fly in the Vandam ointment.

"I don't like the Pendletons being here," protested Milton. "We should keep the sweet pea separate from the *Numero Uno* mess."

"What do you expect me to do about it?" retorted Dick. "I can't throw them out, this isn't our suite."

Nowadays, Jason opposed Cousin Milton on principle. "And it's not a particularly good time to offend the Pendletons," he pointed out. "The lawyers are going to be taking their depositions next week."

Hard on the heels of the editor came a horde of others. John Thatcher and Charlie Trinkam arrived to find Mary agreeing to appear on a local talk show, while other claimants waited their turn.

"I'll be damned if I know what they all see in her," Dick Vandam complained to Thatcher at the bar.

Thatcher, looking across the room at the heroine of the hour, thought he understood. Every generation has produced an ephemeral woman. Once gone forever, she becomes wrapped in the misty tendrils of nostalgia. There was the pioneer mother, there was the Gibson girl, there was the Charleston flapper. In a world where young women were living with lovers, pursuing masculine careers and marching at the head of protest demonstrations, Mary Larrabee was about to be enshrined as the apotheosis of a vanishing breed— the American housewife.

Before Thatcher could outline this theory, the arrival of Dick's father silenced him.

Hendrik was breathing fire. "Do you know who's trying to sign her up now?" He named Shawmut, the country's largest producer of lawn seed, lawn fertilizer, and weed killer. "They want to use her as their television symbol, and they're in direct competition with us!"

"Now don't get excited, Dad." Dick's own control seemed to benefit from someone else's jitters. "We can't expect Mrs. Larrabee to understand the difference between our competitors and people who sell through us. We'll just go over there and explain it to her. You'd better do it. After all, you're the one who handed her the check."

Father and son stalked off, leaving Thatcher to his own devices. He was joined instantly by a stranger who peeled off from a nearby group.

"I overheard that. So they're going to explain things to Mary, are they?" he remarked jovially. "Well, good luck to them."

Then, seeing Thatcher's incomprehension, he held out his hand. "Pete Larrabee's the name. Thanks for taking Mary to the market while I was asleep."

Thatcher examined his companion. When the limelight and a golden shower of dollars unexpectedly descend on a middle-aged wife, the husband normally experiences a momentary spasm of discomfiture. But Pete Larrabee seemed entirely free from any such *gêne*. Thatcher introduced himself and complimented Larrabee on his composure.

Larrabee sounded almost religious. "I told Mary to take them for every penny she could get," he said stoutly.

"Ah!"

That explained it. Larrabee was simply beginning where most husbands ended.

"You see," Larrabee continued, "last month my eldest boy got accepted by MIT."

Again Thatcher congratulated him.

"I thought it was wonderful, too, until I saw how much it was going to cost. Then I went into shock."

What's more, inspection of his family indicated that within four short years Pete would have three children in pursuit of higher education. Now was the perfect time for the Larrabees to acquire a second breadwinner.

"If that's the case, don't you think you should be over there supporting Mary?" Thatcher suggested.

Pete smiled fondly. "Don't let those looks fool you. I'm the guy who was standing at her shoulder when we came to Chicago to redo the living room. She got a decorator's discount, she got free delivery to North Dakota and she got them to go back to the manufacturer and have arm sleeves made up for everything. Listen, when she bought her last car, she negotiated for three weeks. By the time she was done she had so many options thrown in, the dealer was dizzy. Nobody can teach Mary anything about bargaining."

On the other side of the room Mrs. Larrabee was proving

worthy of her husband's confidence. She listened in becoming confusion to Hendrik Vandam's labored explanations. She gave little yips of comprehension at the distinction between competitor and non-competitor. She reacted to familiar trade names with beaming gratification.

Then she twinkled merrily and said, "I'm so unbusinesslike, you'll just have to forgive me, Mr. Vandam. But I don't remember anything about this in the contest application."

With a lurch in his stomach, Dick Vandam realized that there was no such clause in the application or any of the subsequent documentation. Mrs. Mary Larrabee was free to exploit her victory in any manner she chose, and she knew it. Hendrik might go on expecting miracles from his old-fashioned charm, but Dick sensed that nothing was going to stand between the Larrabees and a munificent television contract. In the months to come he could look forward to seeing Mary's image touting someone else's products. Muttering an apology, he left his father to the doomed cause and melted back into the crowded room.

By the time he bumped into Fran Pendleton, he was in the mood to appreciate old friends and proven allies.

"Fran!" he cried with excessive cordiality. "I'm glad to see you. Wherever I go, I hear good things about your floribunda work."

Fran, who had written him off as a cold fish years ago, was surprised.

"And I hope you know that we'll be interested in the results, once you're finished."

Now Fran was even more surprised. It would be normal routine for her to offer the rights to Vandam's.

"I'm glad to hear it," she said temperately.

Then, like everyone striving to spark an emotional response, he went too far. Just before leaving her, he clasped her elbow and said warmly, "And if we do market it, I wouldn't be surprised if we called it the *Mrs. Howard Pendleton* rose."

Fran herself was speechless from a variety of emotions, but a newcomer broke into sardonic laughter.

"Isn't that wonderful! That yo-yo doesn't understand that you name roses after women who've had nothing to do with their development, not the geneticist. Poor Fran! He's not even going to make it the *Frances Pendleton* rose."

"Scotty! What are you doing here?"

He grinned at her. "Why shouldn't I be here? As a matter of fact, the Hogarth people want to talk to Ned about retailing their stuff if we start a mail-order catalog."

Fran had been trying to look severe, but now two dimples appeared. "Oh, Dick Vandam will love that when he hears it," she said, making no attempt to hide her satisfaction.

"He deserves whatever lumps he gets. Apart from everything else, he shouldn't be allowed to name anything. First he hangs that rinky-dink *Numero Uno* tag on my tomato, and now he wants to embarrass you in public."

The dimples disappeared. "*Your* tomato, Scott?"

"That's right." Wenzel looked at her with a challenging gleam in his eye. "You may as well face it, Fran. That tomato is going out under our label. We've got all the proof we need to win."

Suddenly Fran sighed. "I do wish you'd grow up, Scott. You make this sound like a college football game. This isn't a matter of cheerleaders and fight songs. A lot of people are miserable."

"If you're asking me to be a bleeding heart for Vandam's—"

"Oh, forget your obsession with Vandam's," she snapped at him. "I know all about their turning you down five years ago. I sometimes think it addled your brain. You're a lot better off on your own."

"All right, all right, I know that."

Fran swept right over him. "If you stopped thinking about them for a minute, you'd see that there are other people involved. There's Howard, for one. These meetings have been a living hell for him, thanks to you."

"He shouldn't have agreed to whitewash Vandam's," Wenzel said sulkily enough to lend substance to Fran's charge of childishness.

"And then there's Barbara."

"Oh, for God's sake! What am I supposed to have done to her?"

Fran gave him a long level glance. "I'm not sure," she said slowly. "But I know she's wretched at being caught in the middle. You've put her in a crunch between you and Howard, and you know she's not tough enough for that kind of pressure."

"How did I know Howard was going to deal himself in? Why don't you blame him? I was here first."

Fran paid no attention. "And you don't seem to be helping her at all. You're just overloading her with work."

At last they were on sure ground for Wenzel. "I've already told her she can have some time off. And if you'd stop carping at me, Fran, you'd see all this is temporary. Sure, it's a little tough on Barbara right now, but she'll be giving her deposition in a couple of days and then the pressure will be off."

Unfortunately a gap in the crowd swirling about them enabled Fran to spot Barbara, trapped in a corner and listening reluctantly to Milton Vandam.

"Oh, that is just too much," she cried, pointing them out to Wenzel. "Somebody should break that up."

"I'm always glad to have a bash at a Vandam," he volunteered cheerfully.

Fran could imagine Scott's method of tactful intervention. "Not you," she said grimly. "I'll get Howard."

But the first familiar face she encountered belonged to

Eric Most. "Eric, have you seen Howard?" she demanded imperatively. "I need him."

"He's over there with the agricultural attaché from Venezuela," said Most, who was still dazzled by the international reach of IPR. "Anything I can do?"

"No thank you, Eric. I want somebody to rescue Barbara Gunn from the Vandams, and I think Howard had better do it."

Eric Most's reaction to this information more than confirmed her judgment. "My God, what's she doing here?" he asked in disgust. "Are the others from Wisconsin Seedsmen here?"

Why did everybody act as if this were a Vandam bedroom? Fran wondered. "Indeed they are," she said crisply. "I've just been listening to Scotty Wenzel tell me about *his* tomato."

Most reddened. "He's simply trying to get to us. Wenzel knows damn well my notebooks are conclusive evidence. What the hell is wrong with him?"

Fran prepared to move on. "He's conceited," she said with utterly no inflection. "Quite a few young men are."

It was a failing that many of them outgrew, she reflected, when she located her husband and found him both responsive and cooperative. With the ease of long practice the Pendletons traded places, with Howard speeding off to relieve the siege and Fran taking on the Venezuelan attaché.

Twenty minutes later, when she had firmly established the relevance of several IPR projects to agricultural needs in South America, she was once again at leisure to glance toward Barbara's corner. Howard was nowhere to be seen, but he had done his work well. There was not a Vandam in sight and Barbara was deep in conversation with the guest of honor.

Mary Larrabee and Barbara Gunn had found an interest in common the moment Howard introduced them. Mary, after detailing her son's triumph with his College Boards, had uttered a prayer of gratitude for the *Firecracker* windfall.

"Because college costs have gone up so much since our day. You wouldn't believe how much tuition is now."

"Oh, wouldn't I just!" exclaimed Barbara, her eyes brightening. "I'm going back to school myself next fall."

Mary was flatteringly impressed. "I think that's wonderful. I know a lot of women are doing that. Would you believe it, one of my neighbors back home has started going to law school now that her children are off her hands."

"Well, I'm not waiting that long. My little girl will just be starting school. Of course, it's different being a widow."

Sympathetically Mary Larrabee studied this slight, frail girl who seemed far too insecure to juggle the roles of widow, mother and student. But being a kindhearted woman, she provided what encouragement she could.

"It can't be harder than what you're already doing. Didn't Dr. Pendleton say you're working for a seed company? And with your daughter still so young? College is bound to be easier."

But she had said the wrong thing. Because the terrible pinched look was back again.

"It's got to be," Barbara burst out. "I can't go through any more of this. But sometimes I think leaving my job, going back to school, having Tracy at my parents', is all a dream. That it will never happen and this treadmill will just go on and on."

Mary did not like the rising note of hysteria. Maybe Barbara Gunn was simply an overworked, overtired woman. But it sounded more deep-rooted. Before Mary could formulate a cautious probe, her attention was demanded elsewhere.

"Wait a minute, Pete," she said, "I'll be with you in a second."

But turning, she found that Barbara Gunn had taken advantage of her momentary preoccupation to slip away.

"Oh, dear, that's too bad. I think that girl may be in real trouble."

"If she is, she'll find her way back to you, honey. You've got a real gift for the lame ducks. In the meantime, you remember John Thatcher? I think he may be able to do a lot for us."

To her infinite surprise, Mary discovered that Pete felt that among the many new faces entering her life—a manager, an agent, a housekeeper—there should probably be a banker. The talk moved on to trusts, tax shelters, retirement plans. Pete Larrabee, as Thatcher had already discovered, liked to think big.

But Mary preferred concrete details. "Did you say photographers?" she asked, grasping the one familiar word to come her way.

"Sure, honey, you're going to be a news feature. They're on their way up, now."

Mary grabbed a mirror from her purse, took one horrified look and fled to the ladies' room.

She never went farther than the anteroom with its long mirror and vanity table. In the first moment of shock and horror, she realized that the cowardly thought echoing through her mind was: *Why did it have to be me?*

Because twisted in a heap on the rumpled carpet, lying in a pool of vomit, was the body of Barbara Gunn.

15 FAINTLY AROMATIC

ROOTED to the spot, unable to move forward or backward, Mary Larrabee pressed her hands to her eyes and loosed one shrill scream after another.

Her husband was among the group that burst in upon her. Thereafter Mary was the only person in the suite who was not swept up in the crisis of fetching a doctor, calling the police, deciding what to do and what not to do. Oblivious to all the confusion, she huddled in Pete's arms and repeated over and over, "I was awful. I didn't even go to her."

"Honey, stop blaming yourself," he crooned. "What good would it have done? You heard the doctor say she was already dead."

But Mary, consumed with guilt at her paralysis, continued her self-flagellation.

"Then I should never have let her leave that way. I knew she was upset about something—she sounded so depressed."

The police captain in charge had thus far been busy with routine—roping off the ladies' room, organizing a roster of names and addresses, consulting with the specialists. But this sounded too promising to ignore.

"Do you think you feel well enough to talk with me, Mrs. Larrabee? It might be a help."

Over Mary's shoulder Pete Larrabee glared at him, but Mary herself began to straighten.

"I'd like to help," she said. "But I don't see how I can."

"You said she was upset. Do you think she was suicidal?"

This was just the tonic that Mary needed. "She was not! She was talking about going to college next year and making arrangements about her child. Does that sound as if she expected to be dead?"

"You're the one who said she was depressed, Mrs. Larrabee. That business about school and baby-sitting sounds pretty cheerful to me."

"Oh, that was the good part. That was going to happen next fall. It was what was happening now that was bothering her."

"And what was that?"

"I don't know. I'd just met her. But why do you think she killed herself? Couldn't it have been a natural death, or an accident?"

Captain McNabb was diplomatic. "We won't know that for some time," he said. Actually he was merely eliminating outside chances. The police doctor's preliminary diagnosis had been emphatic. This was not a natural death, this was not a homemade abortion, this looked very much like a corrosive poison. Tormented young women take sleeping pills in their own beds after penning a self-justification. They do not swallow painful poisons at crowded business functions.

Coming to a decision, the captain advanced to the center of the room and raised his voice. "All right, you people," he announced loudly enough to still the nervous desultory conversations. "I understand the victim worked for a seed company, and you're all in that line of business. I'd like to get some background on her. Now who's going to tell me about her?"

Ned Ackerman raised his hand, but it was Fran Pendleton

who moved forward. "I think we probably knew her longer than anyone else, Captain," she volunteered.

McNabb brightened as he examined his prospect. A middle-aged lady was far more likely to be a source of personal details than most of the men in the room.

"That's fine," he said cordially. "Why don't you two come over into a corner and tell me how you came to know her."

Fran seated herself with Howard standing protectively behind her. She began by explaining IPR and its Puerto Rican location. "It must have been about seven years ago when Barbara came down. She'd just gotten married and she was very young. Her husband was serving two years in the navy after graduation, and they'd been assigned to the island. We met them at a few parties and everything was new and wonderful to Barbara—the dances at the club, the climate, the beaches. Then the two years ran out. There was a new baby and the Gunns decided to stay in Puerto Rico. They moved off base and Tim began to look for a job. It was then that he was drowned. It's a terrible thing to say, but the timing was all wrong for Barbara. Nobody was responsible for her, she was hard up for money, and she didn't know how to take care of herself. We'd just lost a secretary, so we hired her. And as soon as she'd settled down, we had her over whenever we gave a party." Fran suddenly lifted a handkerchief. "Oh, dear, it all seems so long ago."

"I see," said Captain McNabb. Even in death Barbara Gunn had not seemed old enough for the twenty-seven years her driver's license proclaimed. Five years ago, as a lost, helpless girl, she must have looked like a waif. No wonder she had appealed to Mrs. Pendleton's maternal instincts. He could imagine the string of young men who had been produced at those dinner parties in the hope that Barbara's problem would be solved in the simplest possible way.

"She didn't remarry?" he asked.

"No," said Fran sadly.

Her husband spoke for the first time. "I told you that sort of thing never works."

"Why, Howard! Half the time you were the one who asked her."

"It did her good to get out," he said gruffly.

"I don't know why all men act as if matchmaking is a crime," she retorted before turning to the captain. "But I don't want you to think that Barbara was unhappy. She liked her job and she liked the people at the lab. Then, when one of our researchers went off to set up Wisconsin Seedsmen, she went with him. It was going to be a one-woman office with broader responsibilities and, of course, more pay."

McNabb consulted his notes. "Was that Ackerman or Wenzel?"

"Scott Wenzel."

"Anything between them?" the policeman pressed. "That's a long way to follow a man."

Fran was very confident. "Oh no, Scotty never thought of her that way. I even tried having them over together. It was just that they were used to working together. And the move back to the States made sense for Barbara. Better facilities for the child, closer to her family, that sort of thing."

"Then, if she was so happy about the arrangement, why this business about going back to school? Was it a sudden decision?"

"Oh, no." Fran frowned as she consulted her husband. "When did she first tell us, Howard? It must have been over two years ago."

"Fully that," he confirmed.

"All the young women want real careers nowadays, Captain. I was glad when she told us. I thought she was finding her own feet at last."

Fran had been scrupulously honest. She was sure that Scotty had never thought of Barbara that way. As for Barbara's hopes, let them die along with the poor child.

"But now," she said, "it doesn't make any difference."

McNabb was more interested in something else. "So you kept up with her?"

"Yes, she came to most of the meetings with Scott, and occasionally one of us would be in Madison at the university. We always had dinner with her."

"See her here in Chicago?"

"Yes," both Pendletons replied.

"Know why she was upset?"

"Not really," said Howard promptly. "Wisconsin Seedsmen is expanding, and it's involved in a court case. So there was a lot of pressure on her, particularly when she was trying to arrange things for next year."

Conscious of her husband pressing her shoulder, Fran remained silent but there was a mulish cast to her jaw. She exploded the moment Captain McNabb abandoned the Pendletons to continue his inquiries with Wisconsin Seedsmen.

"Howard! Barbara was probably killed because of the lawsuit. Captain McNabb has to know how important it is."

"Of course," Pendleton agreed. "But let someone else break the news to him. I don't want Vandam's trying to blame this on us, too. I'm sick of their shoving their problems onto us."

"I warn you," Fran said obstinately. "I won't leave this room without the police knowing all about it."

"For God's sake! I'll tell them myself in that case. But you'll see. It won't take more than five minutes with Scott and Ackerman before McNabb is filled in."

Actually things worked out even better from Dr. Howard

Pendleton's point of view. Within five minutes the Vandams themselves were letting the cat out of the bag.

When Captain McNabb confronted Wisconsin Seedsmen, he found two very different reactions to Barbara Gunn's death. Ned Ackerman had shed his customary blandness. His lips were pinched and his nostrils outlined in white. He was in a cold fury. Scott Wenzel, on the other hand, was sitting slackly in his chair, staring at nothing, sunk in the lethargy that McNabb associated with shock. Neither of them seemed conscious of the Vandams, who had been herded into the same corner.

It was Ned Ackerman who supplied the formal details of Barbara's employment.

"You'll have to excuse me if I'm not very coherent, Captain," he apologized. "But we're a small outfit, and we worked together closely. Barbara was a part of our lives and we're going to miss her."

His simple words sparked the proconsular instinct in old Hendrik Vandam. "A great tragedy," he said gravely. "We ourselves did not know the young woman but we would like to extend our sympathy. It is a loss when any life is cut off so—"

Unlike his grandfather, Jason Ingersoll had been among those who had actually seen the body. He had still not recovered.

"Oh, come on!" he said with a snort of derision. "How hypocritical do we have to be? This isn't a loss to those two. It's damned convenient for them."

"And just what the hell do you mean by that?" asked Ackerman with dangerous calm.

"She was giving her deposition next week. Now we'll never know what she . . ."

Jason's voice trailed off. Too late he realized that Captain McNabb was eying him appraisingly.

"And just what deposition was that?"

There was a gleam of satisfaction in Ackerman's eye as he explained. By the time he finished, he sounded like his old self. "It's true we won't have Barbara's deposition, but we've got enough documentation to stuff a horse. As for the Vandams not knowing our young woman, they've been pestering her ever since we got to Chicago!"

"All right!" Dick Vandam said, then turned to Captain McNabb. "My father spoke without realizing that we might have had occasion to encounter Mrs. Gunn. After all, we've been in and out of the same functions for over two days now. I myself spoke with her in the hotel corridor this afternoon. A secretary can be very vulnerable in this kind of lawsuit. I wanted to make sure that she was not being pressured by her employers."

Scott Wenzel had listened to the previous exchange with bewildered apathy. But he had no trouble at all with Dick Vandam's statement.

"My God!" he cried. "You were trying to bribe Barbara."

Vandam's tone became even loftier. "I was merely re-assuring her that she had nothing to fear."

"Because you'd take care of her," Wenzel concluded for him.

"Only if she told the truth."

"Sure," said Ned Ackerman nastily.

Spots of color appeared on Vandam's cheeks, but he was too wily to be drawn into self-justification. That was his story and he was sticking with it, regardless of the implications.

Captain McNabb, when he was convinced that no further spontaneous disclosures would be forthcoming, ceased being an onlooker and became an interrogator. But it did him little good. Everybody had been in the vicinity of Barbara Gunn at some time during the hospitality session. Nobody admitted fetching her a drink. Nobody admitted noticing her glass, except the barman who had supplied her initially. It began to look as if Barbara Gunn had carried the same glass from start to finish.

John Putnam Thatcher was the last person that Captain McNabb came to.

"I don't exactly understand your connection with all this," he began, sketching a wave around the room.

Succinctly Thatcher explained.

"And this bank attachment? Does that make you a party to the suit?"

"By no means. Our only real connection is as bankers to Standard Foods, and that makes the Sloan's interest very tangential."

McNabb nodded in approval. "But you've been in on it from the start. Good. Because there's something that's got me going around in circles, and maybe you can explain it. This Barbara Gunn was just a simple secretary. She wasn't a scientist or anything. And this tomato is worth millions, I guess."

"Easily."

"But from the amount of heat that's being generated and from the way the Vandams were trying to sidle up to her, it looks as if her testimony was central to the whole thing."

"And if she was murdered to prevent her deposition, that certainly reinforces your theory," Thatcher said dryly.

McNabb was scratching his chin thoughtfully. "You'd think if it was that important I could get some handle on it. But I can't. Everybody's stopped making accusations and started being careful. Still, they gave me enough to go on with. As nearly as I can make out, Dick Vandam is claiming that Barbara Gunn could have proved Wenzel stole the tomato. Wenzel and Ackerman are claiming she could have proved it was stolen from them. And this guy, Earl Sanders, is keeping his distance from everyone."

"You must realize, Captain," Thatcher said, "that regardless of whether Vandam's was the thief or the victim of theft, Standard Foods is going to want someone's head for mismanagement."

"Great. So, on the face of it, Barbara Gunn was a threat to everybody. Even Howard Pendleton's neck is on the line, because he's claiming he didn't accept any research data from Vandam's. The Wisconsin Seedsmen people think he's lying."

"Somebody must be. But I agree it's odd how Barbara Gunn's deposition became so critical."

McNabb looked at him hopefully. "That's what I wanted help with."

"You don't want a banker, Captain. You want a geneticist."

"Wonderful. The Chicago Police Department has got a lot of experts, but not in that line."

Thatcher smiled. "Then I may be able to help you after all. At this very moment, Standard Foods has an appointment with one of the most eminent geneticists in the country. I'd talk to Earl Sanders if I were you."

As a result of this information Captain McNabb wore the only pleased expression in the room as he announced that his witnesses could leave.

"All right, folks, I guess that's all we can do tonight in a bunch, and most of you could use some sleep. But I'd be grateful if those of you who had anything to do with Barbara Gunn today would think back over your meeting and then get in touch with me to tell me about it."

Most of the men getting stiffly to their feet looked grim, exhausted, or simply bored. But Fran Pendleton, whom Thatcher encountered in the foyer as he shrugged into his coat, had traces of tears on her cheeks. She was talking to Scott Wenzel.

"I'm sorry about this, Fran," he was saying awkwardly. "I know you liked Barbara. And I did, too. I liked her a lot."

16 EFFECTIVE SCREENS

IN spite of his fair words, Captain McNabb had no intention of relying on the voluntary recollection of his witnesses. Indeed, by the time he had finished consulting the expert suggested by John Thatcher, his witnesses had been upgraded to the status of suspects. McNabb had not profited greatly from the lecture on genetics, but this expert, like all the others, had been awed by the dollars-and-cents value of *Numero Uno*. For McNabb the long dreary night ended at three o'clock in the morning, when he found himself in a deserted lobby staring at a plant and muttering to himself: *If it's worth millions, that's really all I have to know*.

By nine o'clock an army of police had descended on McCormick Place with instructions to talk to everybody they could find—exhibitors, maintenance men, learned professors, hangers-on, the help in the cafeteria and dining room. Eight hours of perseverance produced plenty of ammunition for McNabb. On the principle of first tackling those who were willing to talk, he headed for the Blackstone and the Pendletons.

He entered a scene of chaos. The sitting room furniture had been shoved aside to clear the center of the floor, where two trestles now supported an oversized wooden crate from which husky spikes of greenery protruded. Fran Pendleton was pumping away at a long brass instrument to such effect that she, the crate, and most of the bystanders were enveloped in clouds of mist. McNabb had to wipe droplets of moisture from his glasses before he spied Eric Most on the floor, wrestling with a recalcitrant roll of black plastic. On the other side of the trestles two impatient men in overalls, one clutching the lid of the crate and the other brandishing a hammer, were being held at bay by Dr. Pendleton.

In spite of her preoccupation, Fran welcomed the police captain with open arms. After explaining that the floribunda specimens had to leave for the air freight terminal, she handed her pump to Eric Most and swept McNabb and her husband into an adjoining bedroom.

"I'm glad you've come. I wasn't thinking straight yesterday," she apologized. "But I've got things in some sort of order now."

"You sounded pretty clear to me," McNabb remarked.

"I don't mean when I was talking to you. I mean when I was with Barbara in the afternoon."

"Ah ha! I didn't realize you'd seen her before dinner."

"Yes, but at the time I didn't understand why she was so upset. Now I do."

McNabb was practically purring. "Go on," he invited.

"I was so stupid I could kick myself," Fran said in a burst of self-accusation, before returning to business. "The first thing you have to understand is that we didn't know anything about the lawsuit for months, in fact not until after the catalog injunction."

"That's right," her husband corroborated. "Vandam's didn't see fit to tell us about it."

McNabb was pleased to hear the bitterness in Pendleton's voice. The less sweetness and light between his suspects, the less probability of collusion. Nevertheless, there was such a thing as common sense.

"I thought you were the developers of this wonder tomato," he objected.

Howard Pendleton asked nothing better than the opportunity to continue his indictment. "That's what makes their performance so imbecilic. Just because they'd never heard of Wisconsin Seed, Vandam's decided on their own hook it was a nuisance claim. If their precious catalog hadn't been disrupted, we probably still wouldn't know."

"Even when they told us, we had no idea how serious things were," Fran chimed in. "Remember that day in Puerto Rico, Howard? They called up from Vandamia and told Howard that Wisconsin Seed was contesting the patent. Of course at first I thought that explained everything."

McNabb believed in letting cooperative witnesses establish their own pace. "Now why would that be?"

"We knew Scotty from way back. He and Howard had actually discussed the desirability of a biennial tomato years ago when he was working for us. It was perfectly possible that they had gone out and achieved the same result independently. It wasn't until we got to Vandamia and saw both sets of lab books that we realized it couldn't be."

"Everybody seems agreed that we're talking about outright theft," said McNabb, venturing onto delicate ground.

Fran sighed. "I know, I know. But the point I'm making is that we were so furious at having been kept in the dark it never occurred to us that other people were getting last-minute surprises too. Barbara realized the mess we're all in just as late as we did. That may seem incredible to you, but that's because Barbara was the kind of girl she was."

"Look, Mrs. Pendleton, no matter what kind of girl she was, you can't get away from the fact that Barbara Gunn ran the office at Wisconsin Seed. The two partners must have talked things over, hunted for the right kind of lawyer, decided whether or not to go to court. If they were all such good friends, she heard a lot."

"Of course she did. But it wouldn't mean anything to her," Fran said confidently. "When she was with us at IPR,

Barbara was very conscientious about typing and filing, but basically she never knew what we did there. She liked working for us because she liked the people. And the same was probably true at Madison. Oh, in a vague way she'd know that Scotty was planning to sue Vandam's. But she would never realize that had anything more to do with her than a new experiment. And Vandam's has been just as stupidly tight-lipped with the opposition as they were with us. Even Scotty didn't know about our involvement until we all got together in Illinois. So the implications came home to Barbara very late. That's why she acted so strangely."

"Tell me about that," McNabb prodded.

"It was yesterday afternoon. We bumped into Barbara in the lobby here at the Blackstone. She was terribly upset and I chose that moment, of all moments, to be impatient with her. You see, I was still thinking of us as the only victims of last-minute surprise. Besides I had to go and deliver a paper and Howard had run out on me, so there simply wasn't any time. It ended with Barbara bolting out of the hotel like a scared rabbit."

"What do you mean, the implications had come home to her?" McNabb asked, deferring another question.

Fran had done enough thinking so that she could itemize her points. "First, she was overwhelmed by the sheer commercial value of *Numero Uno*."

"So was I," McNabb muttered.

Fran paid no attention and swept on. "Then, she realized she was going to be a key witness. You know, she was a target for all the gossipmongers at the meetings. I remember she told me everybody was circling around her the minute they saw her name tag. But, most important of all, she knew that her deposition was going to have terrible consequences for at least one of the people she was fond of."

McNabb nodded appreciatively, allowed the Pendletons

ample time to relax and then, almost casually, said, "What was that about your skipping out on your wife, Dr. Pendleton? Didn't you want to talk to Barbara Gunn?"

"No, I didn't," he said shortly. "The gossipers have been giving me the full treatment, too. I wasn't particularly anxious for them to see me closeted with a star witness for the opposition. I didn't know how Barbara was going to testify, and I wanted to keep it that way until it all came out in court."

Instead of continuing the conversation, the police captain leaned back and waited. Under his calm expectant gaze, Pendleton shifted uneasily, then clamped his lips shut. It was Fran who broke the impasse.

"For heaven's sake, Howard. Barbara was poisoned last night. This is no time to worry about telling tales out of school."

McNabb decided to take them off the hook. "You hadn't by any chance heard of certain overtures by Milton Vandam, had you?"

Howard Pendleton reddened angrily. "If you already knew, why didn't you say so?" he demanded. "Yes, Jason Ingersoll overheard Milton making some kind of proposition to Barbara."

"Come on, Doctor, you can do better than that. Exactly what kind of proposition?"

"Jason didn't know." Pendleton paused, then reluctantly continued. "But he did catch a phrase about making her a nice present if she did something."

"Quite a few people heard that one."

"Oh, my God. Do you wonder that I was worried? Barbara was a very straightforward girl, and she would have been fully justified in raising hell. We've already got enough problems. If there was going to be a public scandal about the Vandams trying to bribe her, I wanted it absolutely clear that we didn't have anything to do with it. In all fairness, I should say that Jason was every bit as outraged as I was."

McNabb sounded amused. "I'll bet he was. Tell me, Dr. Pendleton, I don't pretend to know anything about this kind of patent litigation, but doesn't it strike you that the Vandams are pulling some pretty queer plays? They don't tell you about the suit, they don't tell Wisconsin Seed about IPR, and when you all get together, Milton tries some fancy footwork with a secretary from the other side."

"I am not prepared to enter into speculation." Dr. Pendleton's official manner was back with a vengeance. "I have to agree there has been an excess of secretiveness but, in view of their recent merger, the Vandams are probably being overcautious. As for Milton, he has always been an oddity and you cannot extrapolate company policy from his actions."

"Oh, can't I? When Ingersoll was overflowing with outrage, he didn't happen to mention what *he* talked to Barbara Gunn about, did he?"

Pendleton's jaw dropped. "You mean Jason pressured her, too? They must all be crazy!" he cried. "No, he didn't tell me about that, Captain."

McNabb was grim. "Well, he'd better tell me."

After the police captain left and the floribunda had been successfully dispatched, the Pendletons settled down for an indignation meeting. Howard was foaming at the mouth about the selective nature of Jason's disclosures. Fran was loud in her disgust at the attempts either to corrupt or to intimidate Barbara Gunn, attempts which she was certain had led to her death.

But Eric Most, when he joined them, was triumphant.

"Of course it's too bad she was killed," he said perfunctorily, "but it solves all our problems."

Howard, who had been asking the heavens what further

166

insanity the Vandams would inflict on him, stopped in mid-sentence to stare at his assistant. "You think adding a murder investigation to a lawsuit is going to simplify our problems?"

"I'm sure it is," Most said eagerly. "Just because you and Fran were fond of Barbara Gunn, you're letting her death confuse your thinking. It's plain enough what happened. Wenzel faked up a lot of data to steal our patent and got Barbara Gunn to go along with him. Then she got cold feet at the last minute, and he had to kill her to shut her up. What's more, everybody is going to see it that way, so it's really a good thing from our point of view." He ended in a burst of enthusiasm, his face shining.

"Are you out of your mind, Eric?" Fran demanded incredulously.

Pendleton was more lugubrious than disapproving. "You've overlooked quite a lot, haven't you? If you think anything with the Vandams running around is going to be simple, you're living in a fool's paradise, Eric."

It was not easy to track down Milton Vandam. When Captain McNabb finally ran him to earth in a bar at the Hyatt Regency, he was huddled in a corner with a florid man in tweeds.

"This is my publisher, Fred Harris," Milton explained grandly. "He'll be bringing out my memoirs."

"Fine," said McNabb and was unable to get further.

"I'm thinking of including a chapter on my being present at Barbara Gunn's murder," Milton continued. "I think that will add a note of drama, don't you?"

"It'll be wonderful."

But irony, like so many other grown-up responses, eluded Milton Vandam. "Too many people think that life in the seed business is just sniffing flowers. I intend to show them the real story—international travel, big business deals, scientific breakthroughs, even violence. Properly handled"—

here he bent a stern eye on Mr. Harris—"there's no reason it shouldn't be a best seller."

McNabb had a great gift for not fighting the undertow. "Sounds like a sure thing to me."

"And I'm thinking of calling it *My Blooming Life*. Pretty catchy, eh?"

Fred Harris was a long way from deciding on titles. "Well, as I said, Mr. Vandam, we'll be happy to look at the manuscript when it's ready."

"It's the chance of a lifetime for you," Milton told him with simple certainty. "I could have gone to lots of other publishers, but I chose you people because I liked the way you handled those presidential memoirs."

"Glad to hear you say so," said Harris, rising. "And now I have to run along. Nice to have met you, Captain."

McNabb was already formulating his first question when Harris suddenly swung back with second thoughts.

"Say, Captain, *you* wouldn't be considering a book, would you? One featuring the Barbara Gunn case for instance?"

McNabb said repressively that it was early days for that and, not without difficulty, sped Harris on his way.

"Can't imagine why he should want your memoirs," Milton grumbled. "If they're the kind of outfit that will take just anything, I may have to do some rethinking."

McNabb was more interested in his present work than in future literary greatness. "Mr. Vandam, I'd like you to tell me about your talk with Barbara Gunn yesterday."

"It was the merest social obligation," was the airy reply. "We were at the same party, we were next to each other, so I said a few words. Nothing of substance, I assure you."

Not for a moment did Captain McNabb's well-schooled features betray that this was the first he had heard of an encounter at the murder site.

"Fine. But I want to start with your discussion yesterday

afternoon. You remember I asked all of you to review any meeting with the Gunn girl."

"Yes, indeed, and you do right to concentrate on those people associating with her," Milton said with lofty commendation. "I'm sure that the Wisconsin Seed people could tell you a great deal if they chose to. Unfortunately I cannot help you. Aside from those few words last night, the girl was a stranger to me."

"That won't do, Mr. Vandam. Your meeting at the ticket desk was witnessed."

Milton narrowed his eyes and spat one word: "Jason!"

Unmoved, McNabb said persistently, "So, what did you talk about?"

"It was nothing. I just bumped into her," Milton said stubbornly.

"Mr. Vandam, at least six witnesses saw and heard that conversation. I advise you to stop trying to mislead me," McNabb barked, sinking the fact that there had been more seeing than hearing.

Sulkily Milton yielded. He had, he said, decided it was only prudent to discover how the only unbiased witness from Wisconsin Seed would testify.

"You sure you didn't want to write her answers for her?"

"Nonsense," Milton blustered. "I happen to be a man with an unquestioned reputation for integrity. You have no right to make such insinuations. I have a good mind to protest this harassment."

McNabb ignored the babbling. "What about the nice little present you were going to make her if she went along with you?"

"I may have said something like that." Milton gulped. "But in context, Captain, in context!" Reassured by having found the *mot juste,* Milton expanded. "She would have been performing a small business courtesy by giving advance notice of what she was going to say. I intended to reply in kind with the sort of present you give a secretary at Christmas. A box of handkerchiefs or something like that. She understood me."

The rapidly accumulating dossiers at police headquarters had already informed McNabb that Milton Vandam had been living a self-indulgent and apparently celibate life for the past twenty years. McNabb could readily believe it. When was the last time in America that a man had given a woman under fifty a box of handkerchiefs?

In spite of McNabb's open disbelief, Milton refused to amend his latest version.

"I had to find out what was going on," he said over and over again. "It's important to me."

"And it was still important in the hospitality suite, I suppose. So you gave it another try."

Milton had a knack for reliving life's little pinpricks. "If you can call it that," he snapped, still sour with resentment. "I barely had a chance to say hello to the girl before Howard Pendleton came over with some damn-fool woman."

McNabb had only one arrow left in his quiver.

"Let's go back to the ticket desk in the afternoon. Did you leave that part of McCormick Place when you were through with Barbara Gunn, or did you hang around long enough to see Jason Ingersoll talking to her?"

"Jason spoke to her? Why that underhanded, conniving schemer!" His eyes more bulbous than ever, his cheeks purple with congestion, Milton overflowed. "I knew he'd been up to something with those people in Madison. Do you wonder at my trying to find out what? I have a right to know. In fact, you could say it's my duty."

Sowing dissension was all very well, but McNabb would have preferred some hard facts.

He was not going to get them from Jason Ingersoll. That much became apparent to the police captain within five minutes of trailing his quarry to the flower show, where he found the young man leaning against a pillar, his arms folded and his head drooping.

Jason made no bones about his talk with Barbara, but he had other information to impart. Shifting slightly so that a portion of the pillar was free, he invited McNabb to join him in surveying the scene.

"You may not realize this, Captain, but flower shows for seedsmen are like the Paris collections for the fashion business. They tell us what people are going to buy, and that changes every year. Funny how some things go in and out of style. Take hollyhocks, for instance. Nobody's grown them for decades, and now it looks as if they're about to stage a comeback."

Captain McNabb had been walking past the same yellow flowers to get to his front door for over ten years, and he still did not know their name. Nonetheless, he listened to Jason's continuing remarks about larkspur and Oriental poppies with close attention. They told him that Jason found it necessary to demonstrate his complete indifference to police questioning. But, in McNabb's experience, almost all citizens—including quite a few repeat offenders—held it as a God-given right to resent such intrusions. Why was Jason Ingersoll afraid to exercise this right?

To do the man justice, he ran down as gracefully as he had begun.

"But I tend to get carried away by my hobbyhorse, Captain, and I suppose that isn't what you came to hear."

"I came to hear what you and Barbara Gunn talked about," McNabb said stolidly.

"I wanted to find out what Milton had been up to. He could do us a lot of harm in our lawsuit, you know. By now you've probably heard about his offering her presents." Jason's pause for the confirmation that did not come was so slight, it barely broke the smooth rhythm of his remarks.

"Somebody was going to have to put the brakes on him. I thought I should find out how bad things were."

"And what did she have to say to all this?"

Jason shook his head with gentle regret. "Almost nothing. She was so rattled by Milton that she was nervous of talking to any of us, I guess. In fact you could say she was in a cold sweat. I tried to reassure her and left it at that."

"No curiosity about how she was going to testify?" McNabb asked with polite skepticism.

"If she'd volunteered anything, I'm not saying I wouldn't have listened." Jason shrugged. "But I didn't push and, Captain, you're not going to find anyone who says I did."

Unlike his cousin, Jason had not made the mistake of speaking at top volume in the middle of the floor. Whatever he had said to Barbara Gunn, he was rightly confident, had not been overheard.

And all that caution, thought McNabb as he closed the unsatisfactory interview, might be some index to the importance of what Jason Ingersoll had been saying.

"I'm afraid we can't be of much assistance," Thatcher said apologetically. "But we'll do anything we can."

Captain McNabb had not descended on the Sloan contingent until the end of a long and unproductive day. Stifling a yawn, he said that every little bit helped and he was trying to build a picture of Barbara Gunn's last day.

Thatcher obliged with a description of yesterday's cocktail hour. "It was apparent to both of us that she was rendered extremely nervous by any discussion of the *Numero Uno* suit," he concluded. "But I imagine everybody has been telling you that."

"Most of them are too busy impressing me with their own innocence to tell me much about Barbara Gunn."

"Sounds to me as if the Vandams are missing a bet," Charlie said cheerfully. "In their shoes, I'd be pushing the theory that Barbara Gunn wasn't worth murdering unless she was going to blow the whistle on Wisconsin Seed."

The same thought had occurred to Captain McNabb and, in this encouraging atmosphere, he decided to seek clarification of a point that had been bothering him. "I didn't get half as much of that as I expected. That president of theirs, Richard Vandam, mentioned it in passing, but he was more interested in convincing me that nobody in his company had been trying to bribe the girl. As for Jason and Milton, they seem to spend all their time trying to get a line on each other. I thought they were on the same side."

"Ah, now there we can be of some help. Milton used to be head of R&D, with Jason as his assistant," Thatcher explained. "After the merger, Milton was forced into retirement and Jason promoted. No matter how the *Numero Uno* battle turns out, somebody has fumbled. I expect that's what's exercising both of them."

"Great! That's all I need to add to the pot. At least the other two outfits, IPR and Wisconsin Seed, don't seem to have these family quarrels."

Thatcher and Charlie looked at each other before Thatcher spoke. "I don't know about IPR, Captain, but after drinks yesterday Trinkam and I had the distinct impression that Wisconsin Seed is not quite as monochromatic as all that. It was really your idea, Charlie."

Nothing loath, Trinkam recounted with gusto his view of the Hilary-Ackerman-Wenzel trio. "Of course it may simply be a case of the two partners keeping business details from the girl friend. But Hilary Davis knew enough to make sure that Wenzel didn't speak too freely about plant genetics."

In McNabb's view any lawyer tended to suppress social chitchat about an impending lawsuit. He was more interested in the revelations about Ackerman.

"I didn't realize he was so high-powered," he admitted. "I was concentrating on Wenzel."

"You may have picked up that bias from Vandam's," Thatcher suggested.

"And the Pendletons," said McNabb, thinking back. "They didn't even mention Ackerman as a factor."

He repeated Fran's account of Barbara Gunn in the Blackstone. "Mrs. Pendleton saw it as a war of loyalty between the claims of Wenzel and the claims of Pendleton. You would have thought Ackerman didn't exist."

Thatcher recalled all that he had heard about the origins of the biennial tomato, including early dreams in Puerto Rico.

"That may be a natural error on Mrs. Pendleton's part," he mused. "She and Wenzel and Barbara go back a long way. She may have simply overlooked the business manager up in Madison. But I don't think you should make the same mistake, Captain."

McNabb grinned wearily. "No fear. Businessmen are a lot easier for me to take than these crazy scientists." He lifted his coffee cup in salute to his hosts. "Half the time I don't understand what Wenzel is saying. He's clear enough about Pendleton being a has-been but, when I asked him about the Gunn girl's state of mind, he looked at me as if I was talking Chinese."

"A very self-absorbed young man," Thatcher agreed.

As the Captain levered himself to his feet, he carried this thought further than Thatcher had intended.

"That can take people different ways. Make it strong enough, and it can turn a man into a murderer."

17 EXTRA-LONG EARS

ERIC Most's happy certainty that only sentimentality prevented the Pendletons from recognizing Barbara Gunn's murder as the solution to all their problems received one blow after another. First there was the police.

"I'd almost forgotten about that," he told Captain McNabb carelessly, after being reminded of his cafeteria encounter with Barbara.

McNabb, fresh from a night's sleep, was at his smoothest. "Well, now that it's been brought back to you, suppose you tell me about it."

"There wasn't much to it. Actually I was in two minds as to whether I should pay any attention to her at all."

"They tell me you're the one who started things."

"That's right. Seeing her standing there, cool as a cucumber, got my goat."

McNabb invisibly straightened to attention. He had heard many assessments of Barbara Gunn during the last day of her life. *Cool as a cucumber* certainly did not represent consensus.

"So I let her have it," Most continued, seeming to relish the memory. "I told her that she ought to be ashamed, lending herself to a barefaced theft, and did she realize she was stealing five years of my work."

"What did she say to that?"

Most shrugged. "What could she say? But I gave her

plenty to think about, I promise you that. And you can see for yourself what she did."

"Now what would that be?"

"I rattled her. I told her she wasn't going to get away with it. If she backed up Wenzel in his story, she'd go to jail. You can bet your bottom dollar he never told her that." Most leaned forward persuasively. "So she decided to get out while she still could, and she was killed for her pains. It'll all come out in the wash as soon as we get this thing to court."

The police captain held up a restraining hand. "That may be a while yet."

"I'm not talking about your court. I'm talking about ours. Wenzel doesn't have anybody to corroborate him now. It's just his word that he did all those experiments, and that's nonsense on the face of it. He's sunk and he knows it."

"If that's the result," McNabb suggested evenly, "then offhand it doesn't seem like a good reason for murdering her. You're the ones getting all the benefit."

Most waved an impatient hand. "That's irrelevant. Wenzel didn't have any choice," he insisted. "But I'm right, you'll see."

Policeman and witness stared at each other in mutual dissatisfaction.

Captain McNabb, of course, had met this kind before. It was the worst sort of witness to evaluate. Eric Most was so busy convincing himself that it was impossible to tell whether he himself knew when he was lying. The confrontation with Barbara Gunn, for instance, could easily have been a simple case of a weak, vain man seizing the opportunity to bully an even weaker, already intimidated, young girl. Nobody would ever know because of Most's compulsion to rewrite history.

As for Most, he was wondering, as he often did, why

life compelled him to deal with people so stupid they could not see what was crystal clear.

But worse, far worse, from Eric's point of view, was the official reaction of Vandam's and Standard Foods.

"An adjournment!" he cried blankly when Dick Vandam relayed the news. "But that's crazy. We've got Wenzel on the run, and now's the time to stick it to him."

"I agree that this murder has put pressure on Wisconsin Seed, and that's a good thing. They're already operating on a shoestring and the last thing they can tolerate is the introduction of another delay. I've been over all this with Standard Foods and they've come around to my way of thinking. Wisconsin Seed will have to break down and come to the negotiating table."

"Negotiating table!" Eric was speechless with indignation.

No more than most men did Dick Vandam like having every statement received with stark disbelief. "Well, that's what we've decided," he snapped. "That's why I asked Pendleton to come over. But I see he couldn't find the time."

"He's introducing the guest speaker at the Propagation Committee lunch," Most said absently, his thoughts still dwelling on the enormity proposed to him. "Anyway, I'm just as involved as Howard is, and I can't help thinking that you're making a big mistake."

"Nonsense. You don't understand that this is a business decision. And we're the ones who are being sued."

"Everyone at the meetings is saying that it's between Wenzel and me. My whole reputation is at stake."

"Everyone's reputation is at stake."

The words were out before Vandam could stop them. Fortunately Eric did not see the implications, he only saw an opportunity.

"That's why we should get it cleared up fast."

"The decision has been made," said Vandam, rising.

No one could accuse Ned Ackerman of rewriting history. In fact, he seemed barely able to summon any interest in it.

"I had a hard time getting hold of you," McNabb remarked as he followed Ackerman down the corridor to his hotel room. "You didn't seem to be anywhere at McCormick Place."

The police captain had finally succeeded by simply waiting in the lobby of the Drake until his man appeared.

"I had some business downtown."

As they entered, Captain McNabb's vigilant eye noted that it was a pile of government publications Ackerman was depositing on a table.

"Government Printing Office?" he asked.

"Department of Agriculture," Ackerman said briefly as he tossed his coat on a chair. "What can I do for you, Captain?"

"I guess you didn't hear me say I wanted to have a session with everyone who was with Barbara Gunn the day she was murdered."

"Sure, I heard you," Ackerman said without heat. "Sorry I was out of touch for a couple of hours, but I figured Scotty could always fill you in."

Although he gestured invitingly toward two chairs and waited for the police captain to be seated, Ackerman himself stayed on his feet and began prowling the length of the small room.

"You may not have noticed, Mr. Ackerman, but your partner isn't awfully good at fleshing out the human details."

McNabb had intended a small piece of sarcasm. He was surprised when Ackerman stopped dead, cocked his head, and seemed to be studying a dazzlingly new conception.

"You know, you're right," he said at length. "Half the time, Scott doesn't know what people are feeling, and he couldn't care less, which makes him a pretty rotten prophet. I may have been relying on his judgment too much in this business. That's going to change."

The last thing Captain McNabb wanted was to spark an internal monologue in which he had no role. "Let's get back to Barbara Gunn," he directed. "What was she like at the end?"

"Jumpy as hell," Ackerman said promptly.

"Why?"

"Partly that was my fault. When I was describing the deposition process to her, I told her there was nothing to it. She'd just have to tell a couple of lawyers the way things had happened."

"Well, if she was going to tell the truth," McNabb challenged, "that was all there was to it."

Ackerman shook his head. "I forgot the circus atmosphere at these meetings and the way it would affect a timid kid like Barbara. She hated being in the limelight. And then some damn fool scared the bejesus out of her with the crazy idea that she was going to be a star witness at a big trial. That was enough to give her a heart attack on the spot."

Unerringly McNabb pinpointed the one anomaly. "What was so crazy about the idea? It may have scared her, but it was the way things were going to be."

"Hell no," said Ackerman casually. "Barbara was never going to testify."

The statement was so assured, yet so nonchalant, McNabb could scarcely believe his ears.

"Well, that's certainly the way things turned out," he agreed cautiously, "but how could you know in advance?"

The rat-a-tat tempo of their exchange, with Captain McNabb barking his questions at the perambulating figure and Ned Ackerman tossing the answers over his shoulder, had slowed considerably. Ackerman even paused long enough in his quartering of the room to face the policeman squarely.

"The geneticists were going to be the stars in this suit," he explained. "Barbara didn't know enough to be important."

"Come off it, Ackerman. She knew plenty. She knew when and where things were done."

Ackerman held up his hands in a gesture of surrender. "Okay, okay. But come off it yourself, Captain. This was a complex commercial suit with millions at stake. You know damn well that ninety-nine out of a hundred of these cases never see the inside of a courtroom. After everyone's flexed his muscles, the cases get settled in offices by a swarm of high-priced legal talent. I was simply playing the odds."

"But you and that partner of yours have been swearing you'd take this all the way to the Supreme Court."

"People say that all the time," Ackerman said wryly. "They don't always mean it."

And from this stand, he could not be budged. Captain McNabb did not object to pertinacious witnesses. He did, however, object to witnesses who were giving him only a fraction of their attention. Ackerman's mind was nine parts elsewhere. Even his prowling, now resumed, did not suggest nervous tension so much as churning thoughts and schemes that could not be addressed until McNabb's departure. Fortunately there was a sovereign remedy for this situation.

"Maybe it was a mistake for you to take off for the Federal Building today," McNabb began. "If you'd hung around McCormick Place and you like to play the odds, you'd know what the money is saying. That Barbara Gunn decided to welsh on some deal with you, and you killed her before she could sink your lawsuit."

Suspicion will almost always rivet a witness's attention, but nothing works all the time.

"Oh, that. They've been saying it for twenty-four hours," Ackerman said without much interest. "Silliest piece of nonsense I've ever heard."

"If it's that silly," growled an exasperated policeman, "suppose you give me another motive for her murder."

Ackerman brushed an arm across his forehead as if yet another gnat had been added to the cloud already circling him. "I'll be damned if I can figure that one out."

"In other words," said McNabb harshly, "a girl who worked for you has been murdered, you don't know why, and you don't much care."

Ackerman's voice dropped a full octave. "I care all right," he growled, "but that doesn't help me make sense of it."

"You'd better try harder than that. So long as you've got the only apparent motive for Barbara Gunn's murder, you're in this up to your neck."

"I'm not worried about my so-called motive. I'm worried about not knowing somebody else's. Like I told you, Barbara wasn't that important."

McNabb could think of only one explanation for Ackerman's rock-hard confidence.

"You're keeping something up your sleeve," he accused.

The retort was immediate. "If I am, it's none of your business."

"Everything in a murder investigation is my business."

"Like hell it is. We're settling this our own way."

No phrase in the English language is more calculated to raise police hackles.

"Forget that kind of thinking, Ackerman," Captain McNabb warned. "If you and that tin-pot partner of yours get any ideas about vigilante justice, I'll have you inside a jail cell within ten minutes."

This threat achieved what nothing else had. At last he had his witness's undivided attention. Ackerman blinked, readjusted his thoughts, then gave a short bark of laughter.

"You've got to be kidding. You think I'm going to get a six-shooter and gun somebody down in revenge? I'm not an adolescent, Captain. What's more, I'm not a man of violence."

McNabb already knew he had made a mistake. Ackerman, for better or worse, was undeniably adult. His second claim, however, had backfired. It had reminded the homicide expert of that long list of murderers resorting to poison because they simply could not tolerate the sight of human blood.

"I don't know why you say Ackerman is a dark horse," Earl Sanders complained. "And even if he is, I still think Dick made the right call about an adjournment."

"It makes financial sense," Thatcher conceded.

"Of course that's not the reason Dick's doing it," Sanders continued gloomily. "He's covering something. A baby could tell that much."

Thatcher and Charlie, fresh from the death throes of Wenonah Industries, were not encouraging someone else's troubles.

"Time will tell," Thatcher said, glancing ostentatiously at his watch. "Right now we're due at Midwestern Trust."

Sanders trailed after them to the door. "I'll let you know if anything more develops," he promised.

"You do that," they chorused, escaping.

The latest development was taking place that very moment as Detective Ed Dombrow trudged up the steps of a brick bungalow on Armitage Avenue. The steps were bone-dry, although an inch of snow had fallen overnight. Somebody had been out with a shovel, somebody who not only cleared the porch but straight-lined the sidewalk.

Dombrow's brick bungalow on Fullerton was yellow, not red. Otherwise it was a twin of the Norris home, down to the stained glass inserts at the top of the front door. And before he left that morning, Ed Dombrow had carefully shoveled his walk, too.

This in fact was why he was talking to Barbara Gunn's mother and father. The big shots were all downtown talking to other big shots. Phil and Ellie Norris out in Bridgeport had nothing to do with high-powered businessmen, important court cases, or murder—except for the fact that Barbara Gunn was their only daughter.

But Captain McNabb never overlooked loose ends. So Ed Dombrow had been detailed to this chore.

"Sorry to bother you again," he said when the door opened. "They've got a few other questions."

"Come on in," said Phil Norris. Like Dombrow, he was big and solid without any of the thickening that age would bring. "Things are a little better."

"It always takes time," Dombrow replied, following him into the living room.

This laconic exchange bridged the gap between then and now. Late the night Barbara Gunn died, Detective Dombrow had brought the news, the tears, the confusion. Hard-working people caught with their defenses down—newspapers on the floor, stockinged feet before the TV, a small granddaughter sleeping in the bedroom that had once been her mother's.

There was no sign of those ravages, now. The house looked ready for a party. Ellie Norris, who emerged from the kitchen, had newly golden highlights in her hair, while her husband wore a spotless sport shirt and slacks.

Downtown, the body had already been released. Detective Dombrow knew, without asking, about the funeral, the friends and neighbors who would be coming by, the wake, the church, the grave. The long sad pattern had begun and, by the time it was over, the edge of grief would have been dulled.

"We drove Tracy out to Aurora, to Phil's niece," said Mrs. Norris in response to Dombrow's question. "She's got kids the right age and—"

"You didn't want to ask her questions, did you?" Phil Norris demanded truculently.

"God, no!" exclaimed Dombrow.

Ellie Norris looked nervous. "Phil's worried about Tracy."

"She's just a baby," her husband growled.

"Detective Dombrow knows that," Ellie said placatingly.

To the grief in this particular house, there was added rage. Dombrow took no offense, even when Norris turned on him.

"Are they making any progress, finding out who killed Barbie?"

"They're working on it," Dombrow responded.

Suddenly, Phil Norris seemed to crumple within his bandbox-fresh clothes. Stammering something indistinguishable, he blundered toward the kitchen. Ellie started to follow, then stopped.

"He's taking it hard," she said simply.

Dombrow had seen pictures of the murdered woman, and he found himself looking at the same face. There were fine lines around these eyes, the lips were a little thinner. But the same sweetness was there.

"Phil was so proud of Barbie," she said, trying to smile. "You should have seen him at the wedding. She was so beautiful. And Tim was so handsome in his uniform. They were too young, both of them. But—"

She broke off, pressed a handkerchief to her lips. When she spoke again, she turned to the present. She did not trust herself with the unshadowed days of the past.

"And everybody's been so kind. That Mrs. Pendleton came out here yesterday, just to tell us how fond they were of Barbara in Puerto Rico. And her husband would have come if he hadn't had a meeting."

Sorrow could break a man down, Dombrow thought, but women bent. The weight of this tragedy, from care of a granddaughter to comfort of a husband, was falling on Mrs. Norris's shoulders. She would fix her eyes on the sustaining forces—the universal affection for her daughter, the good will of strangers—and somehow she would find the strength.

"Mr. Ackerman's been wonderful, too," she was continuing. "Imagine, he said his wife could put together a case of Tracy's things and drive down from Wisconsin over the weekend. Just to spare us the trouble. There are a lot of good people in the world."

This time when she wavered, she merely gripped the handkerchief tightly. "But you didn't come for that. . . ."

"They want to know if you've talked to the lawyer in Madison yet," he said.

It had already been established that the Norrises knew very little about their daughter's daily life. They had met Scott Wenzel and Ned Ackerman when they drove up to Madison two summers ago for a visit. Otherwise Barbara's life was a closed book to them.

". . . didn't realize what a good job it was," Mrs. Norris was saying. "Of course we knew that Barbie was smart."

For a moment, Dombrow was afraid he had missed something. But Mrs. Norris was talking about what he had come to explore—what Barbara Gunn had left behind.

"Twenty-five thousand dollars," said her mother. "That's a lot of money for a young girl who's supporting herself and a baby to save."

"It sure is," said Dombrow.

With touching pride Barbara's mother read off the details that had been telephoned from the lawyer—the bank, the amount, the dates.

"Of course, we're not going to touch it," said Ellie Norris. "It's all for Tracy's education."

Dombrow nodded approvingly, like the solid family man

that he was. But he was a policeman too. Even as he nodded, he was two steps beyond Mrs. Norris.

Fifteen thousand dollars in one deposit five years ago did not sound like the result of steady saving to him.

18 REMOVE FADED FLOWERS

IT took police specialists less than twenty-four hours to establish the damning facts about Barbara Gunn's nest egg. By the next day, with a little judicious assistance from Captain McNabb, the news had percolated into the board rooms, hotel lobbies and convention halls of Chicago where it unleashed a torrent of speculation, accusation and counter-accusation.

The one place where the subject was not being discussed was a suburban cemetery fifteen miles west of Bridgeport where early arrivals were forced to wait for the long cortège of cars. To those who had known her as a grown woman, whether as naval wife, recent widow, or working mother, Barbara Gunn had been a transient, a bird of passage, never putting down roots. That was not the way she looked to Bridgeport. Phil and Ellie Norris had lived in the community for their entire marriage and, on this sad day, they were supported by relatives, neighbors, lodge brothers and fellow workers. But Barbara herself for many years had been a permanent fixture there, and she was young enough to be a living memory for her own generation. The crowd was swelled by her high school classmates, the boys she had dated, the young people she had once taught in Sunday School. Her funeral was a local event, so much so that the two outside parties, one from Puerto Rico and one from Wisconsin, were almost forced into each other's arms.

This commingling was all the easier because Fran and Ned Ackerman had already bumped into each other during their condolence visits.

"Hello, Fran," Ackerman said somberly. "I think Barbara's parents are looking a little better, don't you?"

"They're over the first shock," Fran agreed. "But I honestly don't see how her father would have gotten through it if it hadn't been for little Tracy."

Scott Wenzel was looking resentfully at the clear blue sky and the clean white drifts lining the roadways through the cemetery. "God, it's as if nothing had happened," he said, with all-too-human frustration at the bland indifference of nature.

When a young person has died, the heavens should weep and the trees should array themselves in long grey tendrils. It is indecent that the sun should shine and a buffeting breeze should toss the bare branches in playful abandon.

"It's hard to believe she's really dead," Howard Pendleton said more temperately.

"And before this damn suit blew up she was so happy," Ned Ackerman recalled. "She really was looking forward to going back to school. I think she felt she was making a new beginning."

Sadly Fran continued the theme. "Yes, it took her a long time to find her feet."

Scott was puzzled. "I didn't know it was such a big deal for her. She didn't say that much about it."

Fran and Ned exchanged glances. They both knew that Barbara had spoken; Scott simply had not been listening.

"What difference does all that make now?" Pendleton reminded them. "Her death is the tragedy."

It was left for Hilary Davis to strike a new note. "The real tragedy was that she didn't get out a year sooner."

"What's that?" Taken off guard, Ned Ackerman was betrayed into asking a question, the answer to which he did not want to hear.

"If she hadn't been around, she wouldn't have been involved in the lawsuit," Hilary relentlessly expanded, "and there'd have been no reason for anyone to kill her."

She had spoken in the tones of a lecturer, without the slightest tincture of any emotion other than the desire to impart information. Nonetheless, such a heavy cloud of self-accusation enveloped the isolated band that she might have been denouncing them from the pulpit.

Eric Most was the one who broke under the strain. "Well, it was her own fault," he burst out.

This appalling truth first reduced everyone to silence, then impelled them into feverish conversation. Howard Pendleton resorted to an old standby.

"I saw you at Maxwell's seminar yesterday, Scott. What did you think of his findings?" he asked.

Scott was a good deal more fluent at picking apart a colleague's work than at dealing with the verities of life and death. As if a button had been pushed, he was soon in full spate, ably seconded by the Pendletons. Ackerman was content to stay on the sidelines, a few alternate subjects at the ready. Hilary, composed and aloof, was contemptuous of this universal failure to face facts. But Eric Most was the chief sufferer. His outburst had sounded childish even to him, and he was mortified by his lack of control. He could not redeem himself with a display of professional bravura because he had skipped Maxwell's seminar. Above all, he was present under protest. His first reaction to Howard's proposal of a mass attendance at the funeral had been that he barely knew the girl. His second was that he could scarcely be expected to put on a big show of grief for someone who had stolen his work.

"Her parents won't know what you're thinking," Pendleton had rejoined roughly, "and I assume you've got enough sense not to air your views at the side of her grave."

By degrees the conversation modulated from Maxwell's mistakes to the future of Tracy Gunn.

"I hope you don't mind," Fran told Ackerman, "but Ellie and Phil let me know what you've offered to do. If there's any difficulty, Howard and I would like to contribute. It can't be easy for a young firm, in its first years, to start a fund like that."

"We'll be able to swing it," Ackerman said confidently. "God knows it's little enough, but it gives them a sense of security for the little girl."

Fran was moved to clasp his arm warmly. "I know it was your idea and I think it's a wonderful thing to do."

"Scott went right along as soon as I mentioned it, Fran," said Ackerman, swift to reject the implied criticism. "You know he's not callous, he's just not used to thinking in terms of people."

"You don't have to tell me that," Fran replied. "I like Scott, I like him a lot, but it's time he did a little growing up."

The process began almost immediately. The final car arrived, the family braced itself, and the simple ceremony proceeded without incident. The Norrises looked drained, their friends looked sad, but when the first symbolic handful of earth fell on the fresh new casket, it was Scott Wenzel who gulped audibly, produced a handkerchief and, with misting eyes, blew his nose.

As they moved toward the line waiting to say a few last words to the Norrises, Scott tried to explain his latest discovery.

"It just hit me," he said, sounding more surprised than anything else. "Barbara isn't going to be here anymore and, my God, I'm going to miss her!"

Hilary was as crisp as ever. "Of course you are."

"But she didn't do anything special," Scott protested, still trying to puzzle things out. "We'll get somebody else easily enough."

"Barbara was a part of your life for over six years. That's why you'll miss her," Hilary said with kindly authority. "Now, I'm going to peel off here with Eric while the rest of you pay your respects. And Scott, remember to tell her parents how much you'll miss Barbara."

This program hit an unexpected snag the moment the two men from Wisconsin Seed approached the bereaved parents.

Even in the midst of her grief, Mrs. Norris recognized that she had an obligation.

"Oh, Mr. Ackerman," she said urgently, "I want you to understand that when we spoke with you the other day, Phil and I didn't know that Barbara had left anything for Tracy. It makes a big difference. We'll be able to manage and—"

"That doesn't change things at all," Ned overrode her hastily, horror-struck at this introduction of a topic best avoided.

"But it does," Mrs. Norris repeated with the persistence of simple-minded honesty.

Ned let her go no further. "We're glad to do it as a memorial to Barbara. We were so fond of her, and we'll never forget her," he said, desperately gabbling a few mandatory condolences while unceremoniously pushing Scott Wenzel past the Norrises.

Just behind them, Fran and Howard Pendleton were equally reluctant to discuss Barbara Gunn's unexpected wealth. They too cut their remarks to a bare minimum, and the foursome cleared the line in record time.

Even so, Hilary Davis and Eric Most had been left alone with each other for far too long.

* * *

"That man is a twit," exclaimed Hilary as she scrambled into the car in a flurry of long, elegant legs.

From the back seat Scott was not impressed. "I've been saying that for years."

Hilary paid no attention. "Do you realize he's talking as if this twenty-five thousand dollars hasn't shifted the spotlight? He still thinks you and Ned are the prime suspects."

"That's just the way Eric would like things to be," Scott reasoned.

"Of course it is. But there's such a thing as using your head. Now that we know Barbara took a bribe five years ago, most people can figure out what she's been stealing and from whom."

Ned Ackerman hunched himself further over the steering wheel. "Could we put a little distance between us and Barbara's grave before we discuss it, Hilary?" he grated.

"You're going to have to talk about it sometime."

"She's right, you know," Scott supported Hilary. "The only reason we didn't do it this morning was because we were in too much of a rush."

The Wisconsin Seed delegation had been among the last to benefit from Captain McNabb's calculated leakage. With Ned Ackerman disappearing into downtown Chicago all day and Scott burying himself in one seminar after another, they were a long way from the central grapevine. It had been Hilary, of all people, who brought back the latest gossip just as they were about to set forth on the long drive to the Bridgeport church.

"All right, all right. So we talk about it," Ned yielded. "What is there to say?"

"Quite a lot," snapped Hilary. "For starters, you two have just been taken off the hook for a murder charge. I don't say I expect dancing in the streets, but you might explain why you're acting as if it's bad news, not good news."

Ned was every bit as irritable as she was. "Just think about it," he advised. "Barbara was into absolutely everything we did. She could have robbed us blind."

"You're the one who isn't thinking." Hilary shook her head reproachfully. "The moment that Vandam's filed for that patent you knew that somebody had stolen the most important thing you had. What difference does it make that the pinching fingers belonged to Barbara?"

Scott Wenzel was as uneasy as his partner. "We took a lot more security precautions after we knew we were a target, but we never tried to protect ourselves against Barbara."

"Yeah," Ned agreed sourly. "She was already inside the fence we were building."

Hilary frowned. She could not help feeling that they were overreacting.

"I grant you that Barbara could have done more damage than anyone else," she said on a calmer note. "After all, she had access to all your private conversations, your correspondence with your lawyers, your strategy for the trial. But there's nothing you can do about it, and there's no point working yourselves into a sweat. You'll soon know if it's as bad as you think."

Ned, the one who had not wanted to discuss the situation, had felt free not only to think about it, but to reach a decision.

"I'm not waiting," he said bluntly. "We're going to force Vandam's into court as fast as we can. I think we'll just make it under the wire."

"You're right, Ned," Wenzel said instantly. "It's the only way to handle it."

Hilary screwed herself around in her seat so that she could watch both men. What she saw—Scott sitting with his arms folded and his jaw outthrust, Ackerman relaxing over the wheel as if the suspense were over—caused her to explode. "Look, I don't pretend to understand what kind of race you two are in, but a child could tell that you're sitting on something. Now, if you don't want to take me into your confidence, that's your affair. I've got plenty of other things to occupy myself with. But stop talking over and under and around me. If you can't come clean, then suppose you shut up about this subject and find another one."

There was a thunderous silence, which Ackerman made no attempt to dispel. After several moments Wenzel politely fulfilled Hilary's last request.

"I'll never understand why Barbara was the one who stuck a shiv into me. I thought we were friends," he lamented. "What the hell was bugging her?"

Ned decided he had relaxed too soon. He himself knew what had been bugging Barbara. Even worse, he was sure that Hilary did too. All they needed now was for Hilary to indulge her didactic streak by explaining the nature of a triangle to poor old Scott.

He was doing the lady a considerable injustice.

"I can't imagine what could have gotten into her," said Hilary in tones of uncharacteristic doubt. "And I don't suppose we'll ever know."

After their unsatisfactory exchange in the cemetery, Eric Most would have liked to forget all about Hilary Davis, but he fell prey to Fran Pendleton's curiosity.

"Of course, I've known about Hilary for years," she said as soon as they were in the car speeding back to the Loop, "but, do you know, this is the first time I've met her."

"She's not very feminine," Eric said primly from the rear.

Fran had long ago abandoned the notion that femininity and masculinity were like universal colorants—something

194

you could plop into any old bucket and count on for uniform results.

"She's feminine enough for Scott and that's what matters," she replied reasonably. "But poor Barbara! She must have been driven crazy by the sight of Hilary. I'll bet that's why she took that money."

Howard had very little attention to spare. Driving in the outback of Puerto Rico had weakened him for the freeways of Chicago, and not until he received assurance that he was in the right lane for his exit could he answer his wife.

"Honest to God, Fran," he said in a familiar complaint, "outside the laboratory you don't have a brain up there, you have a slipped disk. What possible connection is there between the two situations?"

Fran was too accustomed to the accusation to pay any heed to it. "Well, everybody's saying that Barbara took that bribe about five years ago. And Scott and Hilary have known each other for over five years."

"Known each other!" Eric Most echoed sarcastically. "Ha!"

"All right then, Scott and Hilary have been living with each other for five years," Fran corrected herself without much interest. "You know perfectly well that Barbara was a case about Scott. But anyone can see that Hilary is perfect for him in a way that Barbara could never imitate. No wonder the poor girl was aching for a change. I suppose she thought this was the only way to fund it. It would have to be something like that for her to do the dirty on Scott."

Fran was innocently absorbed in the drama of Barbara Gunn. Her companions, each in his own way, seized on other implications.

"There's no reason to assume she did the dirty on him," Eric objected. "Oh, I'll grant you all that other stuff if you like, that she wanted to move on when she couldn't hook him and needed money to do it. But he was beginning his crooked scheme then. He probably paid her to fudge the files over the next five years."

Both the Pendletons were alive to the absurdity of this particular suggestion, but Howard had other fish to fry.

"There's no way we can tell exactly what happened back then. Some people will see it one way, and other people will see it differently. But there's nothing to be gained by listing a lot of wild improbabilities."

"It's crazy, no matter how it happened," said Fran, agreeing with him in spirit if not letter, "but then I've always said that Milton probably was crazy."

"Fran!" It was a cry of agony. "We simply cannot run down the Vandams, one by one, analyzing their potential for every crime in the book. And I don't particularly want to do it with Wisconsin Seed either. It'll be bad enough if we ever know for certain, but at least that will just be one person. Oh God, now you've made me miss my exit. I'm not going to have a moment's peace until I get this damned thing back to the rental agency and never have to look at it again."

Fran, who realized perfectly well that her husband's malaise did not stem from the Chevy Impala, was more than willing to oblige him.

"I really never thought I'd see a woman who was so right for Scott," she mused. "His self-absorption will never bother her. She's just as bad. And when she really wants him to do something socially respectable, she just makes him do it, the way she did at the cemetery. He's awfully lucky to have found her."

"He doesn't seem to think he's so lucky," Eric Most retorted. "You notice he hasn't married her."

"You mean he doesn't value her enough to make an honest woman of her?" Fran chuckled. "That isn't the way it will happen. In about two years Scotty will realize he can't live without her, and he'll go into a panic. For all I know she'll give him a hard time."

Eric Most did not approve of the way the conversation was going. After all, he was a young man under thirty and Fran was a grandmother. Why then was he the one who sounded like a maiden aunt?

Meanwhile Fran had moved to other considerations. "I wonder what they do about meals?"

"I suppose they eat out," her husband said, baffled.

"Oh, Howard, that's so old-fashioned," his wife reprimanded him. "Gourmet cooking is the in thing these days. Probably Scotty makes a mean beef Wellington by now. I'll bet Hilary encourages it as a good relaxation for him."

Howard Pendleton laughed outright and Fran, pleased with her tactics, enlarged on the improvements Hilary had effected in Scotty's wardrobe.

"You remember the way he looked in Puerto Rico? I don't think anybody had broken it to him about dry cleaners."

And so, for poor Eric, it was Hilary Davis all the way back to the Blackstone Hotel.

19 ON SLOPES AND BANKS

DEATH is the ultimate finality for everyone except press, radio and television. Barbara Gunn's funeral, simple though it was, provided raw material for reams of purple prose. "Her name was Barbara Norris. . . ." wrote columnists specializing in pathos. "Bridgeport buried one of its own today," throbbed hard-boiled chroniclers of city life. ". . . her little daughter, Tracy, who is too young to understand . . ." pealed the human Wurlitzers on channel six.

Fortunately, before this outpouring crested, John Thatcher was safely back at the Sloan. The tragedy of Barbara Gunn was bad enough; wallowing in it struck him as either perverted or cynical.

Besides, even without the horror of murder, reassuming his rightful place in the universe was always satisfying. This morning, Thatcher had entered the Sloan with a springy step.

The other inhabitants of Exchange Place were also pleased at his return.

". . . although the weather isn't the best for you," said Billings, who piloted the executive elevator.

"It's better than it was in Chicago," said Thatcher untruthfully. He felt kindly disposed to these stinging pellets of sleet, ice and rain because they were portents of weather to come. "Yes, I was lucky to beat the storm."

Everett Gabler, Grand Old Man of the Trust Department, was above climate.

"John," he said, falling into stride beside his snow-encrusted superior, "Charlie's already here and he said you'd be coming in this morning. Now, I have to talk to you about Section Twelve. If we let it slide . . ."

Gabler was not the only one on the lookout. Walter Bowman pounced as soon as Thatcher and Gabler rounded the corner.

". . . and high time too," he said, attaching himself to the group. "Have you heard what's happening to First Miami?"

Thatcher was not by nature a daydreamer. His attention, like his time, was valuable. Nevertheless, the passing vision sometimes descended. Over last night's high-altitude Salisbury steak, he had idly projected Miss Corsa's reaction to his unannounced return complete with post-Christmas gift.

She was certainly surprised at the crowd scene. But here too, Trinkam had gotten in first.

"Good morning, Miss Corsa. As you see, I finally made it," said Thatcher, deferring present-giving to a quieter moment.

"Welcome back, Mr. Thatcher," she replied. "I've put your current file on your desk."

During these formalities, Charlie Trinkam unhurriedly pushed himself off the corner of Miss Corsa's desk, greeted his colleagues, and prepared to join the procession into Thatcher's office.

Just then sound effects were added. Miss Corsa's phone rang.

"Mr. Thatcher's office. . . . Oh yes, Mr. Sanders. . . . I'm not sure Mr. Thatcher is in yet. . . . Let me check. . . ." she said, cupping a hand over the mouthpiece and semaphoring inquiry.

With a sigh, he stepped over to take the receiver. "Sanders? Yes, I just got in. . . ." If nothing else, he reflected as he stood watching moisture from his overcoat drip on Miss Corsa's rug, he was setting a good example. He listened for a moment, then said, "I see. . . . No, I am not surprised. I assume this means we'll be hearing from you in the near future. . . . Fine. . . . Thank you for telling me."

After this the immediate chances of getting down to Section Twelve or First Miami faded dramatically.

"What's happened now?" Gabler asked acidulously, speaking for all of them.

"No, it is not a progression beyond murder," Thatcher said dryly, answering the implication. "Sanders was simply informing us that Standard Foods is scrapping its delaying tactics. They have decided to push *Numero Uno* through the Patent Office as soon as possible."

In some circles, this might be regarded as anticlimax, but not at the Sloan Guaranty Trust.

"That's a switch, isn't it?" Bowman commented.

"It's an about-face," said Trinkam. "But as John just said, it's not a real earthshaking surprise."

Everett Gabler, although high-minded to a fault, wanted all the distasteful details. "I'm not sure I follow you, Charlie. Surely some sort of compromise—"

"That's what SF thought before Chicago, Ev," Charlie said. "But now, when the can of worms includes murder and bribery, compromise is out. SF wants *Numero Uno* settled fast—before anything really ugly is pinned on one of their boys. Right, John?"

Thatcher, who had been riffling through his backlog, looked up. "That is certainly the line that Sanders and Standard Foods are taking."

The keen-eared Bowman thought he detected a note of reservation. "What about Vandam's?" he asked. "Are they going along with this rush to judgment?"

"That," Charlie told him, "is the hundred-dollar question."

While he would have phrased it differently, Thatcher agreed. At this juncture, SF and Vandam's could well be defending radically different positions. SF wanted *Numero Uno*—no matter what. Vandam's, on the other hand, could be thinking that its loss was a small price to pay for escaping criminal charges.

". . . find it very difficult to believe!" Everett was declaring.

"What do you find hard to believe, Ev?" Thatcher inquired.

"That a reputable firm like Vandam's could be associated with systematic theft, far less murder!" Gabler replied.

"You should get together with Edgar Brown," Charlie said with a grin. "He thinks it's a fine old firm too. But he's met the Vandams, and he wouldn't put anything past them."

Everett was incensed. "I recognize the distinction between the firm and an individual, possibly demented Vandam—"

"They're all a little screwy," said Charlie.

"—however," Gabler plowed on, ignoring this aside, "surely there are alternate ways of interpreting the actions of this Mrs. Gunn, are there not? According to what I have read, the only thing incontrovertible is that some five years ago she accepted a payment of fifteen thousand dollars, presumed to be a bribe."

Walter, a numbers man, had to interrupt. "Twenty-five thousand, Ev."

"I beg your pardon. *The New York Times*—"

It was a needless debate, and Thatcher said as much. "It's not a matter of which paper you read," he said, amused that this point should have to be explained at the Sloan. "Once the unexpected discovery of twenty-five thousand dollars was made in Mrs. Gunn's account, McNabb's people went to work. It was simple enough to determine that five years ago she deposited fifteen thousand dollars in a time account. As she hasn't touched it since—well, I don't have to labor compound interest, do I?"

Since Bowman lived and breathed interest rates, he was visibly discomfited. But not for long. "Have they found out how she was paid?"

"As you would expect, a cashier's check," said Thatcher with no fear of further embarrassment. Jove may nod, but if He worked at the Sloan He could never forget that cashier's checks bought for cash are untraceable.

"And Ev," Charlie interjected wickedly, "the cashier's check was drawn on Midwestern Trust which, in case you've forgotten, is Vandam's bank. Makes you think, doesn't it?"

Gabler was not drawn. "Nonsense. The purchase of a cashier's check can be made by anybody walking in off the street."

"Undeniably," said Thatcher, encouraging him. While he had not hurried back to the Sloan for more of SF, *Numero Uno* and murder, Gabler's idiosyncratic viewpoint was often unexpectedly rewarding.

"So," Gabler continued severely, "despite all the rumor, hearsay and innuendo, the one solid fact appears to be this so-called bribe. All this deplorable confusion would be dissipated if the police could discover who gave it to Mrs. Gunn—and why."

"Well, you can wash out Standard Foods," said Bowman. "They didn't get into the picture until years later."

"I was not thinking of Standard Foods," said Gabler portentously. "I was thinking of Wisconsin Seedsmen."

The pronouncement fell flat. "Ev," said Bowman sadly, "you're letting your prejudice run away with you."

Small companies with more promise than capital might become Wall Street's darlings, but never Everett's. He liked substance, in the form of cash reserves, and he had just reminded himself of another company headquartered in Chicago.

". . . a committee of Wenonah Industries' creditors, meeting with a court-appointed receiver," Gabler was saying when Thatcher managed to clear them all out of his office, with promises of availability later in the day.

Nevertheless, once he was alone, he was irritated to discover that Gabler had left a sleeper behind. What about Wisconsin Seed? Thatcher found himself wondering instead of addressing the material Miss Corsa had prepared for him. Was there a variant reading that pointed the finger of blame at Scott Wenzel?

It was, Thatcher discovered, almost too easy.

If Wisconsin Seed, not Vandam's, had been engaged in commercial espionage, then the bribe to Barbara Gunn took on totally new significance. What if she had been a conduit, not a thief? Scott Wenzel could scarcely nose around IPR without being noticed. But Mrs. Gunn, Thatcher seemed to remember, had friends at IPR. She had gone back to Puerto Rico to close down her apartment. She could have been instructed—and bankrolled—to locate someone privy to Howard Pendleton's work—say, a secretary. . . .

"Mr. Thatcher!"

Standing before his desk was an indignant Miss Corsa. For one confused moment, Thatcher feared she had been reading his thoughts. But his gross libel on the secretaries of America was not what was exercising her. It was his obvious dereliction from duty.

"I'm glad you came in. I was just going to call you," he said, making a brisk recovery. "Sit down, Miss Corsa. Now, as you know, I visited Vandamia last week. While I was there, I arranged something. . . ."

Thatcher outlined his treat, an all-expenses paid VIP tour of Vandamia—for two—at the time of Miss Corsa's choosing. Miss Bohm, of Vandam's, was eager to learn when she should unroll the red carpet.

"Oh, Mr. Thatcher," Miss Corsa breathed when he finished. "My grandfather will be thrilled!"

Thatcher was halfway through Miss Bohm's phone number before her comment registered.

"Your grandfather?" he said weakly.

In a burst of loquacity she told him about her grandfather, about his gardening, his indomitable spirit and his physical infirmity.

". . . but if I go along to take care of him, why it will be wonderful!" she concluded resolutely.

"Fine," said Thatcher, biting his lip. Miss Corsa's choice of companion was, after all, her business. "I think I'd better go upstairs to check in with Lancer for a few minutes."

Talks with the chairman of the board tended to last longer, but Thatcher wanted to give the dust plenty of time to settle before he got back.

Two hours was barely enough for George C. Lancer. He spoke extensively not only of present and future, but of past; he descended from policy to mere personality.

"I've got to get back or Miss Corsa will have my scalp, George," said Thatcher, fighting his way out. He had no one to blame for this interlude but himself. Inauguration of Republican Administrations always acted like May wine on Lancer. Fortunately, they did not come often enough to constitute a major menace, but today, the net result was that Thatcher was running late before he got started.

Back on the sixth floor, he discovered that Miss Corsa had not been doing much better. Despite the work at hand, she had already, so she told him, been on the phone to her grandfather and to Miss Bohm.

And, as he could see with his own eyes, she had also been gossiping with Charlie Trinkam.

"You said ten-thirty, John," said Trinkam unapologetically.

"George is dreaming of balanced budgets," Thatcher explained.

"So, I've just been telling Rose how anybody could have done the dirty in Chicago."

Thatcher had no trouble going from deficit financing to Vandam's current difficulties. But since his most recent source had been Everett Gabler, not the tabloids, he said, "You mean that anybody could have bribed Mrs. Gunn?"

"No," said Charlie, giving him an odd look. "I was just explaining how anybody could have poisoned her."

Belatedly, Thatcher realized that this was the real inside information. Captain McNabb had released everything he knew about cashier's checks and Midwestern Trust to the press. But for a variety of reasons, the salient facts about the poison itself had still not been blared to the world although Charlie, like Thatcher, had heard about Phyllacitin before he left Chicago.

Phyllacitin was a new broad-spectrum fungicide, introduced by Lund Chemical as proudly and publicly as possible. There had been displays all over McCormick Place, and sales to Vandam's and Wisconsin Seedsmen, among others. Lund Chemical was denying charges that Phyllacitin had been criminally available to almost everybody, but they had to admit it was lethal. Phyllacitin would have killed Barbara Gunn within minutes, depending on how much and how fast she drank.

These were the brute technical details, enough for everybody except police pathologists. Thatcher and Trinkam could, of their own knowledge, add the next expert testimony. The Hogarth hospitality suite at the McCormick Inn had been crowded with people in motion.

". . . so anybody could have gone up to her, dropped something in her glass and—pfft!" said Charlie. But he was not all insouciance. "You know, it's chilling when you think about it. I mean, somebody stocking up on Phyllacitin—just in case. Then, watching the poor kid to see how she was bearing up, and if she could pull herself together—or if she had to be killed to keep her mouth shut."

Miss Corsa shivered and Thatcher was deliberately matter-of-fact. "Put that way, it sounds like a particularly ghoulish watching-and-waiting game. But you know, Charlie, I doubt it. After all, everybody seems to agree that Mrs. Gunn could never have been realistically expected to stand up to cross-examination, or even emotional pressure."

"You mean the murderer came prepared to kill?" said Charlie. "But premeditation—and picking up Phyllacitin at the last minute? It doesn't hang together, does it?"

It did not, as Thatcher was first to admit.

Miss Corsa, who rarely put herself forward, waited until she was sure neither man had anything to add, then said, "Do you think it could have been a mistake?"

"Not from what the cops told us about this bug killer—" Charlie began expansively.

That was not what Miss Corsa had meant, as she explained, "I didn't mean a mistake about the poison, I meant a mistake about the murder."

Seeing that both Thatcher and Trinkam were lost, she continued, "You see, I was thinking. Mrs. Gunn was quitting work to go back to college, wasn't she? That's what *Newsweek* said. Well, it seems to me that, if this whole lawsuit came up after she had left, she would never have been called to testify."

"Good God, of course she wouldn't have been called," exclaimed Thatcher, struck by the simple undeniable truth he had completely overlooked. Ex-employees forget details, they cannot read last year's shorthand book, they barely recognize the world they have left behind. No lawyer worth his salt bothers with them.

And if Barbara Gunn had not been called to testify, she would have been no threat.

Charlie was only half-convinced.

"You may be right, Rose," he said slowly just as Thatcher's eleven o'clock appointment came bustling in.

Walter Bowman, overhearing, demanded, "Rose may be right about what?"

He listened critically to Charlie's rendering of Miss Corsa's suggestion, nodded, then swept ahead. "That makes sense to me. And you see what it means, don't you? One way to clarify what's been happening is to go back and see where the legal surprises came from. And they came from Scott Wenzel, the way I understand it. That means that Vandam's must have been caught off guard. Despite Everett, they're still the ones on the spot."

Still digesting Miss Corsa's contribution, Thatcher said, "Actually, Walter, the legal jockeying has been too convoluted for that simple an approach. But I think Miss Corsa has to be correct. The criminal expected events to move less rapidly. Mrs. Gunn should have been off the scene when the fireworks began."

"Even so—" Bowman began argumentatively.

Thatcher was ahead of him. "Don't forget Vandam's announced *Numero Uno* in this year's catalog. That could be interpreted as the precipitating event."

"Which leaves things just as murky as they were, doesn't it?" said Bowman.

After a pause, Thatcher said, "You know, I'm beginning to think not."

20 MUST BE SUPPORTED

UNDER Hilary Davis' critical eye Eric Most seemed almost retarded in failing to recognize the shifting balance in the Barbara Gunn murder investigation. But circumstances had made it possible for Eric to bury his head in the sand. In spite of the fact that he was in the midst of hundreds of co-professionals, he did not share the prevailing camaraderie. Not for him were the enthusiastic reunions of classmates bringing each other up-to-date on who had married whom, who had gone to the Max Planck Institute, who had gotten tenure at California. Not for him were the tête-à-tête lunches between old buddies now separated by three thousand miles. It was no accident that he had ended up on a cafeteria line behind Barbara Gunn, one loner next to another. Since graduate school an unattractive blend of arrogance and ob-sequiousness had kept him from being a general favorite. In addition, his conviction that he should be leading the defense of *Numero Uno* made him stick like glue to his own little group. He was therefore spending all his time with a man who refused to discuss the murder, and a woman pre-pared to go along with that policy.

No such cocoon of insulation was available to Dick Van-dam. Earl Sanders and Cousin Milton, operating from dif-ferent motives, had maintained such relentless pressure that Dick was forced to keep his eye on the ball every minute he was in Chicago. And with his return to Vandamia, things became even worse. The delay in the Vandam catalog, while personally galling, had merely been a comic feature for television. The patent suit, together with its commercial implications, had been of interest only to the *Wall Street Journal* and its ilk. But, with the murder of Barbara Gunn, Dick's troubles became household news, fodder for the national press and in-depth reporting on every network in the country.

And so, for the first time, word of his plight found its way into the homes of all those Vandams who had washed their hands of the family business. Some of the calls came straight to him. In no time at all he heard from Matthew (a ceramics studio in Vail, Colorado) and from Chester (wooden sailboats on Cape Cod) and from Gilbert (repertory theater in Acapulco). Many of the older women in the family, however, followed a time-honored tradition of transmitting their alarms through their nearest male connection.

Jason Vandam Ingersoll had absolutely nothing against his mother's present husband and, after five trials on the lady's part, he was something of an expert. Derek Sommersby was a handsome, lazy, comfort-loving young man with no vices. He was neither over-greedy nor dissolute. Having expended his meager supply of energy on the great effort of his life—finding and marrying a rich older woman—he was now content to sink back and enjoy the good things around him. With his naturally sunny disposition, he found it no penance to run his wife's little errands, support her in her social life, and enter wholeheartedly into a joint conspiracy that they were members of the same generation. Jason was too grateful for the ensuing peace and quiet on the maternal front to balk at a stepfather three years his junior. His only problem was the speech pattern imposed by the couple's life style. Jason's mother, while changing her last name at a rapid clip, had until now stuck with the same first name. With Derek, things were different.

"Binky and I have been out of touch," Derek explained breathily from Malibu. "You know we ran over to Honolulu for the opening of Igor's disco, and we had such a glorious time we stayed on for some surfing. We only got back home last night. As soon as Binky saw the headlines, she wanted to get in touch with you right away."

As usual, Jason's first instinct was to deny acquaintance with this Binky bounding from disco floor to surfboard. Biting down hard, he said only, "The whole family's concerned, Derek."

"Of course they are. But Binky's always had a special feeling for the company, and the poor girl is really upset about this. She says there's never been a murder connected with the family before."

"I know, Derek."

"What's more, Binky thinks that the outfit we traded shares with won't like this at all when they find out."

Jason knew better than to ask what made his mother assume Standard Foods was even more out of touch than she was. "They already know and they don't like it."

"There!" Derek said triumphantly. "Binky was right. So she wants it impressed on Dick that, no matter what else happens, there can't be any drop in dividends. Of course, the best thing would have been to see that this never happened. But now that it has, Binky wants Dick to clear it up right away. You will explain that to him, won't you?"

"I'll do my best."

"I knew we could rely on you, old man. That's why I told Binky it was better to speak with you than to those people at the new company."

Until now Jason had been slumped in his chair, drumming on the desk top, waiting for another feather-brained conversation with his stepfather to end. Now he straightened with a snap.

"What was that?" he demanded.

"You know Binky," said Derek with terrible pride. "That girl doesn't take anything lying down. When she's got a problem, she goes right to the top, and she says Dick isn't the top anymore."

Jason was afflicted with a sudden vision of innumerable Vandams, all accustomed to taking every complaint to the head honcho, all descending on Standard Foods. It looked as if he really would have to talk to Dick, although neither of them would enjoy the discussion.

"You did the right thing, Derek," he said forcefully. "If Mother wants her dividends to stay right up there, this is no time to be emphasizing our difficulties to Standard Foods," he said, relying on the total business innocence prevailing in the Malibu ménage.

"I never thought of that," Derek marveled. "It always pays to talk with you first, Jason."

"Thanks for calling, Derek," Jason said dully.

But Derek always managed to close his conversation on a social note. "And do give our regards to Sylvia. Tell her we've sent a smashing anniversary present." There was a throaty chuckle. "Binky found it in this way-out boutique, and it will shake you two up back there in Illinois."

Poor Jason did not even notice the systematic way he and Sylvia were becoming a pair of old fogies from Binky's past.

Dick Vandam and his wife had worked out a division of labor that had operated satisfactorily for decades. He took care of the family business, and she took care of the family social fiefdom. From the day of her marriage, Gloria had constituted herself a willing and able adjutant to her mother-in-law in matters of the Garden Club, the United Way, the Ladies' Aid and the Friends of the Library. In the richness of time, she had succeeded in most of these responsibilities, which she exercised without requiring conjugal support.

In return, Dick was not in the habit of bringing home his office troubles. But, as one glance at the coffee table told him, they were already there. To the uninitiated, the living room, complete with flames flickering in the fireplace, a profusion of cut flowers, and a silver tray bearing a martini pitcher, might have been designed as a stage set for the ideal welcome home. But Dick saw only the copy of the *Chicago Tribune* lying neatly refolded in its customary position. For all practical purposes, it was as if Captain McNabb and his minions had invaded the house.

The *Trib* could scarcely be blamed for pulling out all stops in its coverage of Chicago's most recent murder. For them Barbara Gunn was a local girl, just as she was to all those high school classmates attending her funeral, and the Vandam Nursery & Seed Company was right in Chicago's backyard. But above all there was McCormick Place and the whole convention business so dear to the Windy City. As far as the *Trib* was concerned, they were dealing with desecration of the temple, and they responded accordingly—with diagrams and maps ("the arrow indicates location of the tomato in the convention hall"), with interviews of hotel personnel ("I was just bringing in a fresh bowl of dip when I heard screams from the restroom"), with photographs of principals ("Mr. Milton Vandam leaving the Hyatt Regency with a friend").

Dick's wife could tell he was upset the moment he entered, but she also knew he liked to set his own pace on such occasions. She therefore held her peace as he carefully poured two drinks, handed her one and sank into his chair with an involuntary grunt.

There was silence as he took his first exploratory sip, sighed approval and laid his glass down. Then:

"I'm afraid we're in for some bad publicity."

But he was going too fast. It was eight hours since Gloria had read the papers.

"Has Father been at it again?" she asked sympathetically.

Dick blinked. When he finally made the connection, he was resentful. "No, Gloria, that's not what I'm talking about. Didn't you read about the murder?"

By rights, Gloria was blameless. Dick had happened to use his code words for a recurring peril. Hendrik Vandam II had been a fly in the perfection of the Vandam ointment for years. His emergence as a household name had been accompanied by serious personality changes. After a lifetime of being safe, sane and stodgy, Dick's father had blossomed into flamboyance, and worse. Those triumphant tours of Japan and Europe were all very well but plaudits were not the only things filtering back home. There were also lurid tales of geisha girls and the Folies-Bergère. The elder Mrs. Vandam naturally turned to her daughter-in-law, and the two of them, over the last decade, had well-nigh exhausted the theme of *to err is human, to forgive divine*.

"I have been reading about it for days," Gloria replied with dignified reproof. "I simply didn't realize that was what you were talking about."

Dick sighed with exaggerated patience. "I would have thought it was self-explanatory."

Not for the first time, Gloria wished that Dick were just a teensy-weensy bit more of a drinking man. With another husband she would have looked to the martini pitcher as all-purpose pacifier. But Dick's pre-dinner drink was simply another meaningless item in the complex daily ritual with which he liked to surround himself. When it came to soothing the beast, there was no substitute for roast beef and potatoes. Surreptitiously she glanced at the clock. Dinner would not be served for another twenty minutes.

And sure enough, for twenty minutes Dick carried on about threats to the family's good name, and how the least he expected was some show of concern from his nearest and dearest. All Gloria could do was play a waiting game. As she expected, translation to the dining room brought a change for the better within minutes.

"Good roast," he said, chomping.

"Yes. I ordered it at Friedlich's."

Silence.

"I like the way Annie did the peas."

"She put mint in them."

Silence.

Before they even reached the weighty question of whether or not he wanted ice cream on his pie, Dick was beginning to unburden himself. As Gloria had never doubted, it was family. She had simply picked the wrong relative.

"All this aggravation has doubled my workload. I simply do not have time for these idiotic phone calls. This morning alone I heard from Jeremy and Gilbert and Baxter."

Gloria clucked dutifully. She knew perfectly well that Dick rather enjoyed being guiding light to his wayward relatives. There was more at stake than inroads on his time.

"Then, to top things off, Virginia—I refuse to call her Binky—has been after Jason."

This time it was not a cluck, it was a sniff. Gloria and Dick were as one in their view of his sister's hectic marital career. "I'm surprised she even heard about it." But Gloria remained true to her ideals of harmony between brother and sister. "I suppose she felt she should express sympathy."

"Sympathy, my foot! She instructed Jason to tell me to clean this mess up right away."

"Now, Dick, you know better than to let Virginia upset you. I'm sure she means well," said Gloria, stretching the truth, "but she doesn't understand your work."

"I would certainly not let her silly views upset me if they were going to end with her. She's threatening to take them to Standard Foods."

They were now well outside Gloria's field of competence. She had never understood the merger, which she regarded as one of those complicated tax shelters that men were so fond of. Instead she clutched at what she did understand.

"But surely they'll see that Virginia is unreasonable. If some secretary has been murdered in Chicago, it's up to the police to handle it. It's terribly unfortunate that you happened to be in the same room. But you simply have to grin and bear it. It would be the same if you were unlucky enough to be involved in a hotel fire or a plane crash. What if Henry Kissinger had been in the MGM Hotel? The whole world would know he'd been spending a weekend in Las Vegas. Reporters always jump on the names they know. But aside from telling the police the little you may have noticed about this girl, there's nothing you can do. And sooner or later it will all die down."

For the first time in years Dick Vandam was almost misty-eyed as he looked at his wife. Good old Gloria! Insensibly flattered by her equation of him and Henry Kissinger, he saw nothing blameworthy in her assuming that Vandams could never be more than witnesses in a murder case.

"But I'm afraid we're more involved than that," he began.

"Yes," she agreed regretfully. "It's too bad that girl worked for the company that was trying to steal something from you. But I suppose she'd still be alive if she hadn't been mixed up with people like that."

All traces of pre-dinner testiness had vanished. Partly this was due to his wife's staunch loyalty. More perhaps was due to Dick Vandam's innate sense of the fitness of things. Faced with the perfection that was Annie's pecan pie, he realized this was no time for small emotions. Unconsciously his voice deepened.

"That's the way it looked at first. But now it turns out that damned girl was bribed to steal some data. So it looks possible—mind you, I'm just saying possible—that someone on our side was crazy enough to buy her."

Gloria did not assimilate new ideas readily. When the process was unavoidable, she found it helpful to do her slow thinking aloud.

"Then, if someone at the company bribed her and it began to look as if she were going to confess the whole thing, then it would be the same person who . . ." Her voice trailed away. The logic was impeccable but the conclusion was so unpalatable that she looked at her husband narrowly. Surely this could not be what Dick meant.

"And these damn women are urging me to clear the whole thing up fast, get the murderer arrested, get the whole thing out of the papers," he burst out. "They don't stop to think what the consequences may be."

Now Gloria was certain that Dick was engaged in a familiar marital game. He had a private bugaboo so absurd he could not bring himself to express it. Instead he would induce her to put it into words and then, by pouring scorn on her fancy, exorcise the demon.

But this time she would not play. "I refuse to believe it," she said flatly. "You can't be serious. We've known Jason since he was a little boy. Virginia may have lost what little sense she ever had, but that's no reason to suppose—"

Dick did not let her proceed. "Virginia isn't the only one who called."

Gloria waited with a sense of foreboding.

"Charlotte did, too," Dick said at last.

"Oh God!"

Charlotte Halvorsen, a forceful old dowager, lived in seclusion except on those rare occasions when she came out swinging in defense of her little brother—Milton Vandam. Suddenly Gloria realized why she was haunted by a sense of *déjà vu*. When Milton had been forced, inch by inch, down the painful road to early retirement, he had called in his most redoubtable supporter. Neither he nor Charlotte was a respecter of Queensberry rules. During the ensuing conflict they had resorted to every underhanded trick in the book, put merciless pressure on Vandams within and without the corporate fold and, most unpardonable of all, refused to acknowledge the non-belligerent status of the womenfolk.

"Lorraine still won't talk to Bernice," she said musingly, conveying in her own terms the magnitude of the disaster. "She wouldn't even come to Bonnie's wedding."

"I know," said Dick somberly.

"But why is Charlotte up in arms now?" she asked, trying to grapple with these unknown forces once again threatening to rend the Garden Club limb from limb.

"Milton must have made her," Dick reasoned. "I'm sure of it. He wants this thing swept under the rug fast."

Gloria's eyes widened. "But surely you don't think . . . ?" she faltered.

Dick avoided her glance. "He might have bribed that girl so that he could stay on at the company," he said unwillingly. "You remember how he felt about it?"

Who could forget? The prospect of losing the dignity and perquisites attached to his position had thrown Milton into a frenzy. It was all too easy to imagine him attempting a mad piratical coup. With growing reluctance Gloria recalled the details about Barbara Gunn which, only this morning, had been of such academic interest. The girl was

217

nervous and guilty, going to pieces in public. Police theorized she was on the point of telling all. If Milton's previous behavior was any guide, how wildly would he meet a threat of disgrace and prison? There must be some alternative.

"Naturally Milton didn't like being forced out. But that was some time ago," she said in a last ditch attempt to retain her blinkers. "There's no reason to suppose he hasn't settled down by now. Are you sure you aren't making a mountain out of a molehill, Dick? I'll bet nobody else has these suspicions."

Dick produced a travesty of a smile—thin, tight and painful. "What do you think has got me going? A week ago Standard Foods decided to play a waiting game with our patent suit in order to put financial pressure on the other company. Today they decided to rush into court no matter what concessions they have to make. Sanders didn't make any bones about the reason for the change. He said they wanted to get the patent situation settled, before there were any further revelations about Vandam's. Those are his exact words."

Gloria stared at him aghast. Like everyone else she tended to undervalue the judgment of those close to her. After all, she had seen what Dick was like when the air conditioning broke down, and she was almost as familiar with the behavior of other Vandams in moments of crisis. But she accepted without hesitation the wisdom of strangers sitting in a board room in Chicago. She could even dimly remember entertaining two of them—solid, substantial men not given to fits and starts. If *they* saw this menace on the horizon, it was no figment of the imagination.

Gloria Vandam prided herself on her cool competence. When her daughters were expelled from select private schools, when they took up residence with undesirable lovers, when her father-in-law threatened to burst into the tabloids, she kept her head. But nothing had prepared her for this moment. Desperately she cast about for a domestic panacea.

"You know, Dick," she said with iron graciousness, "I think tonight we might have brandy with our coffee."

It was in the best tradition of her long reign. Unfortunately the façade cracked with her next sentence.

"God knows I could use it!"

21 TRANSPLANT SHOCK

FRAN Pendleton had been raised in Tennessee, attended college in North Carolina and spent her adult life in Puerto Rico. None of these experiences had prepared her for the rigors of a howling blizzard in Chicago.

"And the way things are going, we'll have to spend the whole winter here," she wailed.

Her complaint was necessarily directed to Eric Most. Howard was doing battle at the airline counter, while his junior stayed in the rear, guarding the mountains of documentation piled on the floor.

Instead of joining in the lamentation, Eric made the mistake of assuming that manly reassurance was required. "It won't be as bad as that, Fran," he said indulgently. "I'm sure they'll find some space for us tomorrow if not today."

"Fat chance," she snapped, nursing her pessimism. "I'll bet Chicago is populated entirely by people so exhausted by trying to leave, they gave up and settled here."

This was their third trip out to O'Hare. The flight on which they had originally been scheduled should have left before the blizzard struck. Unfortunately, it had originated in Denver, and Colorado had been flattened six hours earlier than Chicago. By the time their second flight was due for departure, O'Hare had become an arctic wasteland with record drifts and gale-force winds. They had returned downtown to discover their hotel rooms unavailable, spent a miserable night in inferior accommodations and, at the first hint of one open runway, made their latest break for freedom. So had several thousand others. At the moment O'Hare looked like the airport of a third-world capital, with enemy tanks entering the city.

Every successive frustration made Howard more irascible and Fran grumpier. Now she spotted further grounds for dissatisfaction.

"I hope you realize that this blizzard is going to travel with us straight back to New York."

Fran's depression was not really based on the weather. Most of it was caused by the resumption of legal hostilities impelling the Pendletons eastward instead of southward. Those precious floribunda were going to be transshipped in Miami without her personal supervision. In Fran's opinion, professional meetings were a necessary evil; appearances before the board of patent interferences were not.

Eric was misguided enough to fancy himself as an expert at jollying along middle-aged women. Cunningly he began with agreement.

"Of course, it's too bad we have to make this side trip to New York. I know you're anxious to get back home and I am too," he said chattily. "There's a lot of work that needs my attention. But you can hardly call it a waste of time. I don't really trust those lawyers to understand my notebooks unless I'm there to guide them every step of the way. They're only laymen, and it would be foolish to leave this in the hands of a bunch of New York lawyers. Everything else at IPR is secondary right now, Fran. We haven't come up with anything this big in years and, while I hope the stuff I'm working on these days will turn out a real winner, we've got to go with the odds. After all, there aren't many breakthroughs like this. So you do see that it's essential, don't you?"

He ended with less conviction than when he had started. The look of concentrated venom on Fran's face was enough to give even Eric Most second thoughts. Hastily reviewing his speech, he decided it could bear amplification.

"Of course, it's Howard and me together in this thing. I didn't mean to imply I worked on *Numero Uno* alone." When Fran still did not relax, he laughed lightly to show her how insignificant his omission had been. "That's why we both have to go to New York."

In a voice of icy precision, Fran set him straight. "In case you've forgotten, Eric, IPR was well established years before your arrival. And everything else at IPR is not secondary. My floribunda happens to be a major development that may rival *Numero Uno*. And my delphinium took an All-America just three years ago. Quite a lot is going on at IPR besides your research, and a good deal of it is being done by me."

Eric blinked, then reddened. As Fran listened to his disjointed phrases of explanation, she deliberately refused to unbend. It was time Eric Most learned a lesson.

For over two decades Fran had watched young assistants parade through IPR. Some she had liked and some she had not. It made very little difference as every single one of them left within three years. This turnover was not because of personality conflicts or professional jealousies. The Pendleton establishment was remarkably free of both. Brute economics dictated the revolving-door policy. IPR was too small to support a hierarchy in which beginners could rise through the ranks. Because of the caliber of its research, IPR had a reputation as a solid place for fledgling Ph.D.'s to start their careers, and then move on. Under these circumstances Fran did not usually work up any heat if a young man failed to accord her sufficient respect. But Eric Most's continual remissness in this area was beginning to get to her.

Howard's return saved them both from the prolongation of an awkward moment. He was sputtering angrily, too absorbed in travel arrangements to notice anything else.

"God knows if we'll ever get out of this place," he said, unknowingly echoing his wife. "The best that damned fool could do was give us standby status. So let's get all this stuff down to the boarding area. This may be the only plane that takes off this morning."

With Howard sending off waves of nervous energy, there was no time to talk or think about anything else. Obediently all three snatched up their loads and began the long trek. It was, of course, the most distant boarding gate at O'Hare. Howard, swinging two bulging briefcases, strode imperiously down the bleak corridor. Eric, panting and embracing a large cardboard box, managed to keep up. Fran trotted along in the rear, rounding every corner a little farther behind the pack.

The next half hour was filled with dramatic tension. Ticketed passengers, shrouded in outlandish winter gear, straggled in, one by one. Inexorably the plane began to fill. Then came the exhilarating rumor that a connecting flight from St. Louis had been delayed. If it failed to appear, eight seats would be free.

Fran, who embraced Oriental fatalism when she traveled, had plenty of time for her irritation with Eric Most to be transmuted into something else. Once her attention was directed toward the problem, it was not difficult to pinpoint the reason for her mounting annoyance with him. Almost unnoticed Eric had broken with the pattern of his predecessors. He had already been at IPR for five years and he gave no signs of leaving. At the recent meetings he had been almost embarrassingly underfoot. Not once had he slipped away to canvass potential employers. What in the world made Eric, the most conventional and imitative of men, strike out a new line of behavior?

And the answer was lying there for anyone to see. At IPR, they had all grown older. Fran, at forty-five, sometimes forgot that her husband was twenty years her senior. Now she looked at him, trying to see him with the eyes of an outsider. Howard was concentrating on the final countdown, his watch aggressively displayed, willing the clerk to declare those seats available. To her, he looked exactly the same as he always had. Partly this was because Howard had been forty when she first met him, partly because marriage is the worst vantage point for dispassionate observation. Fran was far more conscious of the changes in herself—from bride to grandmother, from size ten to size fourteen.

"All right, folks. There's going to be room for eight of you."

Victory! With enthusiastic yelps the fortunate eight gathered up their belongings and humped them out to the waiting plane. The seating could not have been better from Fran's point of view. The Pendletons were placed side by side in the tail, while Eric was accommodated on the aisle seven rows ahead. As she watched him make a fuss with the stewardess about the disposition of his box, Fran was granted another insight. It was neither forgetfulness nor bad manners that led Eric to overlook her professional achievements. She was a stumbling block in his path. Eric wanted to become head of the whole shebang. And this golden vision was possible only if Fran herself were relegated to the status of consort, so that when Howard went, she went too.

"Eric wants to take over IPR," she announced, impelled into speech.

"I know," grunted Howard, already immersed in a magazine.

Really! Fran glared at her husband. It was like him to recognize the situation and dismiss it.

"And just where did he get this idea?" she demanded.

"Not from me," Howard said cheerfully. "The poor sap hopes I'm going to retire."

More and more was becoming clear to Fran. Eric's brazen attempts to push himself into prominence, his insistence on a key role in the coming lawsuit, his huddles with the Vandams—all these constituted signals that he was the heir apparent. On the other hand, the signals were all emanating from a closely defined area.

"He's trying to grab credit for *Numero Uno!*" she gasped.

Howard was not cheerful anymore. "He certainly wants Vandam's to know all about his part."

"Then why are you letting him get away with it?"

Juniors trying to corner more than their fair share of glory were nothing new at IPR—or at any other laboratory. But Howard had never been slow to slap them down.

"Actually, Eric did do the lion's share of the work. You know, Fran, he's a better researcher than we thought when we hired him. Of course I kept an eye on him, and I was ready to steer him clear of mistakes. But it's surprising how little supervision he needed. Once I laid out the dimensions of the problem and the direction we'd be working in, he went right down a straight line. I was more and more pleased with him at every one of our weekly conferences. You know, I made a couple of suggestions he disagreed with, and most of the time he turned out to be right."

"Researcher!" said Fran contemptuously.

Fran herself regretted any minute not spent in her laboratory. Years ago she had gratefully resigned the administrative burden to her husband. But Eric Most, in spite of his much vaunted talk, really preferred going to international conferences, receiving foreign dignitaries, holding forth at university seminars.

"You can't fight facts," Howard reminded her.

"If we're talking about facts, you're the senior man on the project and Eric is way out of line."

Howard hunched a defensive shoulder. "It doesn't make any difference," he said, retreating into his reading. "We did *Numero Uno* on contract."

Howard was pretending that since Vandam's would hold the patent on *Numero Uno*, there was no need to deprive Eric of his cherished limelight. This, thought Fran, was so much nonsense. Both the Pendletons had reacted to the murder of Barbara Gunn with the same sense of loss and distress. But when Captain McNabb's last round of questioning had painted Barbara as a paid informant, they parted company. Fran, shocked and appalled, wanted to know more. Howard had gone from disbelief to a refusal to discuss the situation. He would not join Fran in speculation or theorizing. Fran knew that, emotionally, Howard was far more fastidious than she was. Whenever wayward human passions degenerated into a real mess, Fran wanted to clean it up and Howard wanted to get as far away as possible. Now he was simply exercising reasonable foresight. The new view of Barbara Gunn meant that, lurking in the future, was a denouement in which old friends would stand revealed as criminals. When that day came, Howard did not want to be front and center. He would rather let the world think it was Eric Most's discovery that had been stolen.

Fran sighed. Sensitivity was all very well and good, but it was no way to run a research establishment.

"It doesn't make any difference what's going to happen," she said, avoiding dangerous territory. "Eric's getting a lot of the wrong ideas. He thinks we're a couple of patsies."

"He's just ambitious. What's so wrong with that?"

Exasperated, Fran found herself drawing comparisons. Scotty Wenzel had made a name for himself as a firebrand by his loud chafing at subordinate constraints, his determination to be his own man. He had been stigmatized as a youngster in too much of a hurry, with too arrogant an opinion of his own talents. Why was ambition so forgivable in one young man and not in the other? What's more, Scotty had had the decency to be grieved at Barbara's death, Fran remembered on a tide of warmth, whereas Eric had been markedly indifferent. Oh, she knew that Eric liked to think he barely could remember Barbara Gunn. But that was simply Eric being superior. He had carried too many personal messages to Madison to get away with that one. In fact, Eric was a nasty little egotist.

"And what's he so ambitious to be, anyway?" she persisted. "You can't tell me he wants to spend his life in a laboratory. Look at him up there now. That's what he likes to do."

Both the Pendletons were experienced travelers and acted accordingly. Howard had demanded a news magazine from the stewardess before even buckling his seat belt. Fran had provided herself with a thick paperback novel. But rest and relaxation were not part of Eric Most's public performance. He had lowered his seat tray, unzipped a portfolio and was now, to all appearances, lost in his work. And all this play acting was for the benefit of a few passengers whom he would never encounter again.

"He'll get over it," said Howard, continuing his display of unlimited tolerance. "They all do."

"He's about four years overdue."

"Come on, Fran. You just don't like Eric and you've seen too much of him in Chicago. Why don't you break down and admit you're prejudiced?"

She had to admit that there was something in what Howard said. The truth was that Scotty and Howard had struck sparks off each other, while Eric rubbed her the wrong way. Nonetheless she was convinced that Eric, with his surface deference and his unrealistic dreams, posed more of a threat than Scotty ever had. Howard might turn the page of his magazine to indicate the discussion was over but Fran, with a bone to chew, was not that easily silenced.

"It's all of a piece," she grumbled. "You can't tell what he's thinking or what he's planning. At least not until he's halfway there. Then you realize you should have known all along. It's just like Eric to think he can take over IPR and be a big shot. It's just like Eric to steal *Numero Uno*."

The words were scarcely out of her mouth before their dreadful implications came home to her. Hesitantly she stole a glance at her husband. Deep in his article, he had deliberately tuned her out. With any luck that last unfortunate phrase had escaped him.

His next remark reassured her.

"There's hell to pay in the Middle East," he reported. "I'm glad we turned down that desert-growth project when it was offered to us."

"Yes," she agreed absently. "This is no time to be running around a lot of Arab countries."

Second thoughts had prevailed with Fran. Trying to discuss her sudden suspicion with Howard would somehow crystallize it. She would be creating a situation from which neither could retreat, which neither of them could ever forget. The legacy of those words was hard enough for her to handle on her own.

Because no matter how hard she tried, certain images came crowding into her consciousness.

Eric's unexpected talents as a researcher, so self-evident that he could override the skill and experience of Howard Pendleton.

Eric's submergence of all his contacts with Barbara Gunn which, when Fran began to add them up, amounted to a regular, steady trail over the years.

Eric's determination that he should be recognized as the genius behind *Numero Uno*.

And, above all, Eric's unfaltering certainty that he was destined for the top.

22 SEND OUT RUNNERS

THE murder of Barbara Gunn had shaken and horrified everyone unfortunate enough to be present, but not all of them had become entangled in the aftermath. Quite a few had shaken off the tragedy. The representatives of the Hogarth company, for instance, were preparing to inundate the market with bigger and better rototillers. And an improved Shawmut weed killer was about to be unveiled. This in turn meant that Pete and Mary Larrabee could proceed with their plans to fund the next generation.

"I don't have a business manager yet," Mary explained to Thatcher when she arrived at the bank for her appointment. "Pete said I should wait until I saw you. But I have signed these contracts."

He ran his eye down the paragraphs of fine print to get to the meat. Each contract was comfortably inside the six-figure bracket. Mrs. Mary Larrabee was going to be worthy of the Sloan's attention.

That is, unless the Larrabees were planning to make whoopee.

"And how much of this would be for investment?" he inquired tactfully.

Mrs. Larrabee was surprised he had to ask. "Why, all of it. We've decided we can carry Pete, Junior, for the next two years. That is, as long as he's the only one in college."

"I thought you might be considering some of it for immediate expenditure."

"Oh, no." Mary shook her head decidedly. "Pete keeps us going very nicely, and we'd hate to change our style of living any more than we have to. Besides, you'd be surprised at how many extra expenses the sponsor is picking up. Do you realize they've given me a hairdresser?"

By no effort of will could Thatcher recall her coiffure in Chicago. Now, however, artful tendrils descended down her cheeks and cascaded onto her shoulders.

"I expect you noticed," she pressed him.

Cautiously he admitted seeing something different.

"Awful, isn't it? I'm supposed to be part of the back-to-nature movement," she confided.

"I thought you were supposed to be pushing fertilizer and grass seed."

Mary grinned. "It's bigger than that. I'm practically Mother Earth. You should see the clothes they've gotten for me."

Thatcher was pleased that the sane and cheerful Larrabee attitude was surviving good fortune. After striking gold, too many people harped on the pinpricks associated with their bonanza.

This approval continued right through Thatcher's introductory lecture covering paperwork, investment goals and trust officer. His critical faculties revived when he buzzed Miss Corsa and she seized the opportunity to relay a message.

"Mr. Withers called and would like to have lunch if you're free," she reported. "He's just back from Buenos Aires."

As the president of the Sloan Guaranty Trust had been in Argentina for the yachting, Thatcher had a fair notion of what aspects of South American life Brad wanted to describe.

"Just a minute," he directed, shamelessly turning to the nearest honorable escape. "I hope you'll be able to join me for lunch, Mrs. Larrabee, after you're though with Mr. Trinkam."

Upon her acceptance, he reactivated Miss Corsa and was able to say truthfully, "Tell Mr. Withers I'm already engaged. And would you reserve a table for Mrs. Larrabee and me?"

Whenever Thatcher was entertaining clients or guests who were not part of the financial world, he left the choice of locale to Miss Corsa and she invariably produced a winner. How she did it was a wonder. Except for an occasional meal in honor of a departing employee, Miss Corsa was a stranger to Manhattan's expense-account restaurants. Raised in a frugal tradition, she did not waste her money on frivolities. Instead she invested it. It was some years since she had approached her employer about purchasing securities through the Sloan.

Thatcher was not likely to forget the episode. His immediate offer of bank counseling services had produced a long thoughtful silence. Miss Corsa had clearly been appraising the available personnel and their capabilities.

"No, thank you, Mr. Thatcher," she had finally said with her customary composure. "I prefer to plan my own investments."

And there the matter had rested. But recently curiosity had reared its head. Never in a million years would Thatcher have dreamed of prying into either the amount or the nature of Miss Corsa's holdings. But, it turned out, that calm rejection had rankled over the years, and he would have given a great deal to ask the statistical department for a performance rating. In fact, several times he had actually reached for the phone until, at the last moment, sanity had stayed his hand. If Miss Corsa were holding her own or posting a modest improvement over the Trust Department, all would be well. But, God help us, what if she were outperforming the bank two to one? The only logical course of action would be to offer to trade places with her. How much wiser in the long run to let sleeping dogs lie! It was enough that Miss Corsa did her job incomparably well. Let him be grateful for her many excellences, including a sixth sense about restaurants.

Nonetheless Thatcher was rather surprised when he found himself escorting Mary Larrabee to Rockefeller Center and a table with a view of the ice skaters. His qualms were soon allayed.

"I've heard about this," she said happily, "but I never dreamed it would be so much fun to watch."

Indeed she could scarcely take her eyes off the rink and, throughout the meal, kept reverting to the spectacle before them. "I always thought it would be just children and really professional skaters, but there are a lot of beginners out there," she observed. "And some of them are as old as I am."

A chill premonition began to form. All unconsciously, Mrs. Larrabee was edging toward the dividing line that separates spectators from participants. Her next words came as no surprise.

"I suppose they rent skates here," she suggested, toying with a new idea.

"Yes," he said so reluctantly that she read his mind.

"Oh, not you," she told him on a wave of merriment. "But Pete is coming tomorrow, and there's no reason why he shouldn't make a fool of himself. Nobody in New York has ever heard of him."

Thatcher was confirmed in his opinion of Mary Larrabee's good sense. Still, a little insurance is always welcome and he was quite pleased when an early luncher, on his way to the exit, halted by their table.

"Mrs. Larrabee!" exclaimed Jason Ingersoll. "What a pleasant surprise."

Jason extended the courtesies so long that Thatcher was almost forced to offer coffee.

"I'm in New York settling the television contract," Mrs. Larrabee prattled happily as the waiter bustled about. "You have no idea how grateful I am to the Vandam contest for the opportunities it's given me."

Jason was more than cordial. "I'm glad everything has worked out. We were afraid the sponsor might have second thoughts—you know, because of the murder and your finding the body and all that. It would have been a real shame if you'd lost out simply by being an innocent bystander."

It was clear that Vandam's had revised its initial reaction to the Shawmut abduction of Mary Larrabee. Presumably cooler heads had realized that she would inevitably be touted as the developer of Vandam's *Firecracker,* thereby spreading the wealth. But Thatcher was more interested in other modifications of company policy. These casual references by Ingersoll suggested a real departure.

"You see," said Jason with a display of great frankness, "there's no way of avoiding the conclusion that Barbara Gunn's death had something to do with *Numero Uno.* Now that makes it our problem and Wisconsin Seed's, but it's got nothing to do with you. It wouldn't be right if you got caught up in the undertow."

He certainly wasn't getting any argument from Mary Larrabee about that. But, in spite of the engaging smile that he fixed on her, Jason's little speech was really directed toward the Sloan.

And, therefore, Thatcher felt that it was only right that the Sloan should respond.

"Everything I hear from Chicago these days implies the police are satisfied with the motive for Barbara Gunn's death," he said. "And I must say, the discovery of that fifteen thousand dollars seems to support their theory."

Mary Larrabee shook her head sadly. "I realize they've proved that poor girl was taking bribes, but she didn't look the type."

Smoothly Jason used this opening for his own purposes. "She certainly didn't. You know, I spoke with her a few times at the meetings and she seemed to me remarkably young and impressionable."

"That's exactly it," Mary agreed. "I have a nineteen-year-old niece who's a lot more independent and self-reliant than Barbara Gunn was. Patty's used to making up her own mind, and she doesn't take the time of day from anyone. But there's no denying that some of these girls who go straight from their daddy's house to their husband's house never do learn to become grown-ups. Poor Barbara probably could have been talked into anything."

Now that Jason had the conversation where he wanted, Thatcher expected a few pithy allusions to the longstanding association between Scott Wenzel and Barbara Gunn. But no, Jason had other fish to fry.

"I'm afraid so," he said. "She was very close to being a child. I'll bet she would have accepted, almost without hesitation, the views of someone older and more authoritative about what was proper and acceptable."

Thatcher had no intention of playing straight man to somebody else's comedy act. Deliberately he fielded the wrong cue.

"Like Dr. Pendleton, you mean?" he asked, hiding his amusement. "Mrs. Gunn had known him for years, he'd been the head of the laboratory where she worked, he might well have the status of a father figure."

Jason, thrown for a loop, hastened to rectify the error. "Good God, I never meant to impugn Dr. Pendleton's integrity. His reputation alone should—"

Thatcher interrupted the testimonial. "No, of course not," he said innocently. "I meant someone about his age."

But once bitten, twice shy. Jason had now decided to do his own dirty work. "Exactly," he said, refusing the bait.

Only Mary Larrabee was taking every word at face value. "I think you've put your finger on it. Barbara didn't really know what she was getting into. I can tell you one thing. She didn't have any conception of how valuable that tomato is."

For once Jason spoke without ulterior motive. "She can't have," he said crisply. "If she had, she would have gotten a lot more than fifteen thousand."

Thatcher had been waiting for someone to point out the disparity between the value of the bribe and the value of the data stolen. "I've wondered about that myself," he admitted.

Mary, who had constituted herself defense counsel for the dead, seized on this ammunition. "That proves it. That poor girl let someone persuade her to do something she thought wasn't very important and wasn't very bad. He probably told her that it was the kind of thing that goes on in business all the time—about on a par with selling a mailing list."

"And the figure of fifteen thousand was nicely calculated to reassure her," Thatcher decided. "Big enough to be a real temptation, but small enough so it did not suggest stealing the atom bomb."

Even Jason was becoming interested in the reconstruction of Barbara Gunn. "Then, when a big lawsuit sprang up, she went to pieces."

But Mary, gazing into her coffee cup as if she were reading the dregs, disagreed. "It wasn't that simple. A lot of things piled up on her. When she got to Chicago, everywhere she turned someone was talking about the value of *Numero Uno,* and not as a feather in some researcher's cap but in terms of cold cash. She kept telling me she hadn't realized how big a discovery it was, and I thought she was wondering how a plain little secretary got mixed up in something so earthshaking. But actually she was trying to justify herself. Then the day of the deposition was looming, when she'd have to choose between perjury or admitting what she'd done. Oh, she was scared all right, she was probably afraid of going to jail. But she was guilty too, about what she'd done to the man she'd worked for so long. And then, just to make things more complicated, she also felt betrayed. After all, she'd trusted somebody to advise her and they'd taken advantage of her. The poor thing was going around in circles, and anything could have happened. She might have burst into tears and confessed everything to Mr. Wenzel."

As Mary Larrabee innocently disclosed her own conviction as to which way the theft had gone, Thatcher had to admire Jason Ingersoll's response. Smiling wryly, the young man said, "I guess by now the whole world is sure that *Numero Uno* was really developed in Wisconsin. Naturally we've spent a lot of time trying to find alternative explanations, and we've come up with some. But I don't want you to think we're blind. Five years is a long time ago, but the present management at Vandam's is determined to get to the bottom of this business. We've decided to press forward with the patent suit as the best way to bring everything out into the open. I'm confident that presenting the facts and letting an impartial authority decide the issue is the only course open to us."

Like so many ringing declarations, this one, in Thatcher's opinion, addressed the wrong problem.

"Very commendable," he commented. "But I doubt whether a patent court is the appropriate tribunal to determine a question of bribery, let alone murder. And certainly not on the basis of the evidence before it. In this case, I understand, that boils down to two sets of identical lab records. It's hard to see how that is going to result in a flood of light."

Jason took his time formulating a reply while his companions sat silently. Thatcher was waiting and Mary Larrabee, who was not interested in patent suits, had allowed her attention to return to the rink. She was pleasurably absorbed in the sight of a rubicund middle-aged man in a motoring cap coming down hard after an inglorious tumble.

"Not without cooperation from us," Jason agreed at last. "But we're willing to range more widely if that seems promising. So Dick and I have come to New York to help the lawyers get ready for Washington. Even Milton insisted on coming. Of course he's not with the company anymore and I don't really know why he's here, but he seems to feel he has a stake in the outcome."

Rarely had Thatcher seen a knife inserted so delicately. "No doubt after his many years at Vandam's, your cousin indentifies with its interests," he suggested.

"That could be it. And it goes without saying how much we appreciate his loyalty and support," Jason said staunchly before shaking his head. "Although I can't imagine what he thinks he can do."

One of the things Milton was doing was keeping in touch with Earl Sanders, who by now had moved his command post from Chicago to New York. Many of the phrases pouring from Milton's lips into the phone might have been stolen from his cousin—with suitable modification.

". . . talked to the girl myself at the meetings. . . . She didn't have any idea of her own in her head. . . ."

"So what? We already knew she was just a cat's-paw."

"These girls! Only one thing on their minds. . . . Show them a handsome young man and they lose whatever sense they had. . . ."

"Yes, yes."

". . . She came from a very limited background. She'd be flattered by the attentions of someone outside her world . . . lose her head completely and take his word for gospel. . . ."

By the time that Thatcher got through to Sanders, each had a budget of news for the other.

"Jason has just been trying to persuade me that a man like his cousin Milton would have had no trouble bribing Barbara Gunn into a little simple theft. She would have been overawed by an older, authoritative man," Thatcher got in first. "Furthermore, Milton has come rushing to New York because, for some mysterious reason, he has a stake in the outcome of the patent suit."

"What do you know!" marveled Sanders. "Milton has just been telling me how she would have been a pushover for a handsome young preppy type."

When Captain McNabb had said there was skirmishing between Jason and Milton, Thatcher had not realized it amounted to open warfare.

"Tell me," he demanded, "does this precious pair realize the game they're playing? This is not a matter of managerial incompetence we're discussing. Somebody poisoned Barbara Gunn. They're setting each other up for a murder charge."

"Milton doesn't realize a damn thing beyond the end of his nose," Sanders retorted. "That old fool is so hellbent on worming his way back into the company, he'd do anything. But what about Ingersoll? He's supposed to be playing with a full deck."

In spite of his irritation, Thatcher carefully reviewed Jason's program. "He wants Milton firmly saddled with the theft in the minds of Standard Foods and the family. Then, with the patent suit out of the way, he'd like to see the police investigation bog down and Barbara Gunn's death join the ranks of unsolved crimes," he predicted. "To do him justice, I don't think he's trying to railroad Milton into death row."

Sanders had justifiable grounds for displeasure. "That means they both want the court to decide Wenzel developed *Numero Uno*. Boy, that's some subsidiary we've got! Do you wonder I'm going with them to Washington?"

"You'd better do more than that."

"I will! I'm going to read the riot act to Dick Vandam. Then I'm going to bird-dog him every step of the way!"

23 ENCOURAGING NEW GROWTH

EVEN Miss Corsa, a true believer in the priority that attached to any Vandam concern, was growing recalcitrant by eleven-thirty the following morning. Once again the phone had rung, once again she had laid down her dictation book to answer it. For almost two hours she and Thatcher, with the best will in the world, had been unable to make inroads on the pile of correspondence.

"It's Mr. Jackson," she reported. Then, in an uncharacteristic bit of editorializing, she added, *"This* time."

Thatcher had already held long meaningless conversations with Earl Sanders, Dick Vandam, and, surprisingly, an unknown attorney representing Standard Foods. Sanders had pretended to have some questions about SF's current financing program, Dick Vandam had maundered through some disjointed sentences about the enduring affection uniting his relatives despite their surface bickering, and the attorney had rehashed the arrangements governing the frozen Vandam account. To an experienced listener it was obvious that they had all been sending out waves of receptivity. Thatcher was no stranger to this phenomenon. On Wall Street it means that the callers have all heard of some development or rumor that they wish to have confirmed or denied without themselves repeating it. So they telephone someone presumed to be knowledgeable, trail enticing lures, and wait hopefully. If it had been a question of interest rates or bond offerings, Thatcher would have understood their unanimous selection of the Sloan. But under the circumstances, why him?

Miss Corsa, with grandfather's trip in mind, was only beginning to lose patience. Thatcher had irretrievably lost his two calls back.

"What's this all about, Paul?" he began baldly. "You people are supposed to be going into a big huddle before you take off for your patent hearing in Washington. Instead you're all wasting my time. This is the fourth call and nobody's said anything worth hearing yet."

"So the others have been putting an ear to the ground, too? I'm not surprised. Everybody's rattled by this latest wrinkle. Including me."

"If you'd rather not divulge this alarming development, suppose you let us both get back to our work," Thatcher suggested, noting out of the corner of his eye that Miss Corsa was nodding approval.

Good trial lawyers develop thick skins both in and out of the courtroom. Jackson simply launched into his tale. "Wenzel has insisted that I call a meeting of all parties at the Federal Courthouse this afternoon. And, in his usual charming way, he refused to say why on the grounds that I wouldn't understand."

Thatcher knew perfectly well that, even if Paul Jackson had failed to establish his usual supremacy over these particular clients, neither had he become Caspar Milquetoast in his dealings with them.

"So you just rolled over and agreed?" he asked skeptically.

"Of course not! But I'll say one thing for Wenzel, he's got a gift for riveting my attention. He went on to say there shouldn't be any problem getting the others to attend. Not after I told them that Wisconsin Seed would agree to withdraw its petition for an injunction."

"Withdraw!" It was not what Thatcher had expected to hear. Involuntarily he remembered his last view of Wisconsin Seed on the night of Mary Larrabee's triumph. There had been eddies of tension but they had involved the women—Barbara Gunn and Hilary Davis. The men, each in his own way, exuded determination and confidence. But now, suddenly, the first cracks in the wall were appearing. Unfortunately there was no mystery about what had happened in the interim. Barbara Gunn had been murdered.

"Will withdrawing the injunction make a substantial difference to your position?" he asked, searching for a foothold in these murky waters.

"Not really," said Jackson. "The Vandam catalog has already been mailed and, even if they wanted to follow up with an offering of *Numero Uno,* Standard Foods wouldn't let them. If the board of patent interferences comes down in favor of my clients, SF would be liable for whopping damages. That's always supposing my enterprising client isn't planning to withdraw from the patent action as well."

"No wonder everybody's been spinning." Thatcher realized that he had been guilty of the sin of egotism in supposing this morning's calls had centered on him. Sanders and Dick Vandam were probably going down the Manhattan white pages in hope of catching some slight clue as to what was going on. "And I can see why you're disturbed."

"You haven't heard the half of it. I've always realized that Wenzel was some kind of nutboy. After I couldn't get any explanation out of him, I called the Hilton and asked for Ackerman. They told me that he's not there and, what's more, he never has been. Nor has any reservation ever been made for him."

Thatcher was beginning to appreciate Paul Jackson's

plight—one client going crazy and the other one missing. Nonetheless he tried to keep things in perspective.

"Didn't Wenzel come east alone the last time? Maybe Ackerman is still saving plane fares," he suggested.

By now Jackson was taking obscure satisfaction in the magnitude of his confusion. "Sure! So we'll forget that when Ackerman called after the funeral and insisted on full speed ahead, he was filled with what *we* were going to do. We'll even forget that for the last three days Wenzel has been sitting in my office conning me that Ackerman was back there in the hotel room. I said to myself that maybe Ackerman was held up in Madison and I called Wisconsin Seed. Now get this! The dummy on the phone there says Ackerman hasn't been back to the office since he left for Chicago, and she has no idea where he is. Dr. Wenzel, she tells me, stopped by for a day to pick up some stuff for New York. In other words, complete openness about Wenzel's movements and a curtain of secrecy about Ackerman's."

Before Thatcher could ask his next question, Jackson was answering it.

"Then I called the Drake in Chicago. Mr. Ackerman checked out four days ago and left no forwarding address."

There was a long pause.

"It's conceivable that Ackerman has other business somewhere and is planning to join you in Washington," Thatcher murmured, not believing a word of what he was saying.

"It's also conceivable that he's in Brazil by now," Jackson rejoined. "You've met Wenzel. Offhand, can you think of anything that would make him not only start to withdraw but also invite everybody to a conference so he can explain why? Including all the Vandams?"

The scenario had taken place often enough before. The authorities start to close in, one partner vamooses and the other, left holding the bag, has no alternative except a public *mea culpa*.

"But that's not in cases of murder," Thatcher objected, completing his thoughts aloud. "That's in cases of fraud."

"This whole thing started with fraud," Jackson snapped right back. "Suppose Ackerman set this caper up himself, persuaded the Gunn girl to be bagman for data from IPR, then killed her when the heat came on. Wenzel would come apart at the seams when he found out. He's just the sort who'd insist on baring his breast and telling all."

Refusing to be diverted by character analysis, Thatcher considered the facts.

"No," he said firmly. "There's no way Ackerman could have done it without Wenzel's connivance."

"I've always said that Ackerman was the brains at Wisconsin Seed," Jackson insisted.

"He may be a grey eminence, he's not a geneticist. He could never have fooled Wenzel in the laboratory."

For the first time there was a note of hopefulness in Jackson's voice. "You don't think so?"

"Absolutely not."

"Then what in God's name are those two playing at?" the lawyer exploded.

There was only one answer to that.

"Presumably you'll find out at this meeting Wenzel has called. You said it was this afternoon, didn't you?"

"Yes, at three o'clock," Jackson said absently. "Come along if you like."

Under Miss Corsa's reproving glance, Thatcher disdained pretense. "I thought you'd never ask."

The scene at the courthouse was much as Thatcher expected. Paul Jackson was in the corridor, to all outward appearances a man totally in charge of the situation. He had, however, cunningly provided himself with two secretaries and was so deeply engaged with them that he could not be questioned. Directly by the door, Dick Vandam was caucusing with his attorneys. And inside the conference room normalcy still prevailed. The IPR contingent was huddling in one corner, while Earl Sanders seemed to be giving the SF team a pep talk in the other. Jason Ingersoll and Milton Vandam had placed themselves directly across from each other, thereby giving the impression, intentionally or not, of being antagonists.

And at the head of the table, in solitary splendor, Scott Wenzel lounged. He was skewed sideways, with one arm across his briefcase and the other draped along the back of his chair. With a casual nod he acknowledged Thatcher's arrival in the chair next to him. Wenzel certainly did not look like a man bowed down by a guilty secret. But Thatcher had just seen one masterful performance out in the corridor. There was no reason to suppose that he was not seeing another one here.

Within seconds his suspicion was confirmed. A casual shift on Thatcher's part brought his chair into contact with Wenzel's ankle and the whole leg reacted as if to an electric shock. The nonchalant posture was simply a pose. Beneath the table, where no one could see, Wenzel was a tautly wound spring. Fortunately he was spared any further preliminaries.

Paul Jackson, continuing his impersonation of a man who knew what was going on, ushered in the Vandam troops and went to the other end of the table.

"As we're all here, I think we might begin," he called to the corners.

Earl Sanders took him up on this. "We're not all here. Ackerman's missing." He turned to Wenzel accusingly. "And when I called the Hilton, they said he wasn't even in town."

Thatcher nodded at this confirmation of his theory that Sanders had been making wholesale use of the phone.

The outburst had not made a dent in Wenzel's composure. "Well, he is now. Ned called from LaGuardia an hour ago. I suppose he's having trouble with the traffic," he said with a fine display of indifference. "Anyway, we can get started without him."

Dick Vandam asked nothing better. "Jackson says you people are willing to drop the injunction," he began suspiciously.

"That's right."

"And I assume that means you've come to your senses and are willing to drop the patent interferences as well." In spite of all his efforts, Vandam did not sound threatening, he merely sounded like a bad poker player bluffing for all he was worth.

Thatcher examined the young man at his side with interest. Surely now was the time when Scott Wenzel would have to fish or cut bait. He could either laugh contemptuously or surrender.

He did neither. "We could go on with that if you like," he said, shrugging, "but *Numero Uno* is now irrelevant."

Businessmen like to delude themselves that scientists have no sense of money. Other scientists know better. The loudest outcry came from IPR.

"Irrelevant!" Howard Pendleton and Eric Most gasped as one man.

"Have you gone completely crazy, Scotty?" demanded Fran Pendleton.

Before Wenzel could frame a reply, the door opened and Ned Ackerman entered, saying, "Sorry if I kept you people waiting."

Rarely had a man's appearance so much belied his words. Thatcher had never seen anyone looking less regretful in his life. In fact the only time he had seen that expression was on the face of a young bride coming down the aisle. Ned Ackerman—grizzled, paunchy and smelling of cigar smoke—looked so radiantly anticipatory that Thatcher involuntarily expected bridesmaids.

Ackerman did not keep them in suspense. "All right, folks, this is it," he said, planting his palms on the table and peering at them from his cloud of beatification. "I'm just back from Washington, where Wisconsin Seed has filed for a patent on the MF-23 tomato. The war's over."

He then collapsed into a chair as if he had run out of steam.

For a moment it seemed as if nobody would be able to make himself heard in the uproar. What was Ackerman talking about? What kind of fast one was Wisconsin Seed trying to pull? What difference did a name make?

Scott Wenzel behaved very well. He let the din abate before attempting any explanation. Then, in thin precise terms, he told them.

"The VR-117 was never intended as anything but a first approximation. The MF-23 is the final generation. It is a true perennial, hardy in ninety-five percent of the United States."

Ackerman now had his second wind. "It's a tomato *tree*," he said joyfully. "You buy some plants from us and you've got an orchard that starts producing in early spring and goes on doing it, year after year."

The conception was so dazzling there *was* momentary silence. Then:

"I don't believe it," Dick Vandam said flatly.

"I thought you might feel that way about it," Ackerman replied, still breathless with achievement, "so I brought one along. Incidentally, the last generation has been tested at fourteen separate USDA field sites." Heaving himself to his feet, he went to the door. "All right, boys. You can roll it in now."

As the dolly entered, tenderly nursed by four men in overalls, Thatcher felt that a band should have been playing. Even to his untutored eye, agricultural history was being made. The dolly held a vast tub and in the tub was a six-foot tree. Most important of all, the tree was almost obscured by its burden of rich, red fruit.

Ned Ackerman, who seemed to have gone quietly insane, was not content to present visual evidence. With a manic laugh he plucked a tomato and tossed it to Dick Vandam.

"Taste it!" he ordered. And before anyone could stop him he was bombarding every occupant of the table. "Go on," he urged, "you wanted proof Wisconsin Seed was developing a blockbuster. Well, here it is!"

His methods were not without results. After Thatcher had taken one bite from his own projectile, he was ready to discuss Sloan backing for Wisconsin Seed.

The others, of course, were not so detached. The Pendletons were pelting Scott Wenzel with technical questions, the Vandams and SF were muttering to each other in undertones, Paul Jackson looked as if he had been hit on the head.

Only Ned Ackerman was available for conversation.

"I see why you wanted validation by USDA this time, but it must have cost a good deal for a firm your size," Thatcher remarked to him.

"I had to take out a second mortgage on my home."

Thatcher was impressed. "I can think of no higher vote of confidence in your partner," he observed.

Ackerman looked across the table. "I gambled everything I had on Scotty," he growled lovingly, "and the beautiful S.O.B. came through."

Euphoria was, of course, not the general mood at the table. Not surprisingly, Standard Foods and Vandam's had decided to retire.

"An adjournment," one of the lawyers said in an attempt to cast a gloss of control over his party's retreat, "to consider these new findings."

"Of course," said Paul Jackson graciously, still reeling himself.

But there was nothing gracious about his attitude when the opposition had retired. "Why the hell didn't you tell me?" he demanded. "How do you expect a lawyer to handle your case if you keep him in the dark?"

"We got burned once, trusting people," Wenzel shot back.. "That was enough."

Ned Ackerman's explanation, more temperately phrased, was even more damaging to his lawyer's self-esteem. "There never was any case. It was just a feint. If we hadn't pretended to be defending the VR-117, people would have wondered what we had up our sleeve. You were just a distraction."

"A distraction!" Jackson repeated in high dudgeon.

Belatedly, Ackerman applied balm. "We figured if we hired Paul Jackson nobody could doubt we were dead serious."

This view held some attraction for his lawyer. In any event nobody could have been proof against the waves of high spirits emanating from Scott Wenzel and Ackerman. Until the very last minute, they explained, they could not be sure how much Barbara Gunn had stolen. The combination of relief, triumph and expectation would not be denied. Jackson and Thatcher must come with them to the nearest bar.

"We'll take the MF-23 along and christen it," Ackerman proposed exuberantly.

It was not easy to separate him from his cherished tub, and only as they were pushing him through the door did Thatcher realize there was still one occupant left in the room.

Eric Most, his face white and his eyes glazed, was staring unseeingly into space, oblivious to all that was going on.

"Impossible," he was saying, over and over again.

24 BEFORE THEY BOLT

SCOTT Wenzel and Ned Ackerman could afford to go out and celebrate. Their opposition was otherwise occupied. Conference succeeded consultation far into the night. As it assessed the damage, Standard Foods called up lawyers, accountants and marketing managers.

But not Vandam's.

Now, with everything on the line, SF decided to send the Vandams down to the minors. This was a bitter pill for them to swallow.

"When do you expect to hear from Sanders?" Jason asked early the next morning.

Dick Vandam shrugged.

"You shouldn't let him think he can treat Vandam's so casually," Milton chimed in.

"Oh balls," said Jason.

With the best will in the world, the manager of Vandam's cramped New York branch could not provide his visiting grandees with the spacious offices, rambling corridors and crowds of hired help to which they were accustomed. In addition to their other troubles, the Vandams were forced to do their squabbling eyeball to eyeball.

"Where do you get off, telling people what to do?" Jason continued, reverting to his main theme. "You couldn't even manage a competent theft. My God, if you had to land us in this mess, Milton, why let the real prize get away!"

Jason was sitting on a radiator cover so low that his long bony legs were thrust under his chin. Like a small boy, he scowled at the world over a barricade.

Milton, however, was the major sufferer from the inadequate amenities. In Vandamia, he was masterful at using the perquisites of rank to compensate for personal defects. His chair there had been worthy of William the Conqueror. Here, by contrast, his tubby frame overflowed an armless stenographer's stool that had to be shifted every time someone used the door.

"Don't talk to me that way, Jason," he said shrilly. "I was running R&D before you were born."

"Well, I wouldn't brag about it. The only thing you ever came up with turns out to belong to somebody else!" Jason said.

"*I* came up with?" Milton bounced on his deficient perch. "For the last year you've been telling the world *Numero Uno* was your idea. And just for the record, how are you claiming to have gotten it? Are you admitting that you bribed a stupid girl—and bribed her to get the wrong tomato at that?"

"Milton, if you weren't twice my age—"

Behind the small scarred desk, Dick Vandam shut his ears to this exchange. By rights, he should have insisted on order. But Vandam was like a battered boxer, desperately trying to answer the bell. For weeks he had known he was losing ground, but the full extent of the loss had been decently obscured until yesterday afternoon. Earl Sanders' parting words still rang in his head as he surveyed Jason and Milton.

"My God, are you two still at it?" he broke in on their insults. "Don't you realize what Wenzel has just done to us?"

Silencing Milton had never been that easy.

"Wenzel, always Wenzel!" he cried. "Your trouble is that you're obsessed with the man. Now if ever is the time to think about Vandam's. I know you and the rest of the family think Jason here was simply over-zealous. Well, I won't fight. Possibly after assisting me for a while, he may grow into the job."

"If you think I'd work for you, you old fool—"

"Shut up, both of you!" Vandam said wearily. "Get it through your heads that SF is probably going to fire all of us."

If he had not been so disheartened, Vandam could have enjoyed their responses. Milton stared, pop-eyed. Jason, on the other hand, looked as if he had bitten into a sour apple.

Struggling to recover, Milton seized on an old grievance. "Well, you don't have anything to worry about, Dick. You've got a management contract—"

"Oh, God, will you wake up and forget these pipe dreams. Management contracts, who's going to head R&D—they're things of the past." With as much emphasis as he could muster, Vandam continued, "Now that we don't have *Numero Uno*, Vandam's is fair game. And if anybody called Vandam is indicted for robbery, or—God forbid—murder, then SF will wash their hands of all of us. As a matter of fact, I expect—"

"Now wait a minute," Jason objected. "Sure, we're in a hole, but aren't you overreacting? Vandam's is rock-solid. *Numero Uno* isn't that important to us."

Vandam looked at him for a long moment. "You know better than that, Jason," he said evenly.

Flushing angrily, Jason said, "What's that supposed to mean?"

Before Vandam could reply, the door was flung open, buffeting Milton on the shoulder.

"I'm not sure if Mr. Vandam can see you now," protested the girl, clinging to the doorknob.

"He'd damned well better," said Howard Pendleton grimly as he brushed past her.

"Howard!" Vandam exclaimed apprehensively. "What's this all about?"

"What's this all about?" Pendleton repeated with savage mockery. "You were in the courthouse with us, weren't you? What do you think it's all about?"

Pendleton had shed his customary self-control. He was openly enraged. Ignoring everybody else, he stalked straight to Vandam's desk and loomed over it.

"Of course I was there," Vandam said, stung. "I simply wondered . . . Well, at any rate, I assume you're upset about this latest announcement of Wenzel's. We all are— that's what we've been discussing. But Howard, we've come to the conclusion that it would be wise to reserve judgment. Wenzel's claims haven't been checked out. For all we know, this is another one of his con games."

Pendleton laughed humorlessly. "Sure," he snapped. "And pigs can fly!"

All the confidence Vandam had built up as he spoke collapsed, leaving him helpless. Milton shrank away from Pendleton's oversized fury. Only Jason was capable of a coherent reply.

"Now calm down, Howard. There's no use going off the deep end until we're sure that Wenzel isn't simply grandstanding."

With a brusqueness more offensive than anger, Pendleton dismissed him. "You think I don't intend to check that out myself? I put Fran onto the night plane to Washington so she can look into all this field testing. No, I'm not in the habit of leaping to conclusions, and I don't intend to start now. But it's a waste of time. We're just going through the motions, and Fran knows it as well as I do."

He broke off. Then: "Vandam's must be feeling pretty pleased—the way you led me down the garden path. What did you promise Eric Most? His own research funds? His own laboratory? Or were you so stupid you thought you could deliver IPR to him?"

For a moment, nobody took in what he was saying. When the light finally dawned, Vandam was dumbfounded.

"I don't know what you're talking about," he mumbled.

"Like hell you don't!" Pendleton shot back. "Scott Wenzel developed *Numero Uno* and while you've been diddle-daddling in Vandamia, he's perfected the next generation. How he managed it, I'll never understand. But one thing I do understand—that you and Eric Most have been playing games for years. And if you think I'll let anybody pull the strings at IPR, you've made a big mistake."

Again, it was Jason who spoke for Vandam's. "Making a lot of wild charges isn't going to get us anywhere. Suppose—"

"Wild charges, hell! I may have been blind, but Fran practically drew me a diagram. How often Eric was in contact with Barbara, how he called the shots on the basic research. But one thing she couldn't tell me—how Vandam's was funneling data stolen from Wenzel to my assistant."

As Pendleton paused to draw breath, Dick Vandam inconsequently noted how deceiving looks could be. Pendleton was not a tall, tweedy scientist but a human battering ram.

His words packed a punch too.

"If you goddamn shits were so hellbent on stealing research, why didn't you do it on your own territory? But no, you wanted to keep Vandam's hands clean, so it was IPR, wasn't it? You probably enjoyed hearing me tell you how well the work was going. How did you keep straight faces?"

Vandam made an anguished attempt. "I assure you, Howard, that whatever may have been done—and I regret it as much as you do—it was not with the connivance of the company. Possibly some misguided individual—"

"Oh, God, are you trying that old line?" Pendleton snarled. "Do you seriously believe that you can sacrifice one or these two"—he jerked a contemptuous thumb toward Milton and Jason—"then make everything all right? Forget it. As far as I'm concerned, you're all up to your necks mud."

"Howard, even making allowances for the fact that you've had a blow—"

"Blow?" Pendleton interrupted. "You should hear Fran on the subject. It's bad enough that you spread your filth around IPR— but what sticks in her craw is what you did to Barbara Gunn. And it makes me sick to my stomach too. It wasn't enough to corrupt that poor child, you set her up to be killed."

Vandam floundered in an appalling position. He could scarcely deny that Barbara Gunn's murder was linked to *Numero Uno*, nor could he expand on Jason and Milton. He could only retreat into platitude.

"We are all deeply disturbed by the tragedy, as well as by the discovery that, however innocently, we have been trying to exploit someone else's findings. But we've got to keep our perspective, Howard. Vandam's has always valued its association with IPR and I certainly hope we can put all this behind us and work together again."

The olive branch was shot from his hands.

"You're out of your mind," Pendleton rasped. "Or else, you think I am. Vandam's will never set foot in IPR as long as I live. That's what I came here to tell you. And once I track down that little prick Most, he's getting thrown out on his ear. So you can forget about your inside man. From here on, the only way Vandam's touches anything IPR develops is at open auction."

Having delivered this statement, Pendleton wheeled and headed toward the door so fiercely that Milton nervously ducked out of his path, chair and all.

There was a silence after Pendleton's turbulent passage. Then Jason grimaced.

"Whew!" he gasped. "I've never seen him like that before. I didn't know he had it in him."

Still looking after Pendleton, Vandam said flatly, "He doesn't like the dirt piling up inside his own operation. Neither do I."

Milton began a bleat of protest, but Jason cut in ruthlessly. "You know, Dick, he gave me an idea with all that ranting of his."

Vandam was not encouraging, but Jason persevered. "I'm beginning to think we don't have to take the heat for what's happened."

"Then you haven't been listening," Dick retorted. "We're not geneticists, and Pendleton is. You just heard him. There's not a snowball's chance in hell that Wisconsin Seed is faking. Where does that leave Vandam's?"

Jason dismissed this objection. "No, that's not what I'm talking about. Let's say Wenzel did develop *Numero Uno.* . . . Oh, pipe down, Milton. If Pendleton is right, Eric Most found a way to steal Wenzel's findings. But why does Vandam's have to come in? This could all have been Most's bright idea, something he pulled on his own. My God, Dick, we're as much innocent victims as Howard Pendleton."

Dick Vandam was pitiably eager to grasp at anything that exculpated Vandam's, particularly anything that kept criminal indictments a long way from Vandamia. As Jason spoke, his uncle began to see possibilities.

His cousin was less enthusiastic. "That means nothing wrong happened at Vandamia, so everything stays the way it is," he said sourly.

"Milton," said Dick with some of his old forcefulness, "get it through your head, you're never getting your job back. Right now, concentrate on staying out of jail—and keeping your dividends up. Go on, Jason."

"It makes a lot of sense," said Jason, marshaling his arguments as he went on. "There's no obvious reason that Eric Most couldn't have swung it alone."

"What about the fifteen-thousand-dollar bribe?" Dick asked quickly. If there were flaws in this theory, now was the time to find them. "Pendleton runs a tight shop. There's no way Most could have siphoned off that much money."

But Jason was ready. "What if he paid the girl out of his own pocket?" he said persuasively. "Why not? He was going to be the big winner, after all. He made sure that everybody in Chicago thought he was the brain behind *Numero Uno*. And it was his notebooks and records used to support the application. If Most had pulled this off, he'd be an established name before he was thirty. That's a pretty good return for a fifteen-thousand-dollar investment."

"And Pendleton did say that Most occasionally met the Gunn girl. We don't want to forget that, either."

Even Milton got caught up. "Didn't Most graduate from the University of Wisconsin? No doubt, he returned to visit while the Gunn woman worked in Madison."

Jason nodded, then hammered the final nail. "And it makes more sense if she was murdered because she was mixed up in a one-man show. With her out of the way," he said significantly, "with her out of the way, there are no witnesses."

Vandam considered. Then slowly, he said, "I like it. I

like it very much, Jason. But you see what it means, don't you? We all have to stick together."

Carefully, they avoided looking toward the weak link. "Oh, all right," said Milton ungraciously.

For the first time that day, Dick Vandam smiled. "You know," he said, "I think it would be wise for me to give Earl Sanders a ring. Immediately."

25 CUT BACK HARD

ONE reason that Earl Sanders constantly turned to John Thatcher in moments of turmoil was his lack of confidants within Standard Foods. A year ago Sanders had hogged all the credit for arranging the marriage between SF and Vandam's. Now that the happy couple was having trouble, his colleagues were conspicuously aloof. And the Sloan, after all, was paid to simulate interest in the problems of its clients.

But payment or not, Sanders was unable to reach Thatcher with his latest communiqué. By the time that his secretary buzzed through for the fourth time to announce that Thatcher's line was still tied up, Sanders had reached the point of accepting surrogates. Fortunately two of them were sitting on the other side of his desk.

Not that the meeting with Ned Ackerman and Paul Jackson was going as planned. After a futile morning with the experts, SF's front office had accepted the demise of *Numero Uno,* and Sanders was hoping to score Brownie points with Wisconsin Seed by a prompt and generous waiver of all patent claims. But Ackerman, suffering from a richly deserved hangover, was unimpressed.

"Is that all you wanted? Hell, we could have handled this on the phone and saved the trip," he said, reaching for his overcoat.

Sanders decided to put more meat on the bare bones of his announcement. "I speak for everyone here at Standard

Foods when I say how much we regret this entire mis-understanding. Of course we acted in good faith throughout. We had no reason to doubt the claims of—"

"Sure, sure," Ackerman cut him off. "How could you know what was going on in Vandamia?"

"That's just it," Sanders persisted. "When it all comes out in the wash, it may develop that Vandam's was an innocent victim of this misrepresentation as well."

Paul Jackson was openly skeptical. "The bad fairy at work again? Come off it, Sanders. You bought a lemon and you're stuck with it."

"That isn't what Dr. Howard Pendleton thinks," Sanders retorted.

Jackson and Ackerman had suspended their leave-taking activities and were waiting.

Sanders, on reflection, decided to adopt Dick Vandam's interpretation of the evidence. "You know that assistant of his, Eric Most? Well, it seems that Most has been running up to Madison during the last five years and seeing Barbara Gunn regularly. What's more, Most rejected a couple of Pendleton's ideas during the research. Said he knew a better, faster way to get results. He had an inside track all along."

Ackerman was blunt. "It sounds like a whitewash to me."

"I assure you that Standard Foods intends to get to the bottom of this. Our interests are identical, Ackerman."

"Like hell they are! SF wants to bury this mess so it doesn't stink anymore. I want to find the creep who poisoned Barbara. But I'll run your theory past Scott and see what he says."

As the door closed behind his visitors, Sanders could not convince himself that he had made any progress in wooing Wisconsin Seed. In fact, a few more stumbling blocks had been strewn across the road. There was only one thing to do.

"Try Thatcher again, will you?" he barked into his intercom.

Ever since assimilating the glories of MF-23, John Thatcher had seen one indisputable way to establish the identity of Barbara Gunn's murderer. He was not surprised that nobody else had been vouchsafed this vision. His technique was unlikely to occur to anyone except a banker.

His first step had been to institute a series of long-distance calls. This morning the return calls had been filtering through for over two hours. The last one had hit the jackpot.

The voice on the line had belonged to Santiago Cruzman, a valued Sloan correspondent, and the tempo had been stately enough to require self-restraint on Thatcher's part. No matter how impatient you are, you do not rush your fences south of Key West.

". . . exactly as you anticipated, John," said Cruzman with creamy congratulation. "As you asked, I have had the records for the year in question examined, and there is no doubt at all."

"Ah," said Thatcher, expelling the breath he had been holding. The outline of two crimes had been horrifyingly clear to him since yesterday. Nonetheless, Cruzman's confirmation ended the suspense. Documentary proof beats insights any day.

". . . sending you the photostats," Cruzman continued. "And of course I need not assure you that I—and Hector Montoya, who remembers the transaction most clearly—will be ready to testify, if that should be desirable."

Thatcher roused himself to utter the requisite gratitude with all proper embellishments. When this time-consuming process was over, he instructed Miss Corsa to get police headquarters in Chicago.

There was a good deal to say, but Chicago marches to a different beat than Puerto Rico. Captain McNabb was ready to roll within ten minutes. He had been surprised by Thatcher's methods, but not by his results.

"That explains why she went to the Blackstone," he grunted before going on to discuss probable ETAs.

When he cradled the receiver, Thatcher produced a summary of the conversation for Charlie Trinkam, who had been sprawled in a chair for the last hour.

"He seemed like a pretty bright cookie," said Charlie, more subdued than usual. "I wonder how long it will take."

They could only stare at each other. Putting the police on the trail of a killer is a sobering experience.

It was during this emotional letdown that Earl Sanders finally broke through. From his point of view, the conversation was strangely unrewarding. Thatcher reacted with a series of noncommittal monosyllables, repressed all attempts to theorize, then rang off abruptly.

"After all, I'm going to have to discuss this in great detail with Sanders sometime in the next twenty-four hours," he justified himself to Charlie. "Why waste time fabricating evasions now? Particularly when the first thing he'll do is pass them on?"

"These people all talk too much," Charlie said disapprovingly. "Vandam natters to Sanders, then Sanders lets it all out to Ackerman."

Thatcher nodded. "And Ackerman is on his way back to the Hilton to tell Wenzel."

Rhythm has its own seduction. Almost automatically Charlie continued the chant. "Where they'll no doubt bump into Most. He's at the Hilton, too."

As the words sank in, Thatcher was suddenly disquieted. "Are you sure?"

"Mary Larrabee told me. The Pendletons are on the same floor she is." Even as he spoke, Charlie was straightening. "You know," he continued slowly, "I don't think it's such an awfully good idea for this bunch to meet up right now."

"You're right!" said Thatcher, who was already on his feet.

Events might have turned out differently if Ned Ackerman had not had a headache. But there was a crowd in front of the SF building waiting for taxis, New York was enjoying a respite from dirty weather with a clear, dry, bracing day, and Ackerman decided to blow away the cobwebs by walking back to the Hilton. He therefore arrived at his destination an hour later than he might have.

As soon as he rolled into the crowded Hilton lobby, he was set back on his heels. There, emerging from the Kismet Lounge, was Scott Wenzel.

And, at his heels, was Eric Most.

Ackerman blinked at this unlikely duo. The seed that Earl Sanders had planted began to germinate. With a muttered oath, he stumped across the lobby to Wenzel's side.

"What's Most doing here?" he demanded.

"Don't ask me," Wenzel said irritably. "Ask him. He seems to think I'm his father confessor or something."

If Ackerman had not been blinkered by suspicion, he would have realized that Wenzel was more amused than exasperated. The triumph of MF-23 had softened some of his cutting edge.

"What's he confessing to?" Ackerman demanded.

"You've just got to understand how I feel," Eric Most intervened earnestly. "God, when I see what happened I don't know how I can face you or anybody else."

"Great," said Wenzel without interest. "Why don't you just roll away then?"

But Most wanted more than confession; he wanted absolution.

"I didn't realize what I was doing or how it would all end up," he said in a cracked voice. "You can believe that, can't you? But *Numero Uno* was so big I just lost my head. I've only come to my senses now."

To Ned Ackerman, every word was chilling corroboration of Dick Vandam's theory. To Scott Wenzel it was all a distracting buzz from a contemptible worm.

"You never had any sense. You just had an inflated— Ned! For Christ's sake, what are you doing?"

With an inarticulate noise in the back of his throat, Ackerman had reached past Wenzel to clutch Most's shirt.

"I'm going to shake the truth out of him," he threatened.

As his other hand had doubled into a clublike fist, Wenzel abandoned attempts to reason with his partner. Instead he shoved himself between the antagonists. Unfortunately Most accepted this reprieve as another opportunity. When Ackerman thrust him loose so roughly that he staggered, he did not retreat to safety.

"Look, I know you two have got a right to be mad at what I've done," he said with a pathetic stab at dignity. "I'm apologizing to both of you. What more can I do?"

"I'll tell you, you little turd!" Ackerman thundered.

By now Scott Wenzel was expecting the hotel security forces to start converging on their corner.

"Could you hold it down, Ned—" he began before being cut off.

"Hold it down?" Ackerman gulped. "He's doing a lot of bleating about what he did to us. What about what he did to Barbie?"

Most went white. "Barbara? What are you talking about?"

"Pendleton's blown the whistle on you, Most. You're lucky not to be in jail right now. But that's where you're going to end up, I swear it," Ackerman vowed.

Most tried and failed to say something, his mouth working soundlessly.

"Are you going to explain any of this or do you just want to stand there and yell?" Wenzel challenged his partner.

With deadly economy Ackerman outlined Howard Pendleton's theory.

"That's crazy," Wenzel said instantly. "Most going directly to Barbara? Never in a million years."

"Stop being so hipped on the Vandams that you can't see straight."

"I'm not hipped on the Vandams!"

In spite of his surface eccentricities Wenzel was incapable of losing his temper as thoroughly as Ned Ackerman. Instinctively Ackerman recognized that, with Scott, the i's would have to be dotted and the t's crossed.

"All right, all right," he said more calmly. "I admit that Dick Vandam wants his people off the hook so he's trying to make it sound as if the whole rotten deal never passed through Vandamia. But you only have to listen to this little rat to see that he was involved. And how many people were likely to be in on it? You said yourself it was easier to fake up something in a small lab than in a big one."

"If you were listening to me then, why the hell won't you slow down and listen to me now?"

"Because I don't want Barbie's killer to get off scot-free!"

For a moment it looked as if Scott Wenzel would resort to some shaking of his own. "Her killer isn't going anywhere," he promised.

Their altercation absorbed them so totally that neither noticed when Eric Most, still ashen, took one last look—then slipped away.

Whatever John Thatcher expected to encounter at the Hilton did not include a pitched battle between the two partners of Wisconsin Seed.

Charlie Trinkam had a knack of taking things as they came. "Looks like they can't stand success," he said, observing the hostilities judiciously. "But at least this way of passing the time keeps them from fingering anybody."

Thatcher was only momentarily taken aback. There were endless reasons for Ackerman and Wenzel to quarrel, but they were unimportant. He and Charlie were here for only one reason—to be absolutely sure that Howard Pendleton was safe in his room. Or, better yet, safe somewhere else.

Without hesitation he approached the combatants. "Ackerman! Wenzel!" he snapped to claim their attention.

Wenzel was glad to see him. "You're just in time! Will you try talking sense to Ned? I think he's losing his marbles. I had to stop him from strangling Eric Most with his bare hands."

"Eric Most? You've already seen him!"

"Uh-oh!" said Charlie. "I knew this wasn't going to be as easy as it looked."

Ackerman was still seeking supporters. "Wait until you hear what Sanders has come up with," he began urgently.

"I already know about that," Thatcher cut him off, "but where's Most?"

Wenzel was more interested in his own complaint. "And Ned won't stand still long enough for me to set him straight."

Ackerman, however, had responded to Thatcher's question with a discovery. "My God, Most's gone. He's making a run for it."

"I can think of something else he may be doing," Thatcher said grimly. Memories of past efforts to get information from the Hilton desk rose to haunt him. "Let's pray Pendleton isn't in. Because they'll never give us his number in time."

"Four-oh-six," said Wenzel immediately. "You don't think—"

Thatcher did not pause for thought. Wheeling, he headed for the elevators with Wenzel right at his side.

The others were just in time to tumble in after them.

"But Pendleton's already told everybody his story," Ackerman protested. "What would be the point?"

"No point at all," Thatcher said sadly. "We don't have to depend on stories anymore. There's written proof on its way from Puerto Rico. But he doesn't know that."

The fourth-floor corridor was long and claustrophobic. The door to 406 was at the far end.

"Christ," said Charlie, breaking into a dogtrot to keep up. "You don't think we're too late, do you?"

But as they pelted ahead Thatcher could hear voices, angry voices, behind that door.

Where there were voices, there was life.

Then two things happened almost simultaneously. Scott Wenzel brought his fist crashing down on the door and there was the shocking explosion of a gun firing.

With a lazy protest from its hinges, the door swung open and a man, clutching his shoulder, staggered into the corridor and collapsed into Scott Wenzel's arms.

The uproar was immediate. Hotel guests seemed to pour out of every room on the floor, Charlie rushed to help Wenzel and Thatcher stepped over the threshold.

Time is relative. There was only one occupant of the room and he still held his gun pointing at the door, his face convulsed with despair. To John Thatcher it seemed as if he had hours to repent his folly before the barrel turned away. To those in the corridor it seemed only a moment before the second shot resounded.

"Mr. Thatcher!" a familiar voice cried in alarm.

"I'm all right, Mrs. Larrabee," said Thatcher, shaken, "but Dr. Howard Pendleton has just blown his brains out."

26 EASY TO PICK

HOWARD Pendleton's suicide was a confession, not an explanation. Eric Most, recovering at Mt. Sinai Hospital, was the major beneficiary but the other actors in the *Numero Uno* drama also profited. They could now stop circling each other warily, suspicious of every move. The great clarification had even made it possible for Scott Wenzel to help Dick Vandam arrange for the withdrawal of the Vandam patent application.

Or so Ned Ackerman reported.

"Scott was pretty damn cordial. He agreed it was only natural for Vandam's to have been fooled by Pendleton. For him, that's the equivalent of kissing and making up."

Earl Sanders surveyed the dinner table with disappointment. "I thought Wenzel was joining us."

For a full week Sanders had been nagging Thatcher to provide a casual background against which Standard Foods could renew its overtures to Wisconsin Seed. Thatcher had been at a loss for the proper atmospherics until another Sanders ambition surfaced. The first public reaction to Mary Larrabee's screen debut had made her a hot property. Standard Foods yearned to cast her as queen of their TV kitchens. The embryo Larrabee account at the Sloan was looking better and better. Tonight Charlie Trinkam was sitting on one side of the table, hosting the Larrabees. On the other side, Thatcher balanced him with Sanders and Ned Ackerman.

"Scott's coming. He wouldn't miss this for the world," Ackerman promised. "But he's visiting with Mrs. Pendleton right now so he may be a little late."

It was not Earl Sanders' desire to criticize Scott Wenzel but compassion for the bereaved made him protest. "My God, doesn't the lady have enough trouble on her hands?"

Ackerman grinned. "That's what I thought myself. But Scott's been over there every day this week and she hasn't thrown him out yet. So he must be doing something right."

"Mrs. Pendleton is the wife of the man who killed that girl in Chicago," Mary Larrabee explained to her husband.

In her own eyes Mrs. Larrabee had redeemed her failure of nerve in Chicago. Faced with Eric Most bleeding all over the Hilton, she had brushed everybody aside and gone to work. Without a woman like her, the paramedics said, Most would have died.

"I'd like to find out what it's all about," said Pete, as amiable as ever in spite of the bandages circling his brow. He had already explained these decorations as mementos of the ice rink at Rockefeller Center. "Back in Chicago everybody was saying that either Vandam's had stolen something from you or you'd stolen something from them," he added to Ned Ackerman.

"God knows that's the way it looked to me," Sanders supported him.

Charlie saw why everybody had made this mistake. "Bound to look that way," he commented. "The whole thing started with a patent suit. You had two companies, each maintaining that the tomato belonged to it. It looked as though one of them had to be lying. So the basic problem seemed clear, and we all got started on the wrong foot."

"You may have put your finger on a weakness in the whole judicial approach," said Thatcher, attracted by this tempting byway. "The adversarial process necessarily begins by boiling everything down to a two-sided contest. If you reduce your quarrel to the wrong two principals, you can miss the boat entirely."

"That's very interesting," said Mary Larrabee kindly, "but it doesn't explain anything."

Thatcher hastened to make amends. "Let me start at the beginning. Six years ago the big canners and soup companies lost their last-ditch battle, and it became legally possible to patent a tomato."

Sanders was pained by this formulation. "You make it sound as if we were trying to rob somebody, when we were trying to ensure the rewards of competition to the American consumer," he said piously.

Charlie hooted, Ackerman guffawed, and the Larrabees looked incredulous. But Thatcher's reaction was worst of all.

"What you managed to do," he said, "was convince Scott Wenzel there was gold in them thar hills. He realized the tomato was so central to the giant food processors that the man who developed a real breakthrough could name his own price."

Ned Ackerman had undergone a transformation since the successful unveiling of the MF-23. He had always affected a casual style but now he was really unbuttoned, leaning back and watching life parade by with infinite indulgence. His genteel surroundings were certainly not inhibiting him. Mary Larrabee might be sipping a distinguished white wine (lovingly chosen by Charlie), Earl Sanders might already be on his second round of some exotic aperitif, the other men might be upholding solid conservatism with straight Scotch, but Ned had insisted on plain old Pabst.

"You still haven't got Scott figured out," he corrected after taking a swig. "When I got hold of him, he was still wet behind the ears commercially. All he wanted was to do his own kind of work. He was babbling about being able to write his own ticket with one of the big labs if he got his name on that patent. It was news to him that he could have his own big laboratory." Ackerman smiled benignly at the gathering. "In fact, you could say I'm the one who's money-minded."

Thatcher had no doubt that Earl Sanders was going to discover that for himself when the negotiations between Standard Foods and Wisconsin Seed began in earnest.

"Good for you!" said Charlie enthusiastically.

Before Mary Larrabee could call them to order once again, Thatcher hurried on. "But Wenzel had already mentioned the idea when he was still working at IPR. Pendleton of course saw the economic possibilities but he dismissed the notion as more empty talk from his bumptious assistant. Imagine his jealousy when, later, Barbara Gunn innocently told him that Scott was making great advances on the project. He immediately realized that, if anybody was going to patent that tomato, it had to be him."

This evoked a chorus of protests.

"Now wait a minute," growled Ackerman. "I know our society is supposed to be filled with corruption—my son keeps telling me about the rotten world I've brought him into—but there are still lots of honest people around. I don't say they might not be tempted by something smack in their path, but you're saying Pendleton took off from a standing start. Why should a successful accomplished scientist turn crooked overnight?"

"That's what they want to know over at Vandam's," said Earl Sanders, underlining the fact that Standard Foods had merely inherited Howard Pendleton. "He'd never stolen anything before."

"Surely it's staring you in the face. Scott Wenzel kept telling us that Pendleton was a . . ." Thatcher paused to remember some of the choicer epithets that had peppered

Wenzel's descriptions. "A has-been, a bag of wind, a professional joke, were some of the expressions I recall."

Ackerman snorted. "You know the kind of swollen head that Scotty's got. You have to take his descriptions with a grain of salt. For God's sake, if he'd been a young physicist twenty years ago, he probably would have described Einstein as a has-been."

But Charlie, more detached, was slowly shaking his head. "I don't know if I go along with that. Sure, that kid of yours has got a damned good opinion of himself. But that doesn't mean he's wrong calling the shots about other people. Look at IPR. He said Eric Most was a dumbbell, and he certainly seems to have been right. And he's always been respectful about Pendleton's wife."

"Exactly," said Thatcher. "Just because Wenzel is overflowing with confidence doesn't mean his professional judgment is invalid. And quite apart from that consideration, we had a good deal of confirmation. After all, Sanders, you've told me that Jason Ingersoll was constantly saying that under Milton's guidance R&D at Vandam's hadn't come up with anything big in years."

"Well, yes, but—"

Thatcher swept over him. "And Eric Most dinned into the ears of anybody who would listen that *Numero Uno* took priority at IPR because it was the only major breakthrough in ages."

"And he was wrong!" Sanders retorted triumphantly. "Fran Pendleton had produced a winner with her delphinium. It's true that it didn't go to Vandam's, but it was there all the same."

"You're missing my point. I agree that everybody was grinding his own ax. Jason was interested in undermining Milton. Eric Most was so self-absorbed that he forgot there was any other work going on at IPR. That's why we missed the remarkable unanimity coming at us from all directions.

272

Scott Wenzel, Jason Ingersoll, Eric Most, were all saying the same thing—that Howard Pendleton hadn't produced any important research for a long, long time."

He had convinced his audience, but they all reacted differently.

"You know, Scott's got more sense than I give him credit for," Ackerman murmured approvingly.

"What the hell were they doing at Vandam's, not to notice?" Sanders demanded.

"It must be a wonderful business to be in," marveled Pete Larrabee. "Nobody cares whether you're winning or losing. It's a lot different in hardware."

Remorselessly Thatcher returned them to the straight and narrow. "So this was not an overnight collapse by Howard Pendleton. IPR looked all right to outsiders because the other sections were doing well. But he knew he hadn't had a major idea in ten years. And he was at a critical stage. Only vigorous, productive scientists go on working into old age. Has-beens are supposed to retire at sixty-five."

Sanders chuckled. "You should hear Dick Vandam on the subject. He's having more trouble with his father."

"What's wrong with retirement?" asked Ackerman. "Lots of people like it."

"Not Howard Pendleton. He was too fond of playing the great man. He didn't intend to sit back and watch someone else lord it over IPR. Of course I doubt if he thought all this out until Barbara Gunn unwittingly showed him a simple way to continued grandeur."

"Now that's what interests me," said Mary Larrabee, leaning forward so eagerly that she knocked over her neighbor's glass.

"Watch it, Mary," exclaimed Charlie as a waiter rushed to mop up the damage. "Flourishing those nails of yours is like waving around a couple of pitchforks."

"They're not mine," she replied indignantly, viewing the long talons with disfavor. "They put some kind of gel at the end of mine to make them like this."

Little by little, Mary's sponsor was turning its attention to every visible inch of her body. No doubt she was soon to be sporting eyelashes that constituted a public peril.

Pete Larrabee voiced the thought in everybody's mind. "They look god-awful, don't they?" he remarked affectionately.

Mary was making the best of a bad job. "At least they're not fragile. Once the cement sets, they're like iron."

"Wonderful for you, not so hot for the rest of us," Charlie said, moving his replacement glass to the other side of his setting.

"Never mind about that," she directed. "I still want to know about Barbara Gunn."

"We'll never know exactly what Pendleton said to her," Thatcher reminded them. "Both parties to the conversation are dead. But I doubt if he had much trouble. He was a high-pressure salesman and she was used to accepting his judgments. He probably delivered all the usual clichés about being in the right place at the right time, doing what everybody else in business does. She was genuinely ignorant of the value of the tomato and, of course, the money was a temptation."

Sadly Ned Ackerman agreed. "I'll go along with that. But how come he took the chance? He must have realized that the minute the pressure came on, Barbara would go to pieces. Are you telling us he intended to murder her all along?"

"No, no. There wasn't supposed to be any pressure. You've been associating with Scott Wenzel too long," Thatcher argued. "I think you still don't appreciate the magnitude of the miracle he pulled off."

But Ackerman was beyond the reach of such barbs. "You

274

haven't forgotten that I'm the one who keeps the books?" he asked gently. "I'm the one who's made the cash-flow projections for next year."

"You sure weren't exaggerating when you said you were money-minded," Charlie rebuked him. "John is talking about the experimental miracle."

"Charlie's right," Thatcher said. "Howard Pendleton was overly respectful of Vandam's. The basic laboratory work was pretty much a one-man operation. By feeding stolen data to Eric Most, Pendleton could keep IPR synchronized with Wisconsin Seed. Once it became a matter of extensive field testing, he assumed as obvious that there was no way Scott Wenzel could keep up with the manpower, the money and the other resources that Vandam's could lavish on the project. He never considered the possibility that by using high school boys and botany students, that by working like a dog himself, that by never making a mistake, Wenzel could bring in his final results on the same schedule as a giant corporation."

"That boy was a slave driver. He damn near killed us all," Ackerman recalled fondly.

Mary Larrabee was confused. "What difference did the timing make? Dr. Pendleton still stole the tomato, didn't he?"

"Yes, but researchers are quite often independently working on the same development. If Vandam's had filed for its patent two years before Wenzel was ready to do so, he wouldn't have had a leg to stand on. It's very hard to claim that somebody who's far ahead of you is picking your brains. What's more, his suspicions wouldn't even have been aroused. So there wouldn't have been any lawsuit and there wouldn't have been any pressure on Barbara Gunn. It was the neck-and-neck finish that put the fat in the fire."

"If you say so." Mary was still dubious.

"After all, it's the reverse situation that came about. When Wisconsin Seedsmen revealed the second-generation tomato, Vandam's threw in the towel because it was clear Wenzel was the one who was way ahead."

Ned Ackerman was willing to buy this. "That means Pendleton didn't have to be completely crazy. Only a damned fool. He didn't even get progress reports from Barbara about the field testing."

"Apparently not," Thatcher agreed. "IPR was no longer working on the tomato in Puerto Rico. Pendleton was confident that Vandam's would give him the necessary lead time—there was no point in increasing the danger by needless transmission of information. Far better to let Barbara forget her part in all this."

The whole picture had suddenly become clear to Sanders. "Sweet Jesus," he muttered. "Then it all broke on him from out of the blue. First the patent suit by Wenzel, and then Barbara Gunn going to pieces all over the place."

"Precisely," said Thatcher. "My secretary put her finger on the solution when she reasoned that the killer's timing had been thrown off by the actions of others. We wasted that insight by considering minor surprises. But Pendleton was the one who had a major surprise at the last moment."

Sanders was remembering the Pendletons' hurried side trip to Vandamia. "And Barbara Gunn wasn't even there. He didn't have a chance to see her until Chicago."

"Yes, he got to her by the skin of his teeth."

"You know, I wondered about that." Mary Larrabee's brow was furrowed in thought. "After we found out about the bribery, I was thinking over the night she was poisoned and it seemed to me that the murderer was taking an awfully big chance."

Charlie was always ready to listen to the ladies. "You mean killing her in such a public place? But it worked out well from his point of view. Anybody could have done it."

She waved this away. "No, not that. I mean leaving it until so late. She could easily have broken down and told all that last night."

"That's a very important point," Thatcher congratulated her. "In fact, it more or less cleared the Wisconsin contingent of suspicion."

"I'm glad to hear it," Ackerman said, "but why?"

"Barbara had been deeply disturbed ever since she realized she would have to testify. What's more, she'd been talking about her trouble for days. The murderer wouldn't have waited if he'd had access to her before. Howard Pendleton killed her at the first opportunity. You and Scott Wenzel would have done the same thing and you probably wouldn't have had to pick up poison at the convention. You would have come prepared."

Ned Ackerman received this without a blink. "All right, but once we were cleared out of the way, that left Vandam's. They were in the same position as Pendleton. They hadn't had easy access to Barbara, although God knows they kept trying."

This reminded Earl Sanders of a grievance. "Those damned fools did everything they could to look guilty. Actually, they were just running their own cozy little war, but that wasn't how it looked to the rest of us. Hell, I know for a fact that Dick was damned worried about how far those two might have carried it."

"The Vandams were a godsend to Pendleton and not just because of their activities," Thatcher replied. "First, there was Scott Wenzel's prejudice. They had filed for the patent, they were trying to steal from him and, hence, they were responsible for everything. Even when he knew the work had been done in Puerto Rico, he continued to assume that Pendleton was nothing more than a cat's-paw. And the Vandams themselves were not prepared to think the unthinkable. Pendleton had been a star in their firmament for so long they never suspected him."

"And I wasn't too bright," Ackerman admitted. "I was so hellbent on protecting the security of the MF-23, I didn't have time to think about anything else. I just went along with Scott's suspicions."

Charlie pointed out that he'd done a fine job on security, and it was just as well to leave the expertise to the experts.

While giving lip service to this principle, Thatcher had a reservation. "I'm not surprised about the rest of us, but I would have thought that Wenzel would have grown suspicious very early in the game. Certainly Pendleton must have been afraid that he would. I suppose that's why he began to disassociate himself from the work on *Numero Uno* as soon as he got to Chicago."

"You mean he was setting up Eric Most as a patsy?" Charlie asked intelligently.

"I think at the beginning it was instinctive. *Numero Uno* had turned into a mess and he therefore, very uncharacteristically, let an assistant push himself front and center. But Wenzel, of all men, would have known how uncharacteristic that was. Why didn't he smell a rat?"

Ackerman was at no loss for an explanation. "I'll tell you why. It would never occur to Scott to steal somebody else's work. He could accuse a bunch of businessmen in a big corporation. But the worst he could think of Pendleton was that he was trying to curry favor by helping with a whitewash."

Mary thought this spoke well of the young man, Charlie deprecated such innocence in a naughty world, and Sanders was inclined to suspect simple stupidity. The subject of their discussion arrived in time to defend himself.

After greetings, the first questions were about Mrs. Pendleton.

"Fran'll be all right," Wenzel said confidently. "She's ridden the first shock and now she's facing up to the consequences. But it's been a long week. I'm glad her daughter is here now."

Mischievously Ned told him they were all wondering why he hadn't spotted Pendleton's guilt early on.

"Me?" Wenzel did not regard himself as in any way to blame. "I want to know how the hell Fran could have been so blind. Howard pulled this off right under her nose. He didn't get her out of town until the last act."

"Oh, come on!" scoffed Ned. "You told me yourself Fran met him when she was a graduate student. She was young, she was impressed by his professional stature, she went on that way."

Wenzel wasn't giving an inch. "What does that have to do with it? I was young when I met him but I didn't stay snowed for long."

Ackerman was outraged. "You didn't fall in love with him, you didn't have children and grandchildren with him."

"I don't see what difference that makes," Wenzel insisted stubbornly.

Thatcher could see that Scott Wenzel still had much to learn about life. "When you share vested interests with someone over the years, it is profitless to continually search out their defects," he informed him. "You spend your time concentrating on the ones that surface by themselves."

"It happens to the best of us," Ned Ackerman said slyly. "I've noticed it happening with you and Hilary. There's a lot you're learning to live with."

Now it was Scott's turn to be outraged. "I'm fully aware of Hilary's defects," he said stiffly.

Mary, of course, wanted to know who Hilary was. She was more curious than censorious when she found out.

Scott shrugged off this digression. "All right, so Fran was turning a blind eye to the fact that Howard was through as a scientist. But I wish she'd get off this guilt kick. She seems to think she's responsible for the attack on Eric Most, just because she let herself be sent to Washington. And she says she gave Howard the idea in the first place by beginning to suspect Eric."

"He was already using Most as a stalking horse. After all, there wasn't that much choice," Thatcher said dryly. "And when you unveiled MF-23, he knew Most would eventually put two and two together. So Pendleton took the bull by the horns, marched over to the Vandam office, and rather cleverly presented them with a palatable solution to the crime. After that, it was only a question of time before Most confronted him under circumstances that could be twisted to look like an attack."

"What was so clever about it?" Wenzel demanded. "I heard he went over and raised Cain about Most."

Thatcher continued his education of the young. "If he had gone over with simple suspicion of Most, it would have looked self-serving. By storming in and accusing Vandam's of participation, he directed their attention to Most and then let them figure out for themselves how to get off the hook. There's no persuasion like self-persuasion."

Sanders decided to make his own confession. "You're right about it's being palatable. I didn't like to say so before, but once I realized that the Vandam bank in Chicago had been used to bribe Barbara Gunn, I was afraid of what we were going to dig up."

"Good heavens!" Thatcher was astonished. "That was what convinced me that the Vandams were out of it. If you're trying to arrange an anonymous transfer of funds, the last place you go is a bank where you're known."

Sanders was chagrined that this thought had never occurred to him. While he was recovering, Ned Ackerman produced his own doubts.

"But with the Vandams and us out of it, that left Pendleton and Eric Most. How come you were so sure which was which when you went to the Hilton?"

Thatcher grinned at him. "Because I'm a banker. Once it narrowed down to two people, there wasn't much difficulty spotting which one was the killer. I simply lifted a telephone, called some contacts in San Juan and asked which one had liquidated fifteen thousand five years ago."

Charlie was amused at the general reaction. "And you people call yourselves businessmen," he chided Sanders and Ackerman and Larrabee. "Don't you know money always leaves a trail?"

"And if you think that's simple, consider what narrowed the field for Captain McNabb. The only suspects staying at the Blackstone were from IPR. Barbara Gunn had been avoiding Eric Most and fled from Fran Pendleton. What did she have to say that Dr. Pendleton was determined not to hear?"

But Thatcher's audience was turning its attention elsewhere. Pete Larrabee was bringing Mary up-to-date on family news.

"You know Betty's gone to West Point to see her boyfriend a couple of times," he reported. "She came back in seventh heaven. She's really wild about army life."

Mary paled. "You tell Betty she's too young to get married—or whatever it is they do these days. She's got to go to college first."

"Hell, that isn't what she's thinking of. I keep telling you, you've got to keep up with the times, Mary. Betty is going to apply for the Air Force Academy."

While Mary was speechless, her husband beamed around the table. "That girl of mine really has her head screwed on right. Do you know she may get an engineering degree without costing me one red cent?"

Earl Sanders had begun his tactical approach to Ned Ackerman, who was looking so guileless that Thatcher pitied Standard Foods.

"No," said Ackerman blandly. "That wasn't the arrangement I was thinking of. Not at all."

Scott Wenzel had so much confidence in his partner that he wasn't even listening. Instead he chose to make Thatcher his confidant.

"What Fran needs is to bury herself in her work," he announced. "I told her that."

"You may be right," Thatcher agreed, the first to admit that Scott and Fran were probably very much alike.

"So what if she is gun-shy about having anything to do with Vandam's again? I told her there are other outfits. For instance, there's Wisconsin Seedsmen."

It was Ackerman who was now listening to him.

"We'd be proud to handle her floribunda," Wenzel continued. "We're going to have to broaden into flowers anyway. By the time she's ready, we'll be able to handle production and distribution. And just to avoid any more talk about underhanded tactics, that's what I told Dick Vandam."

Thatcher was the first to admit that he was too ignorant to understand the coup that Wenzel was pulling off. But an old hand from the Department of Agriculture was ready to guide him.

"Boy, I'll say one thing for you, Scotty," Ackerman whispered admiringly. "You sure learn fast!"

Wenzel went on to prove it. Turning graciously to Thatcher, he said, "By the way, Dick mentioned that your secretary is bringing her grandfather to Vandamia for the royal tour. Of course in Madison we don't have that kind of Disneyland yet. But I'll tell you what. Send them up to me and I'll give the old man an MF-23. He'll have the only tomato tree in New York."

Captains of industry, Thatcher had always known, are made, not born.

ABOUT THE AUTHOR

EMMA LATHEN is the nom de plume shared by Mary Jane Latsis, an economist, and Martha Henissart, a lawyer. The authors met at Harvard, where they were doing graduate work. Miss Henissart went on to practice law for twelve years, and Miss Latsis worked as an agricultural economist for the United Nations and the United States government. Their first book written together, *Banking on Death*, was published in 1961. *Green Grow the Dollars* is the nineteenth novel by Emma Lathen.

A MR. & MRS. NORTH MYSTERY

THE CLASSIEST COUPLE EVER TO SOLVE A CRIME— MR. AND MRS. NORTH

Pam and Jerry North, a charming, witty and sophisticated pair who like nothing better than a very dry martini and a very difficult murder.

Enjoy all these Mr. and Mrs. North Mysteries

DEATH TAKES A BOW 44337/$2.95
THE JUDGE IS REVERSED 44338/$2.95
MURDER COMES FIRST 44335/$2.95
MURDER IN A HURRY 44336/$2.95
MURDER WITHIN MURDER 44334/$2.95

FROM
POCKET BOOKS

Agatha Christie's *favorite*

THE REMARKABLE MISS MARPLE

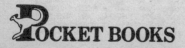

POCKET BOOKS